RUNAWAYS

John,
always appreciate
fellowshipping with
you. You are a
man of integrity

RUNAWAYS

When it's easier to just get away...*fast.*

and one that runs to
God in all situations.
Hope we can continue
getting together.
Your friend + Bro in
Christ,
Tim

TIM BENNETT

SEL PUBLICATIONS
Syracuse, New York

DEDICATION

To all the people currently serving the Lord in France
and to all the wonderful French-speaking people,
from many different nations, who allowed us into their lives
and befriended us. Our lives were enriched because of you
and we will never forget you.

**"Let us not become weary in doing good,
for at the proper time we will reap a harvest
if we do not give up."**
(Galatians 6:9)

Acknowledgments

The first person I want to thank for helping me get this story to print is my Lord and Savior Jesus Christ. Without His gentle whispers to my heart over the last 20 years: "It's a good book . . . keep going," I would have thrown in the towel long ago. In fact, I did throw it down on several occasions, but I always found myself picking it up again, wiping the sweat off my angst-ridden face, and getting back to the task at hand.

The second person I need to thank is my wife, Veronique, who has listened to me tell this story for two decades, a test in forbearance few could tolerate. Merci Chérie pour ton soutien et amour tous ces années. Tu es un don de Dieu que je ne mérite pas.

Next up are the people who read my novel and gave me valuable suggestions on how to improve it. They are as follows: Joe Michelini, Tim Bleecker, Erika Rudl, Abigail Komhaus, Anne Knittel, Howie and Janet Brittain, Mary Dawes, Jeremy Schep, Faheed Haddad, Lee Simmons, Dareese Dunbar, Greg Barnes and Veronique Bennett. Thank you, Pat Joyce, for reading the hospital chapter for medical authenticity, and the kind man (sorry I forgot your name) from the air charter company near Albany airport who told me what I would see if I took a flight from Albany to Montreal. If you don't see your name, but you read the book and gave me feedback . . . please forgive me. It's been a long time. Just let me know and I will include your name in the next printing.

Thank you, too, Dave Danglis, for being such a great layout professional and exhibiting such incisive editing skills.

You were, indeed, my last line of defense and I am grateful for all the things you caught. You did not withdraw. You did not retreat. You charged right in and told me what you thought needed changing and the book is better for it.

I would be amiss if I also did not express my gratitude to Faith Chapel, Elim Fellowship and all the churches that graciously supported my family when we were ministering in France. Thank you. They were precious, wonderful years (though not without their challenges) and it was a great privilege serving cross-culturally in one of the most beautiful countries in the world. We could never have done it without you. Of course, it goes without saying but I'll say it anyway—I could not have set part of the novel convincingly in France had I not lived there for almost ten years.

The last word of thanks goes to Terry Bish and Mary Sorrendino who helped make this project financially sound. As a creative person you do not want to think about money, but the reality is . . . sometimes you need it to bring your dreams to reality.

Preface

A novelist once wrote about his book: "All of it is fictional . . . except where it's true." I can honestly say the same thing about the book you are now holding in your hands (as a paperback, on an iPad, or Smart Phone, tablet, etc.). It is based on my experiences or those of someone I have met along the way. As a reader, I will let you guess what is fact or fiction.

When you reduce things down to their lowest common denominator, however, the following story is essentially the story of us all because in the circumstances of life at some point(s), we've all run away from the God who loves us.

Thankfully, over the centuries, there are millions, including myself, who have discovered a remarkable truth—changing directions can make all the difference in the world.

Chapter 1

A Routine Day Gone Berserk
Monday, May 19, 2003
Albany, NY

If Ace Parks had known what kind of day was ahead of him, he would have stayed in bed. It was a fairly cool day at 59 degrees, but spring had indeed sprung and people were finally getting outside. Driving to work he chuckled to see one guy in shorts and flip flops already barbecuing something outside, completely oblivious to the grey clouds overhead. Ace wore his favorite hoodie, a gift his Uncle Jerry had bought him at Niagara Falls a year earlier, to ward off the slight chill in the air. He hummed the classic rock song, "Eye of the Tiger," as he pushed open the glass door with the word *Luigi's* written on it in bold, black italics. The familiar smells of garlic, tomato sauce, and baking pizza greeted him like old friends.

Bill Stanley, the manager, was throwing pizza dough in the air at the far wall counter while two girls with phone headsets and red tee shirts with Luigi's spelled out in large white letters across the backs were taking orders and tapping keyboards in front of two flat screen monitors. Three other stations remained empty since it was not quite supper time yet. Valerie, the girl closest to the door, smiled when he came in. She mouthed a silent "Hi Ace" and fist bumped him while the other stared straight ahead listening intently.

"Hi Ace. What's happening?" Stanley yelled over his shoulder while spreading the tomato sauce evenly on the uncooked pizza with the underside of a ladle. "Pete called in sick, so could you help with some deliveries tonight?"

"No problem, Bill."

Ace walked briskly down the short corridor to his left and grabbed an electric Luigi's sign from the back room. Piles and piles of empty Luigi pizza boxes stood like white towers against the back wall. Stanley always encouraged the drivers to put together the boxes during slow times so they would be ready when orders started. They came flat and it only took ten seconds to put them into shape. Sometimes the drivers had contests to see who was the fastest. Ace had it down to a science so no one came close, but they tried anyway.

Ace picked up a spray bottle on the floor and moisturized the suction cups dangling from the thin metal arms on the sign and then went outside. He quickly put the clips from the sign on the passenger door window of his black 2001 Eclipse, threw in the electrical cord, pushed the suction cups against the glass, and then came around to the driver's door. He leaned in and pulled the lighter out of its place and stuck the plug from the sign in the opening. He also turned on the key, which illuminated the sign, and pushed the button to raise the passenger window to the top to hold the clip fast.

He walked quickly back inside the store and looked at the computer-generated strip of paper hanging from the top of the aluminum counter. He read the name: Wilson, address: 675 South Lincoln Ave., the price: $7.99, the order: large cheese pizza, and the time the order was given: 4:29 PM. Ace winced involuntarily when he saw the address. He ripped it down quickly and smoothed it to the side of the pizza box until it stuck. He then stuffed the box into a brown vinyl insulated bag that he pulled up from under the counter and closed the flap with the sound of Velcro.

This wasn't his favorite area to deliver in. A young black man was killed in a nearby state recently by what some believed was police brutality by white officers. To Ace, this neighborhood was a time bomb waiting to explode. He'd heard of drivers from other pizza places being chased by gangs, or even physically assaulted and robbed. Places like Domino's, Pizza Hut, and Little Caesar's had stopped delivering there, which meant, of course, more orders for Luigi's, but he sometimes feared for the drivers. He tried to convince Stanley to stop going there like the other stores, but he could tell his manager liked all the extra orders from the lack of competition. As long as nothing happened to his drivers Ace doubted anything would ever change. Ace was happy Stanley at least listened to him about only sending guys there, but he was wondering how long the manager would hold out with some of the girls complaining about fewer deliveries and threatening to contact the corporate office about him discriminating against them because of their gender.

But there was another reason he didn't want to go to that area, and he wasn't about to tell Stanley. He hoped another driver would come in so he could hand it off to him, but none appeared and Stanley kept waving at him to get going.

Ace made it to the address in less than ten minutes and turned into the driveway. Immediately he noticed a lively group of dishevelled men sitting on the porch of a nearby house holding paper bags with glass bottle necks protruding from the tops. The drivers had mentioned this group before and even nicknamed it the "Ignited Nations," because of the mixed nationalities present. A fellow driver named José Gonzales from Puerto Rico always asked anyone who went down there, "Hey, my man at the meeting? We need some representation you know," as a standing joke. A boom box blared out of a window somewhere, oblivious to the possibility of offending anyone's musical taste or tranquillity.

As soon as Ace stepped out of his car with the pizza, a voice cried out, "Hey, boy, that's my pizza!" The big, burly black man in the middle just stood up and put out his hand. A smaller white man to his right with a Boston Red Sox baseball cap, then spoke up: "What you mean by that, Sonny! That's my pizza." The tall man just pressed his hand on the other man's cap pushing it down over his eyes and the man back into his lawn chair. "I got a better idea, Boston. Why don't you just sit down and shut up!"

On the other side of the street, little boys and girls were riding bikes and zigzagging up and down driveways with their roller blades. Ace got out of the car, smiled in the direction of his spectators, and ran to the door and rang the doorbell. After a few minutes a forlorn looking woman in a ragged housecoat appeared and gave him the exact change in rolls of quarters, nickels, and pennies. He ran back to his car amidst mild protests from the onlookers next door. He looked in his rear-view mirror and saw nothing. He put the car in reverse and began moving. *That's odd*, he thought. *That little bump wasn't there before.* He heard a whimper and then silence.

The big man yelled out from the porch. "He's killed little Henrietta! Look! She's not moving."

Ace felt a cold sweat envelop his body. How had someone gotten behind the car? He could have sworn he had looked carefully. Pandemonium exploded. Mothers were screaming. Children were crying, and those men on the porch were coming at him full speed with the big man out in front. Out of nowhere he also saw a band of four gang members with red bandanas and black jackets appear from around the side of the green house across the street. One yelled out, "Hey, that's his car!" and pointed in Ace's direction. That gang was the chief reason Ace was nervous about coming to this area. In unison they all began to sprint in his direction. The lead runner looked like he was digging for something in his right pocket.

Ace put the car in drive as a reflex. The big man was getting closer and he was chanting something like, "I'm gonna take care of this myself right now. Yes, sir. I seen that white boy do that on purpose and . . . and I'm gonna get 'im."

Before Ace knew it his driver's door flung open and a hand, the size of a baseball mitt, grabbed his shoulder. Ace didn't hesitate. He quickly shifted into "Drive," pressed down hard on the accelerator and turned the steering wheel hard to the left. He felt the strong grip on his shoulder release as the car spun into the yard and over the curb to the street. The door clacked shut from the momentum. The arriving gang members jumped out of his way, cursing. A few of them were able to get off some loud punches to the car as a parting gift. Ace glanced into his side view mirror and saw a small girl in roller blades lying on the street and the big man clutching his arm. The man's eyes were red and menacing and he shot up his middle finger and shouted, "We're gonna get you, white boy!"

Chapter 2

The Escape
Monday, May 19, 2003
Albany, NY

As Ace sped away from the accident his mind raced as his sweaty palms lubricated the leather steering wheel. This couldn't have happened. It was like a living nightmare from which he could not awake. Did he in fact kill a little girl? How did she get behind him so fast? Why didn't someone see her and yell at him to stop? He was sure he had looked in his rear view mirror. What could he do now? If he'd gotten out of the car he may have been killed. Now he was guilty of leaving the scene of an accident. Who would believe a pizza delivery boy?

And who in that neighborhood would testify on his behalf —a white boy! Everybody knew pizza drivers drove too fast. He remembered an accident a couple of years ago out west where a pizza delivery guy ran over an old lady and killed her because he wanted to get the pizza to the customer within a half an hour. Of course, the company quickly abolished the half-hour-or-it's-free rule, but the damage was done. A woman had lost her life. He could forget about being the assistant manager at that new store now. And what about his dream to have his own store in two years?

But how could he even think about himself when a child could be dead? But she wouldn't want revenge, would she? She was just a little girl. Children forgive quickly. It's the adults who like to hold grudges and punish severely. She wouldn't want his life to be ruined. They might even put him in jail, being on probation and all for cutting up that gang member in the bar. The way things were going along racial lines the judge might even jail him for political reasons. He could call his lawyer, Uncle Jerry, who had helped out a lot when he had to check his mom into the nursing home while she waited for the kidney transplant, and two years ago when she had died.

No. No use getting Uncle Jerry involved. He'd already done enough. Go to the police? Fat chance he'd get a fair trial. Better to just get far away as quickly as possible. That gang now had two reasons to get him and he knew they would eventually track him down, especially if that kid didn't make it.

One bad move and his life could be limited to a five-by-seven cell somewhere. Too bad this wasn't a chess game. He regularly had fierce matches with the number one player at Albany High and could usually figure out how to get out of most messes, but this was different. It was real life. *Just think*, he kept telling himself. *You can do this. There is a way out of this.* He pulled over on the side road by the Big M truckers' diner and took the Luigi's sign out of the window. He threw it in the back seat. He sat back down in the driver's seat and grabbed his cell phone. It rang once. Twice. He muttered under his breath: "Please. Oh please, Gabriella. Be home." Finally the soft, gentle voice he knew so well came through the receiver.

"Hello."

"Gabby," Ace whispered, although no one was anywhere close by.

"It's me, Ace. Listen. The plans have changed."

"What do you mean, Ace?"

"I mean something has happened and we have to go now," Ace said. "Please don't ask questions now. I'll explain later."

Gabriella didn't argue, and least not now. Ace was in trouble and she had to help. "Okay. What do you want me to do?"

"Tell your dad you are going to sleep over at Mary's tonight.

Pack a light suitcase and then take your bike and ride over to my house. Don't forget the dress. The front door key is under the rock by the mailbox. Go into my room and get the envelope with the $3,000 in cash and the passports. There's also the small box on the top shelf of my closet. Bring that too. Then get the key to my mom's Oldsmobile that's hanging on the key rack in the kitchen. Meet me at the parking lot at the river near the bus station downtown. Did you get all that? "

"Yes. I think so. But Ace, I'm scared. What is going on? I only have one month left of school. I thought we were going to wait until my graduation before going to France and everything?"

"I'll tell you as soon as you get here. Please hurry, Gabby. Something serious has happened, but I think everything will be okay if you can get here quickly. Please Gabby. I wouldn't ask you if I didn't have a good reason. Try to be there in fifteen minutes. Our future depends on it. Oh, and don't forget to get a suitcase for me. It's in my closet. Just grab a bunch of clothes from my drawers and my toothbrush and stuff, okay?"

"What if my dad comes home early and says I can't go?" Gabriella said, her voice shaking.

"In that case, just go in your room, turn up the stereo, and climb out the window," Ace said resolutely.

"I'm coming, Ace, one way or another. I love you."

"I love you, too, Gabby. Please, fifteen minutes."

They both hung up the phone. Gabriella sat up straight on the bed and took a deep breath and let it out slowly. She got up and took her suitcase out from the attic and quickly packed her things. "The dress" Ace had referred to was the one she was going to wear when they eloped. It wasn't a typical wedding dress but more of a white business woman's ensemble with a skirt just above the knee and a beautiful silk blouse with lace at the top. She had to ruffle through ten dresses hanging in her closet to get to it.

She felt like a butterfly shedding its cocoon. She was light-headed and moved like she was in a dream putting clothes and accessories into her suitcase. It was finally going to happen. But, why now? What was so important that she had to drop everything and not even graduate? It wasn't like Ace to panic like that. Maybe she could talk some sense into him once she knew what was really going on. Now she had to act fast. She ran to the window. *Good,* she thought, *the Explorer's not in the driveway. He's not home from work yet.* Recently her father, who owned a successful general contracting business, had been coming home earlier to start his beer consumption. *This will be easier.* She went to the vinyl note pad on the refrigerator and took the marker hanging on the string and wrote: *Dad, I'm over at Mary's house. She asked me to stay over. We have a physics project we're working on together and I thought we could start tonight and finish it tomorrow morning. I'll call tomorrow. There's left-over ziti in the fridge. Gabby.*

She hurried back to her bedroom and put on a sweater and her brown suede jacket. She left on her jeans and slid on her sneakers, grabbed her purse and suitcase and ran out the side of the house to the garage. She went in through the side door and found her bike in the corner and pressed the button to open the garage door. She pushed the red ten-speed to where she placed the other things, ran back into the garage, pressed the button again and then sprinted out before it closed.

She pulled out an elastic from her purse and put her long black hair through it to make a ponytail. She grabbed the suitcase with her left hand and got on the bike. For fear that she might be seen on Fowler Road, Gabriella rode through their perfectly landscaped backyard around the in-ground pool until she reached Simpson Road, which was parallel to Fowler where they lived. She knew her father would be taking Fowler, especially since Simpson was under construction. She hoped no one saw her. She then jumped on the ten-speed and shifted into gear. It felt a little awkward since she hadn't ridden on it in months and she had a suitcase in her left hand, but soon she was travelling fast enough to arrive at Ace's on Kirby Avenue in five minutes.

She found the key under the rock and then went to the back of the grey Cape Cod house and pushed the bike under the deck. Then she ran around to the front and up the wheelchair ramp to the front door. Her feet made loud dull sounds on the wood and she could feel her heart beating rapidly almost in unison. She opened the door and quickly gathered all the things that Ace had instructed. She went out to the garage and lifted the door. The springs vibrated nosily as if announcing to the world that she was there. She opened the rear door of the grey Olds and threw the suitcases in the back. She placed the passports and the cash in the glove compartment, put the small box in her jacket pocket and turned the key. It turned over several times but didn't start. Obviously it hadn't been used in quite a while. Gabriella stopped and took a deep breath and said under her breath, "Please God" and tried again. The engine coughed a few more times and then roared into life. She jammed the automatic into reverse and stepped on the gas and shot out of the driveway.

Fortunately, the road crew had left enough driving space for the residents so she could drive fairly fast down Simpson to Kirby. From there it was just a left and shortly thereafter the entrance to the highway, which would bring her to the parking area where Ace was waiting.

Chapter 3

Albany Bus Station
Monday, May 19, 2003

After Ace talked with Gabriella he pulled back out into rush hour traffic and merged into the rapid flow of cars in the direction of the bus station, but not too fast so as to attract unwanted attention. He heard the blasts of the rescue vehicles just as he parked the car outside of the Greyhound station. He fought off the fear that tried to paralyze his thinking. He made sure he left his Luigi's hat on and pushed through the glass door. He was relieved to see only a few customers in the ticket line in the bus station and a bus marked NEW YORK CITY in the bus port. "Next," a 30ish heavy-set black woman with frizzy hair barked. "Destination?"

"New York City, please. One way," Ace said.

"That's a little far to bring a pizza, isn't it?" the woman said with a smile.

"Oh yeah. But they're big tippers," Ace retorted.

"No doubt," the woman said, resuming her professional manner. "That'll be $34, please."

"You take checks, right?" Ace asked.

"Yeah. As long as it's local and I can see your driver's license."

"Sure. Here you go." Ace took out his license and handed it back to her. The woman copied down the number and gave it back to him with the ticket.

"You better hurry. It's leaving in about five minutes."

Ace ran out the door and up the stairwell of the waiting bus. Halfway up he stopped and looked to see if the woman at the counter was looking his way. She wasn't so he turned around, went down the steps and sprinted in the direction of his car.

At that moment the bus driver was coming out of the bus station entrance with a cup of coffee in his hand. Ace brushed by him and the hot coffee spilled onto the bus driver's chest and arm. The driver yelled, "Hey kid, why don't you watch where you're going!" and then muttered under his breath, "Those stupid pizza guys are always in a hurry. It's a wonder more people don't get killed."

Ace cursed under his breath and jumped into his car. He hoped the driver wouldn't remember he saw him until at least the next morning. He drove out of the parking lot onto the main street and made a left that took him underneath 790 and over to the river park just three minutes away.

Chapter 4

Albany Tribune Office
Monday, May 19, 2003

R obert Palmer, veteran reporter for the *Albany Tribune,* slouched at his desk. He yawned and sighed in relief for a little breathing room when his phone rang. He whispered, "Oh great, just what I need," and picked up the receiver. "Hello, Albany Tribune, Palmer speaking." The voice was a familiar one from the north side.

"Bob, I think I got a good one for you. Some pizza driver from Luigi's just ran over some little girl down on Lincoln Avenue— she could be dead. He just drove away. Better get here quick."

Palmer responded without enthusiasm, "Thanks Charlie. I'll get right to it."

Another hit and run story, Palmer thought. *Maybe it would make it to the last page of the local section, but who knows? Luigi's was a national chain, so maybe they'd put his title and a few lines in a side bar on the front page.* It wasn't that he was calloused to the tragedies that he wrote about. He just wanted a change of scene and a salary increase. The more front page stories he did, the more valuable he looked to potential bigger city papers. He had found the more detached he was from the unpleasant stories, the more objective he could be. After all, he was paid to be factual not sentimental, and one thing he knew Bascom couldn't tolerate was sentimentality. The editor had said it so much every reporter could complete the sentences for him: "We want to be salt to this town, not sugar. Leave the sweet stuff for the weeklies." Since many weeklies relied on advertisers for their source of income and gave away their papers for free, they were obligated to write positive things about those businesses. Palmer knew, however, that powerful political forces could influence their editor's choice of subject, or how a story was written.

Palmer picked up his grey suit jacket from behind his chair and shot his hands through the sleeves. His salt and pepper hair betrayed his age and his big belly his bad eating habits. He saw Editor Norman Bascom out of the corner of his eye and tried to duck out the side door, to no avail.

"Hey, Palmer! Where are you going? You just got here, didn't you?" Palmer's shoulders hunched up involuntarily and he felt a slight irritation in the back of his neck. *Why did this guy make him react like he used to when his old history teacher in high school hovered over his desk?*

"Yeah, Norman. I just got back, but I also just received a call from someone. Evidently there's been a hit and run down on Lincoln Avenue. A little girl could be dead. A Luigi's driver just beat it out of there."

The editor's eyes narrowed in interest. "A Luigi's driver, huh? That's a bad break for them. They've got that super high tech store opening up next September in Delmar. Make sure you get some good pictures this time, will you? And call the Luigi's manager for details about the driver. I think the New Scotland store covers downtown. The cops should get 'im pretty quickly."

"Thanks," Palmer said. For some reason Bascom loved to state the obvious.

"And Palmer," Bascom continued, "how about bringing a large pepperoni back with you? I'll even let you have a piece." He laughed jovially. Palmer knew Norman liked picking up the pizzas himself. That way he didn't feel obligated to give a tip. He hated it when some counter people started putting paper cups or cans labelled "tips" by the cash registers. "Why should

I give them a tip?" he'd complain. "All they're doing is taking my order and taking my money."

Bascom pulled out a wad of bills and peeled off ten ones. "Here you go, Palmer."

"It could be a while though, Norm," Palmer said, trying to avoid the extra duty.

"That's all right, Palmer," Bascom assured him. "I don't mind cold pizza. I can always warm it up in the microwave."

Palmer shoved the cash into his right pocket and pushed his way out the door under the EXIT sign. It was raining lightly and he pulled up his collar and walked to his green 1991 Volvo.

Unfortunately, the driver's window was still broken and would only go up to three inches from the top. The wind blew in just enough rain to irritate Palmer and cause him to promise himself to fix the window. For some reason, whenever it was nice out he would forget about the window until the next time it rained, but then it was usually while he was working, so he couldn't take it in. He'd grumble and make promises to himself when he sat on a wet seat in the morning, but it did little to motivate him to actually make a plan to drop it off at Vinny's. Instead, he just carried a roll of duct tape and put a strip across the top if it got too bad.

Within five minutes he was at 675 South Lincoln Avenue, the scene of the accident. The ambulance had already arrived and the workers were huddled over the small body of the girl, completely blocking her view except for her calves, white socks, and roller blades. What looked like the girl's mother stood a few feet away in a catatonic-like state staring blankly to nowhere in particular as neighbors and friends tried to console her. Every resident from a block away was standing on their front porch, or milling close by, shaking their heads and talking in hushed tones.

Palmer got out of the car and recognized the burly black man talking to a reporter from a competing paper. He didn't remember where he had seen him but the face was familiar. The black man was talking in an animated fashion using his hands and then holding his arm indicating how the driver got away. Palmer moved closer and overheard the conversation.

"I'm telling you, mister. That boy purposely ran over that girl. See that porch over there. I saw the whole thing. I tried to stop him from driving away and he just took off."

"Do you know what kind of car it was?" the reporter asked.

"Car? Uh, I think it was a blue Camaro." He then turned and yelled to a man on the porch. "Hey Boston! What kind of car was it?"

The man hesitated and then yelled back. "It was a blue Pontiac!"

"Look, it all happened like that," and the man snapped his fingers. "We were looking at the girl, not the car. But you can get that info from Luigi's, can't you?"

The reporter nodded and said, "Yeah, I can. But let me see if I understand you correctly. You believe this driver did this on purpose?"

"No doubt in my mind. He should be punished to the full extent of the law. That's what I say."

"Could you write down your name for me please?" The big man grabbed the pen the reporter handed to him and scribbled on the note pad.

"So I'm going make the news, am I?"

"There's that possibility."

"Hear that fellas? I'm gonna be in the paper."

Palmer pursed his lips, shook his head, and walked toward the ambulance. He lifted the camera from around his neck and took a few shots of the emergency workers surrounding the little girl with her calves showing and her red roller blades sticking out from underneath the huddle. The four uniformed men then lifted the stretcher with the unmoving form of the girl covered with dark-colored blankets and slid her into the back of the ambulance and shut the two doors.

Palmer caught a glimpse of her pale face. Her eyes were closed. *She's obviously in shock or dead*, Palmer thought, but he couldn't be sure. After the worker closed the rear doors he walked toward the driver's door when Palmer intercepted him.

"Excuse me, sir. I'm with the Albany Tribune. Could you tell me if she's gonna be okay? She's not dead, is she?"

The driver was obviously upset by this accident and said curtly, "No, but she's in critical condition and I'm sorry I can't say any more. This girl's got to get to an emergency room fast." With those words he opened the driver's door and jumped in. The siren erupted into its loud wailing sound and Palmer watched it pull out from the curb and speed down Lincoln Avenue in the direction of Albany Medical Center.

Palmer looked over to the big man and thought to himself: *There is more to this story than meets the eye.* He interviewed a few other bystanders, but most had not witnessed the accident. He asked a woman standing next to him who the man was who had talked to the reporter. "Oh, him. That's Sonny Jackson." Palmer wrote down the name and decided to talk to this one later. He approached the woman who seemed to be the mother of the child but thought she must be on drugs by the strange look on her face, and decided against it. He got back into his car and drove to Luigi's on New Scotland Avenue. He was happy that he beat the other reporters to the store. They might have thought the other store on Main Street covered the Lincoln Avenue area. Easy mistake to make. Nice break though.

As he pushed his way through Luigi's glass door, it was like walking into bee hive. A number of uniformed boys and girls were performing a wide range of duties. Two were throwing dough up in the air. Another one was putting toppings on several pizzas in front of her and five were answering phones as quickly as possible and typing the orders on the computer keyboards. One motioned with her index finger that it would be just a minute until she got to him. He shook his head and raised his hand to indicate he didn't mind the wait. Meanwhile, other employees were taking pizzas out of the oven while the rest were putting them into canvas bags and running out the door.

Three carry-out customers were seated on the wooden bench on the left as he entered. He asked the Puerto Rican boy running out of the door with a brown canvas bag where he could find the manager. The boy pointed around the corner to the office, looked up to the large clock on the wall, shouted out how old the order was, and sprinted to his car. Palmer turned the corner and immediately saw the blue uniform of Phil Pierce from the City Police Department standing in the doorway to the office obviously talking with someone.

When Palmer approached Pierce turned his head and said to the person inside, "Guess what, Bill. Your worst nightmare has arrived. It's the media. May I present Mr. Robert Palmer from the Albany Tribune."

Palmer came abreast of Pierce and looked in the closet of an office and saw a middle-aged balding man with a silver name plate on his Luigi's shirt. It read *Manager Bill Stanley*. Stanley turned to face him. The man was obviously distraught and at a loss for words.

Finally, he said, "I'm sorry but I'm not authorized to say anything yet for the company. I should have a public statement soon. All I can say is Ace Parks was my best driver. Has a great reputation with us and I don't have the slightest idea how this happened and why he would leave the scene of the accident. His driving record is impeccable. I can't say anything else at this time. To tell you the truth I haven't even told the crew yet what happened."

Palmer lowered his note pad and said, "I understand, Mr.

Stanley. I'm sure it has been very unsettling for you. Can I call you later to get some more details?"

"Sure. I should be able to say something soon. I just need a little coaching is all from the main office. Nothing like this has ever happened in my store before." Stanley turned back to the table, lowered his head in despair, and pushed his hands through the little hair he had left on the sides of his head.

Palmer looked at Officer Pierce in a questioning way and Pierce nodded like he understood and winked at him like he would talk to him in a few minutes. Palmer went back out front and noticed the bench was now empty. He sat down and wrote a few lines in his note pad. He then got up and ordered a large pepperoni pizza and sat down again.

A few minutes later Pierce walked around the corner. Palmer followed him out the door and over to the police car. Pierce opened the driver's door, leaned over, picked up a black receiver, said a few words into it and set it back down. He turned to Palmer and sighed, "I don't have a lot to give you but the kid is 19. He's worked for Luigi's for four years and he was going to work at that new store in Delmar next September. In fact, he was in training to be the Assistant Manager. Apparently, he's a bright kid. No parents on the scene though. His mom died two years ago and his dad walked out on the family when he was a kid. Tough situation yet he was making the best of it. I just called a car to go over to his house off of New Scotland. We should have him in custody in no time—two hours max. I mean where is he gonna go? He just panicked. That's all."

"Do you know what kind of car it was?" Palmer asked.

"Yeah. It was a 2001 Eclipse. Black."

"We'll get his photo from Motor Vehicle for you for tomorrow. Call me at the police station in two hours. I should be able to give you some more details by then."

"Thanks Phil. I'll do that. Don't get too cocky though.

Sometimes the fish get away, you know," Palmer said good-naturedly. He knew the policeman was usually accurate on things like this. He just wanted to bust his chops.

"Okay. I'll give you two and a half," Palmer said as the officer started his engine. He patted the police car driver's door as to signal a goodbye and went back into the store. He grabbed a Diet Coke out of the cooler and waited for the pizza.

Chapter 5

An Unusual Guy
Monday, May 19, 2003

abriella kept looking at the speedometer on Route 90 to make sure she wasn't going more than five miles over the speed limit. She couldn't afford to be stopped by the police now. She and Ace had secretly planned their get-a-way for the last three months. Ace had even blocked it off at Luigi's as a vacation. Why postpone her graduation? It didn't make sense, but she knew Ace wouldn't ask her to come now if there wasn't a good reason. What could have happened?

She still remembered the day that she first became aware of this unique male specimen. She was in her freshman year and sitting with a few friends in the cafeteria. She was picking at her bowl of canned fruit salad when she overheard the conversation of a group of junior and senior boys who were just in back of her. As usual they were discussing girls and sex and, at first, she just wanted to get out of earshot—but something stopped her.

She heard the deep mellow voice of the boy who apparently was directly behind her. He said, "No. I'm going to wait 'til I get married before I have sex with a girl." At that the whole table laughed, but he waited until they stopped and continued. "To me sex is kind of like a fire. It can burn your house down or it can keep your house warm, contained in a fireplace. The way promiscuous sex has gotten out of hand it has also brought about a lot of serious diseases—and I'm not just talking about AIDS—I mean many kinds of sexually transmitted diseases that you don't hear about. I just think it's smarter to wait. That makes it more special. I mean, if you saved that experience for the one you are really committed to."

Bret Peterson blurted out, "Haven't you heard of condoms, man? You can have fun and not worry about that stuff?"

"You think you're safe with condoms?" Ace countered. "You gotta be kidding. That's a bunch of crap that those planned family clinics tell you to keep you coming to them so they can get those federal dollars. Look at it this way. Condoms are not even 100% effective in preventing pregnancy and that can only happen a few times a month. AIDS is something you can get every time you have sex and AIDS can kill you."

This information was something that Ace had learned at an almost all black (except for him) youth retreat he went to with Elijah Williams, the all-star fullback for the varsity at Albany High. He couldn't buy into all the God stuff, but he thought the speaker had made a lot of sense. Somehow he couldn't believe in a God that would let his father desert him and his mother die when he was so young. His mom kept confessing her faith to the end, radiating love and peace, but he was devastated. No. He was on his own now and he knew it. Still, some arguments just made sense, nothing to do with religion.

Gabriella couldn't believe what she was hearing—a teenage boy saying he believed in commitment and saving sex for marriage! She wanted to turn around and see who it was, but she didn't dare. She knew she would probably get the brunt of the other boys' jokes if she did. In fact she heard the school clown, Craig Shaw, crack after a few minutes of awkward silence, "He just says that 'cause he's gay," and all his cronies laughed—that is, except this mystery boy. Then he said politely, "If you boys will excuse me I've got a class to go to." But he must have been a little nervous because he backed his chair into Gabriella's. She looked up shyly into his face.

He said, "I'm sorry" with a sincere, almost embarrassed, look, but their eyes met for a few seconds like they understood each other on a much deeper level. Of course, this hesitation sparked off another round of catcalls. "Hey Gabby, you wanna get married?" Craig bellowed. "We've got just the guy for you." Gabriella turned a deep red that really got them going. He had just announced to the world the dream and desire of Gabriella's heart. She just knew that she was going to get married young. She didn't want to fool around with a lot of boys. She wanted to find the right one early and settle down. She'd seen enough of her friends get hurt, used, and abused. She just hadn't found the right one . . . yet. But . . . maybe.

She left her two green grapes and the pineapple chunk in the bowl and got up shortly after him. These boys wouldn't understand her feelings. But this boy was different. He might be someone worth knowing. She had seen him in school before but never really talked to him. She thought he must be a transfer student. He wasn't the most handsome but he was tall and had a good build. His nose was a little long and narrow but there was something honest and vulnerable in those blue eyes. She'd notice his dimples when he smiled later and the way he tossed his head to get his blond wave out of his eyes, but that would be much later.

When she discovered he worked at Luigi's she developed a much keener appreciation of circular meals, and began asking her father if she could order a pizza at least one night a week. Sometimes it would take some work because her father loved her cooking so much, but when she complained that she had a lot of school work he would relent. If Ace wasn't the pizza driver, she was very disappointed. When he was, they both were a little timid, but she always made sure he got a good tip, even if she had to slip in a few extra dollars of her own on top of what her dad gave her to pay him. Of course, Ace would respond enthusiastically to her generosity, but it was clear the money wasn't the only thing that excited him.

"Thank you, Gabriella. Any time you want to order just ask them to send me."

One time she betrayed her feelings when she pouted angrily, "I do, but they don't always listen."

That was the time she noticed his dimples, because his smile brightened and he said, "Yeah. Sometimes they just give it to the next driver up. I could be on the road with another delivery. They don't want it to get cold on you."

What she didn't know after that confession was, Ace always made sure he was the right man up when her address appeared on the pizza box. If not, he would just ask to change with someone so he could have the honors.

Gabriella heard some sirens and rescue trucks speeding by in the opposite direction that broke her out of her reverie. She saw the sign for the riverside park and put on her blinker.

Chapter 6

A Different Kind of Girl
Monday, May 19, 2003

A fter Ace parked the Eclipse, he pulled off his Luigi's shirt and threw it in the back seat along with his hat. He left the motor running but got out of the car and moved the cement blocks bordering the grass and wooded area of the park. He jumped back into the driver's seat and drove a short distance onto the grass. He opened the door again, leaped out and ran to where he left the cement blocks and moved them back into their original position. He got back into the car again and drove around a clump of shrubs and trees. From the parking area the car was barely visible.

Ace rolled down his window and turned off the engine. He listened to the sounds of the traffic from the highway. Then he turned the key just enough so he could have power to listen to the radio. He pushed the second button for the all news channel. He desperately wanted to know what happened to the little girl, but all he heard was the weather for the next couple of days. "Light showers for this evening and for the rest of the week," the announcer predicted.

Ace sat rigidly still hoping to hear something about the accident and that the girl was not seriously injured. Next was world news. Ace thought he heard a car approaching and quickly turned off the radio. A slight wind blew through Ace's hair and he felt a chill. He suddenly realized that he had been sweating even though he now wore only a tee shirt. He stoically calmed himself and tried to think through this problem like he would a chess game. He had just played a gambit at the bus station, and now he had to see if the police would go for it. He quickly got out of the car again and opened the trunk and took out an old Luigi's poster. He ran around the rear fender of the Eclipse to the passenger door. He jerked the door open and turned the knob for the glove compartment. His hand shuffled through the papers and cassettes until he found what he was looking for—tape and a red marker. He took the top off the red magic marker, turned over the Luigi's poster and began printing in large letters *Just Married* and laid it on the driver's seat. He thought about Gabriella. He knew that she would come, but he wondered how she would respond when he told her what had happened. He couldn't afford to lose her. He was sure she would understand but would she leave everything to go with him?

He still remembered the day she discovered him crying inside his mom's room at the hospital where she volunteered as a candy striper. She had been walking down the hall when she saw him. His vulnerability compelled her to go into his room and sit down beside him. His mom had just been wheeled away for another test of some kind and suddenly he couldn't take it anymore and had an emotional meltdown. At first she didn't say a word but then very gently touched his knee and asked, "Ace, it's me, Gabriella. Are you all right?"

Ace looked up all bleary eyed and wiped his tears from his face. He was happy to see it was her but a little embarrassed that she saw him crying. Gabriella grabbed a tissue from the box on the table and handed it to Ace. He was touched deeply by the intense compassion and concern that he saw in Gabriella's eyes. He knew then that she was someone that he could trust and be open with. "Thanks, Gabby. The doctor just told me that I have no choice but to keep Mom in the hospital to see if her body is going to accept the new kidney or not."

Gabriella put her hand on Ace's forearm and said quietly, "I know how you feel. My mom's been in and out of mental hospitals for years and it's hard when you feel like there is nothing you can do to help. Let me know, though, if there is anything I can do. I'm a good listener. I gotta go now. I'm supposed to take a patient to the gift shop." During those few minutes Ace felt that a strong bond had formed between them. As she got up to go, Ace smelled the sweet scent of her perfume and wished it would never leave. "I mean that, Ace. Let's talk some more some time, okay?" Gabriella said.

"Sure," Ace replied. "I'd like that." After that brief exchange, Ace knew she was the only girl he wanted.

He was overjoyed later that year when he discovered they were in the same French class. At first he signed up for the class because his mom loved the language so much, but he soon discovered that he liked it too. Pretty soon Ace and Gabriella were officially dating—that is, until Gabby's father found out.

"You don't mean to tell me, Gabby, that you're interested in that guy that brings us pizza!" her father had shouted at her. "I thought Anthony who works for me would be perfect for you. Now that kid has got a future in masonry. But this kid, forget it! He's a loser. I forbid you to ever see him again. Do you understand?"

Gabriella had no choice but to agree. What her father said was law and final. So over the last few months they had to see each other secretly. Last Christmas they went out to the mall and picked out a ring. They had worked out a detailed plan for their itinerary in France for a honeymoon and they had saved several thousand dollars. Didn't hurt, of course, that Ace's mom had a life insurance policy of $250,000.

Ace had never met a girl like Gabriella who didn't like to flirt with boys and lead them on, or try to seduce them by wearing provocative clothing. She played oboe in the orchestra and expanded Ace's horizons to cultural events he would never have attended otherwise without her influence. He'd usually come in late for her concerts because of his pizza delivery schedule, but he always clapped the loudest after her solos if he was able to hear them. She was a real complement to his personality and he knew it. While he was prone to just tell people what he thought, she was always considerate of the other person and sensitive to what they were going through. Her current job, a receptionist for a general practitioner, was perfect for her. She sympathized with the patients and knew them all by name and the names of their children. She also knew how to maintain her gentleness when people got angry about a bill, or were just snappy because they were sick. He was amazed how she was able to work that out with the school and get out early so she could work from 1:00 to 4:00 Monday through Friday.

Ace thought about what a mistake it would have been to get tied up with Cindy Trola. She was the beautifully bronzed captain of the cheerleading team, thanks to in-door tanning salons, that had basically gone out with him for a few months on the rebound. Matt Peterson, the varsity quarterback, had dumped her and, in reaction, she started looking beyond the sea of shoulder pads and helmets for someone totally different.

She started to come on to Ace in computer class and ask for his help, but he thought it was out of a genuine interest. He got suspicious, though, when she always asked for free pizzas for her parties. The truth hit home the night she got drunk and started punching him hard on the arm. At first he thought it was a joke but she just kept hammering away. "Uh, that hurts. Do you think you could stop?" he asked, but she was relentless. He was bewildered. Supposedly this girl liked him and here she was pounding on him like he was a piece of meat. He couldn't punch her back because of the way he was brought up, and yet he didn't appreciate being a human punching bag either. He solved the problem by moving quickly to the side as her fist was in mid-air. She fell on the floor and cut her lip and started yelling at the top of her lungs as though Ace had hit her. A couple of linebackers showed up and threw him out in the snow. Not a pleasant experience. Now Cindy was back with Matt and everything was supposedly hunky dory. Who knows, Ace thought, maybe they had a future together posing in muscle magazines.

Although Ace wasn't thrilled with the rejection, he eventually came to the conclusion that for him the attraction was purely physical. Sure, she was beautiful, but he just couldn't feel relaxed around her. She was always telling him what to wear and how to wear it and their conversation was usually forced and superficial. The jock crowd she also hung around with wasn't exactly warm to his intrusion into their inner sanctum, except for the free pies and the hot wings. It didn't take long for him to figure out he was being used big time.

Elijah Williams, however, was not your typical jock. Even though he went to some of their parties, he didn't drink. Ace knew Elijah felt almost as uncomfortable as he did. Ace had first met Elijah when he'd asked him for help with his computer skills. He knew Ace was at the top of the class and wanted to get up to speed with his technology. From then on, they had become friends despite coming from completely two different worlds. At the parties, he'd pull Ace into a corner and say, "Ace. Let's get out of here, man. I'm tired of talking about football statistics. Wanna go bowling?" That would always get him to lighten up, because Elijah and Rhonda had gone on a double date bowling one time with he and Cindy, and Elijah was hilarious. Every time it was his turn, Elijah would loft the ball high into the air and it would come down with a thundering crash. He still remembered the mortification on Cindy's face when the manager came running out from behind the bar screaming, "Hey, you! Whatta ya think this is, a track meet?! That ball isn't for shot put, you know!"

Ace remembered watching Elijah's huge shoulders sloop down and his big eyebrows go into a puppy dog expression. "Oh, I'm sorry, sir, I'll try not to do it again." Ace laughed until he cried while Cindy kept pulling on his shirt and whispering in his ear that she wanted to leave. Ace just couldn't stop thinking that here was the best fullback in the league, who could easily destroy anyone in a brawl, humbly saying he was sorry he couldn't control his bowling ball. It was one of the only sports he didn't excel in, and that was probably due to the fact he couldn't find a ball with holes big enough for his fingers. When the manager finally realized who it was, it was his turn to be embarrassed. "You're Elijah Williams, aren't you? I read in the paper that you received a full scholarship to Michigan University? Is that true?" Before he could respond in the positive the manager was talking about this game and that play. They ended up getting the games for free.

Elijah told Ace later he made a good decision to dump Cindy. He didn't want to say anything to him while they were dating but he saw through what she was doing to Ace and had absolutely no respect for her. When he noticed Ace and Gabriella together, however, he winked at Ace and told him, "You're on the right track now, bro."

Ace shivered and rubbed his hands over his arms to warm himself up. Why was Gabriella taking so long?

Chapter 7

The Decision
Monday, May 19, 2003

ce could hear the familiar sound of the Olds. It had a small hole in its exhaust pipe and made a little louder noise than he appreciated at this moment. He grabbed the "Just Married" sign and the tape and was at the driver's rear side door before Gabriella could stop. He jumped in the back and quickly taped the sign to the back window and then opened the suitcase Gabby had brought for him. He pulled out a blue short-sleeved polo shirt, a pair of black jeans and a black denim jacket. He put them on while Gabby looked straight ahead, biting her lower lip, and waiting for the worst. She slid over to the passenger side as he climbed over the seat to take the steering wheel. He put the automatic transmission into reverse, put his right arm around the back of her seat, and backed up into the parking lot. People often used this lot to park their cars and then bike to Troy on the paved bicycle path that ran parallel to the Hudson River. Gabriella and Ace had even done it a couple of times, but a leisurely ride of any kind was definitely not on his mind. Only one word was: ESCAPE.

When he got to the road leading to 790 he gunned it, leaving a patch of tire in the tarmac. The traffic was still pretty heavy with commuters at 6:17 and Ace slowed down to go with the flow. He wrestled with the idea of getting off the highway but decided to stay on it knowing the police would be looking for a different vehicle. He took 90 West, which said Buffalo. He heard the sirens, too, and hoped his plan would buy him time. Gabby kept looking at him to judge the right time to ask for an explanation for this radical change of plans.

Suddenly they heard loud honking and screaming. *An undercover police car?* Ace thought. Instead of being pulled over, however, the car, a red BMW, swerved perilously close to their car and two college-aged girls in the back and a long-haired guy in the front hung out the open windows laughing and yelling in unison: "Happy honeymoon!!!!" and then the car swung back into traffic.

Ace hadn't counted on this attention and his heart tripled in beats per second. When he regained his composure he said quietly, "Ah, Gabby. Could you take that out of the back window, please?" Gabby quickly unfastened her seat belt, dove over the seats, re-emerged in the back seat, looked at the sign and then tossed it on the floor. She returned to her original position.

When they passed the exit for Everett Road, Ace said softly: "I'm sorry, Gabby, for all this."

"So, what's going on, Ace? Tell me." She squinted her eyes, revealing both deep concern and a dread of what she might hear.

"Well. It's not easy to explain but to put it bluntly . . . I backed over a little girl and a guy tried to pull me out of the car to beat me up, so I just took off."

"Oh, no. Ace. That's terrible. Do you know how bad she was hurt?"

"No. I've been trying to listen to the radio for some idea, but it's probably too recent to make it for the 6 o'clock news. I just knew I had to get out of there. The guy was huge and drunk and there was no way I wanted to hang around and be his punching bag. I also saw that gang I told you about coming after me too."

"But Ace, isn't it serious to leave the scene of an accident?" She shifted her weight on the seat.

"Yeah. It is. But it was better than being beaten to a pulp or worse. You remember that case of that pizza delivery guy in Texas, don't you? He accidentally killed an old lady and went to jail. I can't take the risk, Gabby. I think it's better to just clear out and let things die down. Maybe the girl won't die and we can come back eventually. Maybe we'll just love it in France." He looked over to Gabriella with a forced smile as if to move the conversation to a more pleasant topic.

Tears came to Gabriella's eyes. "This is so terrible, Ace. It's nothing like we imagined it would be." Ace turned to her as he bore right to get on the Northway in the direction of Montreal. Tears were running down both her cheeks and his heart went out to her. He resisted the temptation, however, to dwell too much on the circumstances. Someone had to be strong and decisive. Yes, things were bad, but they were together and that's what counted. The first order of business was to get away—as far as possible. He had to think like he did when he played Henry, the top chess player at Albany High. What were his opponent's next moves, and how could he avoid walking into a trap? What would the police do? He abruptly swerved the car to barely make the Wolf Road exit. Gabriella came sliding over next to him from the force of the turn.

"Ace! What are you doing?" she cried as she moved back to her place on the passenger side.

"We have to go to the airport and take a plane to Montreal. It would be too easy for the police to call ahead and block all highways. They won't be expecting us to take a plane. You got the small box? Open it and put on the ring. We just got married and we're taking our honeymoon."

Gabriella took the box out of her jacket, opened the lid and took out the slim gold wedding ring and put it on her finger. She still remembered the day they had picked it out together at Colonie Center. She wiped her eyes with her two hands to clear the moisture from her face.

"Looks great on you," Ace said as he turned left on Albany Shaker Road from Wolf. He clicked the radio on to see if there was any more news, but the airwaves were dominated by talk show hosts who thought they had the last word on everything. Both sides of the fence used heavy sarcasm and liked to make the other side look stupid, never conceding anything. Ace sometimes wished they would just admit it when the other side had a good point. He felt if you had to rely too much on "look how dumb they are," you had a weak case. He clicked it off. They passed the Americana Hotel, which looked as though a committee of architects designed it with a variety of building styles for each addition. They arrived at the airport and Ace drove into the parking area for longer stays.

He grabbed the suitcase from the back seat and got out of the car. He waved for Gabriella to come but she stayed motionless in the front seat. He opened the driver's door and said, "C'mon, Gabby, we gotta go. We don't have a lot of time."

Gabriella looked at him and her wet eyes became more intense and adamant. "Ace, please get into the car. We need to talk this through a little bit. You're asking me to leave everything behind and just come with you to France. The police are looking for you and there is a big chance that we will not make it. Is this really the best thing we can do right now? And, you haven't asked me if I even want to go with you. You're just assuming."

Ace opened the driver's door and squatted down in the opening, and looked Gabriella straight in the face. He tried to understand her dilemma, but he also knew valuable time was fleeting. He dropped his gaze momentarily to the ground, pursed his lips, and then locked eyes with Gabriella once again. His blue eyes had their familiar warmth but also a steely shine in their resolve.

"Gabriella, I love you. I want to marry you. This accident

has messed up our plans. It's obvious that I no longer have a future with this company. If the girl dies, I could go to jail. I never told you the whole story, but during Mom's sickness I did something stupid. I got drunk one night and got into a fight at a bar. I know how you feel about alcohol because of your father and all, so I didn't want to tell you, but this guy was coming at me with a chair and I broke a bottle and cut him pretty bad. Even though the guy wanted to press charges, my uncle, Jerry, who is a darn good lawyer, was able to get it reduced it to five years probation with youthful offender status.

"With all the racial tension in that neighborhood where I had the accident, the judge will probably put me in jail. I know it is not easy, but there is a good possibility that they will not catch us. I went to the bus station and bought a ticket for New York City. With luck, the lady at the bus station will put two and two together and call the police and say she sold me a ticket to the city. The police will then concentrate their efforts in that direction as we escape north to Montreal. They also will not be looking for a couple, since your father will not find out until tomorrow that you are gone.

Hopefully, we will be able to get on a flight stand-by to Paris. It's not tourist season yet and there may be two seats available. If not, we can go farther north into Quebec and get married. We've saved plenty of money and with my inheritance it should last quite a while. When things have settled a little I can contact Uncle Jerry and see what my options are. I've made up my mind, Gabby. I'm going." He hesitated slightly, inhaled slowly, and continued, "I understand if you want to stay. Graduation is just around the corner. You have a good job waiting for you. But for me . . . I gotta go and I'm not sure when I'm coming back."

Gabriella listened intently. She had always admired Ace's practicality and sense of direction in life but this . . . she had never imagined in her worst nightmares. If she stayed, their relationship was probably over. How could she let him go now? All her plans for the future included him. How could she abandon him now when he needed her most? Her head said to stay but her heart ached to go. She lowered her eyes, smiled weakly and said, "Okay, Ace, I'm with you. What do you want me to do?"

Ace stood up and leaned into the car, drew her close to him and kissed her on the forehead. "Thank you, Gabby. The first thing you can do is try to look happy. We're newlyweds, you know."

Gabriella tried to perk up and said, "OK Romeo. Lead the way. I will follow you wherever you may go."

Ace took her black suitcase and his own from the back seat.

"My first act of husbandly kindness is to carry your *valise, Madame.*"

"Will you stop it, please," she said. "You use the word *Madame* here in America and people get other ideas."

Chapter 8

Capaldi Home
Monday, May 19, 2003

The 2003 black Explorer turned into the long winding driveway with the sound of tar and gravel. The driver picked up
the plastic automatic door opener from the passenger seat,
pushed a button, and one of the garage doors hummed and rose
slowly upward. The SUV glided into its sanctuary, idling more
loudly within its walls, indicating a powerful engine built for
the open range. The sound stopped abruptly. A short but stocky
man with a barrel chest and white hair sticking out from a
yellow construction hat exited through the same air space the
vehicle had just entered. He pointed the remote control at the
garage and the door jerked and hummed once more and began
its slow descent. He walked slowly but purposefully past the
carefully manicured lawn and up the steps to the front door,
opened it and went inside.

After placing his windbreaker and hard hat on a wooden
coat tree near the door and taking off his work boots, he padded
on the rug to the dining room floor tile and straight to the
refrigerator, opened the door and took out a six-pack of beer
with a German label. He then pulled open a drawer, withdrew
a bottle opener with his free hand and pushed the drawer closed
with his hip. He walked to the kitchen table and sat down. He
ripped a brown bottle from the pack and popped the cap,
emitting cold vapour in the process. He took a gulp. He took a
few more swigs and then yelled at the top of his voice, "Hey,

Gabby! You here? Gabby? You home?"

He then got up and bee-lined it to the fridge to see if she had left a note. He read it with the beer in his hand and grunted when he understood the gist of it. He couldn't complain though. She was there most of the time and helped out with everything. He was thankful that she took over all the home responsibilities in addition to her studies after her mother went into the psychiatric hospital—she cooked, took care of the house, and even worked at a respectable doctor's office in town.

The only time he had reason to complain was when she was sweet on that guy from the pizza place, but he had nipped that baby in the bud and she seemed to be over it. He scooped out a mountain of pasta from the plastic Tupperware container with a wooden spoon, spread it evenly onto a plate and put it into the microwave. He flicked on the TV while he waited. It was too late for the evening news; he'd have to catch it later at 11. Maybe he'd call some of the guys and get in a couple rounds of poker.

Chapter 9

Albany International Airport
Monday, May 19, 2003

With both of their suitcases in hand, Ace turned to Gabby and said, "We better run! This is one place where nobody will question why we're going so fast!" At that he bolted in the direction of the airport entrance with Gabby lagging sadly behind. Ace reached the double doors first and waited for her to catch up as he stayed just inside the building to keep the automatic doors opening until she arrived.

As she crossed the threshold he said in a louder voice than normal, "C'mon, honey, hurry or we might miss our flight!" Together they ran into the main room and up to the nearest overhead monitor to see if any planes were scheduled for Montreal. Air Canada Flight #204 was scheduled for 7:15 p.m. It was 6:20 p.m. Gabby spotted the Air Canada counter. She yelled, "Ace, it's down . . ." and then caught herself. They both looked around nervously, hoping no one had paid attention and heard his name.

Ace scanned and scrutinized the faces to see if there was anyone he knew. Businessmen in suits were heading down to the gate for the commuter plane to New York City. A guy with long hair and a black guitar case with stickers plastered on it from everywhere he'd been was leaning against a pillar and sipping from a can of Coke. Porters were looking for someone to help. No one looked familiar, but with all the customers he served in the Capital District he couldn't be sure that someone didn't recognize him. He nodded to Gabby and they walked briskly to the counter behind which a blonde woman in a blue uniform was staring intently into a computer screen. When they approached Ace managed to say, "Do you have two empty seats to Montreal for the 7:15 flight?" Ace spoke in a calm casual voice, trying to be as unassuming as possible.

"Kind of late aren't you?" the woman replied.

"Please Ma'am," Ace stuttered, "we just got married and it was hard getting away."

"Congratulations to you and your wife but I'm sorry, the flight is full. There's another flight at 10:20 p.m. if you'd like."

"Aren't there any other flights we could take?" Ace pleaded. "We'll miss our connecting flight in Montreal if we don't leave soon."

"No commercial flights but you could try Fast Flight. It's a charter company in the next building over. They might be able to take you. They're kind of expensive though. You can ask at the information desk over there to call them for you."

"Thanks. We'll give it a try. If it doesn't work out, we may be back."

"Just make sure you are here early enough this time, okay?"

"You bet," Ace said.

Ace picked up the suitcases he had let down on the floor and nodded to Gabriella, who gave him a disappointed look. They walked briskly to the information booth located near the entrance where they had come in. A tall thin man around thirty looked at them with raised eyebrows expecting a question.

"Excuse me, sir, but my wife and I are looking to get a flight to Montreal as soon as possible. The lady at Air Canada said Fast Flight might be able to take us."

The man whistled and said, "They might be able to, but it will cost you a pretty penny, I can tell you that."

"That's okay. A number of people gave us cash for a wedding present and we don't want to miss our connecting flight for our honeymoon," Ace replied.

"Where are you going?" the man asked.

Ace looked at Gabriella and then blurted out, "Oh, it's a secret. Nobody knows."

"All right, Romeo. But you can't say I didn't warn you," he said in a fatherly tone, implying he thought it was a waste. "I'll give them a call and see."

"Might want to consider Geneva, Switzerland. Beautiful mountains. Clean country. I went to a public, heated swimming pool there once, just outside the city, and they had a part that opened up to the outside and you could see the white caps of the mountains from the pool."

"That sounds pretty cool. Thanks for the tip. We'll have to talk about that. Right, honey?"

"Sounds wonderful," Gabriella said. "Maybe we could do some skiing too."

The man winked at them and picked up the telephone, hit some numbers, and waited.

"Yeah. I have a couple here wanting a flight to Montreal real quick. Is there anyone available? Really? Great. I'll send them right over. Oh, by the way, how much is it? Really? Wow. I'll ask them if they can swing that." He then looked at Ace and Gabriella. "Ah . . . she says it'll be $1,012.73. Still want it?"

Ace's eyes widened in shock, but after they returned to normal he just pursed his lips and nodded his head. As soon as he mentioned the price, Gabriella gasped and put her hand to her mouth. Ace whispered confidently, "it's okay, Gabby. We've got it." She just shook her head and said, "I'll tell you outside."

The man redirected his attention to the phone and said,

"Yeah. He says it's okay. All right. I'll send them right over."

The man turned to Ace and said, "Yep. There's a pilot who just got in. The operations manager said he can take you in about 20 minutes. You just go out the entrance you came in, turn left and it's the first building on the left. It looks like a corporate headquarters with big glass windows and doors. You go into the foyer and you'll see their door with their logo on the right. They charge a lot because they return empty. Well, have fun in Geneva if you go, and don't forget to buy their chocolate. Best in the world! Tell Jacques Chirac I said hello."

"You bet!" Ace retorted. "I'm sure he'll have a band waiting for us."

"Oh, and by the way, be careful in the subways in the big cities over there. There are some pretty professional thieves there. I knew a guy whose wife had her purse snatched right from her shoulder in the subway in Paris. The guy just ripped it off and leaped over a turnstile and disappeared."

"Ah, thanks," Ace said. "We'll keep a sharp lookout. But, we're not going to Paris."

"Oh, yeah. A secret. I remember. Well. Wherever you go, have a good time."

"Thank you," They said in unison. They both hurried past the airline counters with Ace carrying the two suitcases. As soon as they were far enough away from the booth, Gabriella whispered, "I left the money and everything in the glove compartment in the car."

"Oh, boy. Good thing you thought of that now."

When they reached the outside sidewalk the sky was grey and it was getting toward twilight. Ace said, "Just stay with the luggage, Gabby. I'll get the stuff."

He let down the two suitcases and ran like a man with a swarm of bees chasing after him. When he arrived at the car he was out of breath and sweating profusely. He jammed the key into the passenger door key hole and opened the door. He then placed his knee on the seat and turned the knob to open the glove compartment. He grabbed the white envelope and opened it to verify its contents. Everything was there—the three thousand in cash, the passports, and the travellers' checks. He took out his wallet, stuffed the cash into it, and put it in his back pocket. He flung the envelope on the floor. He then shoved the passports into his front jeans pocket. He was about to open the door when he heard the familiar classical music coming from the back seat of the car where he had left his cell phone. Who would be calling him at this moment? The police? Mr. Stanley? He didn't want to know. He closed the door with Beethoven's Fifth still ringing in his ears as he ran to join Gabriella on the sidewalk.

"C'mon, Gabby. We've got no time to lose." They arrived at the entrance of the building five minutes later. Before entering, however, Ace stopped and said, "Gabby, let's be calm and try to look happy. If the guy sees that we're nervous he might get suspicious." Gabriella put her handbag on the sidewalk, waited until she stopped breathing heavily, stood erect, and said, "How's this, Mr. Parks?" Her stomach felt tense like before a concert but on the outside she wore the serene expression she often adopted in greeting patients at the doctor's office.

"Perfect," Ace said smiling, "you're my eye of the hurricane." The first set of glass doors opened automatically while the second set he had to pull open. Immediately they found themselves in an office foyer. He saw the name, Fast Flight, and the words Air Ambulance as well as the logo of a red plane with lines indicating speed on another glass door. Ace pulled it open and immediately saw a young woman with brown neck-length hair at the counter.

"Hello. You must be the couple wanting to go to Montreal," she said with an affable smile.

"Yeah, we are," Ace said, putting down the suitcases. He pulled out their dark blue passports and the cash and laid them on the counter. She opened them and began to write their numbers on her Fast Flight paper. She finished and slid them back to him. He then peeled off ten 100 dollar bills from the wad and pulled out another twenty from his wallet. He was glad that it wasn't the end of the night or else he would have had all the money from the deliveries instead of just the one. Still, he wondered, would he be charged with stealing as well for taking the $7.99? The woman took the money and gave him the change.

"If you will just sit down in the waiting room over there, the pilot will be right with you. He just has to check a few things on the plane before take-off. You can see it through the window there. You are not authorized to go out there unless you are with the pilot. And here is a little brochure that tells you about our company." She passed the pamphlet with Fast Flight written across the top and a photo of a Cheyenne Turboprop jet just below it.

Ace picked it up, said, "Thanks" and started to turn around. He changed his mind, faced her again and asked, "Oh, how long does it take to get to Montreal?"

"Not long. About thirty minutes."

"Really. That's great. We might even make that connecting flight to Paris after all." He instantly regretted giving their final destination.

"We certainly hope so, Mr. Parks," the woman said smiling again, obviously proud that she had already memorized his name.

Ace hoped she would forget what she had just said as fast as she had memorized it. Their escape could depend on it. Both he and Gabriella went into the side room. Ace put down the suitcases again and went to the water cooler, picked up a paper cup and got some cold water. Gabriella sat down on the nearest leather chair and shuffled through some of the glamour magazines. Ace looked at the round clock on the wall above the water cooler. It was 6:30 p.m.

"Hey Gabby, you want some water?"

"No thanks, I'm not really thirsty." She picked up a *Glamour* magazine with Gwenyth Paltrow on the cover and started flipping through it.

Ace sipped the water and walked to the window. He watched the pilot busily checking the propellers, wings, and tires. Although he only took fifteen minutes, it wasn't fast enough for Ace. He would only be happy when they were on their flight to Paris. After finishing his tasks the pilot lowered the stairs, which led to the side door of the plane, and kicked the wood blocks from in front of the tires. He then walked toward the door, which opened into the waiting room. He was wearing a white shirt with the red Fast Flight logo, black pants and black dress shoes. He had a full head of grey hair with more white in his short sideburns. The brochure mentioned that he retired early from the commercial airlines after 20 years and set up his own company five years ago. He smiled when he entered.

"Hello, you must be the couple dying to get to Montreal. My name is Michael Bradshaw. I'll be your pilot this evening."

"Yeah, that's us," Ace replied. Gabriella stood up and Ace picked up the two suitcases.

"Oh, let me carry those," the pilot said grabbing them both from Ace. "Just follow me and we'll get you going." As their shoes hit the runway he continued talking: "You'll find the ride very comfortable. The turbo engine doesn't make too much noise as compared to the piston engine planes. The weather isn't too nasty so we should be there around 7:30. You'll know we're halfway there when you see the red beacon flashing from on top of Mount Marcy. If you're hungry or thirsty there's some Coke and chips in the plane. Just this way."

Ace understood his cheerfulness. A thousand bucks an hour would put anyone in a good mood. In fact, with those prices they should have fresh jumbo shrimp with hot sauce and champagne. The man pointed to the stairs and let them go up first. As they entered the cabin they saw two seats in front for the pilot and possibly a co-pilot and two leather seats with backs to the ones in front and then another two facing them. Ace chose the seats farthest away from the pilot. He let Gabriella sit near the window. Bradshaw put the suitcases in a cargo hold and then mounted the stairs. After he came inside he clicked a switch to bring in the stairs and, once they were in place, closed the door with a thud.

"Okay. We'll just need to get the go-ahead from ground control and the tower and we'll be off. I'll let you know just before we take off so you're ready. It takes off pretty fast." They taxied out in the direction of the runway while Bradshaw lifted a receiver and said, "This is Alpha Charlie 334. Ready for take-off. Tell me when."

A voice answered, "All right, Alpha Charlie. Go for it. You're clear." A few short minutes and Ace and Gabriella were forced into the backs of their seats as the plane sped down the runway and began the powerful ascent into the night.

As the plane levelled off, Ace motioned for Gabriella to put her head on his shoulder. "Gabby, won't you try and get some rest. It's been a stressful time." Some of her long black hair cascaded across her face. She automatically lifted it and put it around her ear and then closed her eyes. Ace feigned sleep as well but was about as tired as a boy with his finger stuck in an electrical socket. His mind raced going over every detail of their escape. Suddenly, his eyes popped open and he whispered to the top of her sweet-smelling head, "Gabby, Gabby. You left a note for your dad, didn't you?"

Gabriella's green eyes blinked and she moved her head up slightly, "Yes, yes, Ace. I told him I was going over to Mary's house. Don't worry."

Then, thinking the pilot might be listening somehow, she added, "Just try to get some rest, honey. We have a long flight in front of us."

"You're right, darling," Ace replied, wondering if all the

sweet talk sounded natural or forced. He wasn't usually a sentimental kind of guy but it seemed the circumstances demanded it. In fact, his lack of tender words was sometimes a sore point between them. Gabriella lifted her head from his shoulder, looked him straight in the eyes and smiled. She didn't mind this change at all. Ace just said, "What? Muffin."

"No Ace. Muffin does nothing for me. Try *mon petit chou chou.*"

"Oh no. Not yet. You'll have to wait until we get to France."

Despite their playful teasing, Ace could not get the tense knot out of his stomach. A girl might be dead because of his carelessness. He had to find out somehow what happened to her.

Chapter 10

Uncle Jerry
Monday, May 19, 2003

Jerry Jensen sat behind his mahogany desk that was littered with piles of unattended files, a black cordless phone to his ear. He was muttering to himself: "C'mon, Ace. Answer. C'mon. Do it. Pick up the phone." After around 20 rings he jammed the receiver into its cradle in frustration. He had heard the police communication on his pager in his car coming from his office and quickly called the police station to see if Ace was involved. He thought he could talk some sense into Ace's head if he could only get hold of him. Jensen knew it would be much better legally if Ace turned himself in, rather than being picked up by the police. Where was he? What was he thinking? Why would he leave the scene of an accident?

Jensen knew there had to be a logical reason. He also knew Ace was no slouch, even though he had a derelict for a father. Hadn't he told his sister over and over again that the guy was a loser? Ever since the man had left Ace and his mom, Jensen felt responsible to help in any way he could. At first, he tried to convince Carl to check himself into a rehabilitation center. When Carl refused to do that, and called for small loans to fund his drinking and gambling obsessions, Jensen told him flat out he would not fund addictions. The calls soon stopped.

For years he hadn't heard from Carl, or known of his whereabouts. He wouldn't be surprised if he had migrated to a big city somewhere and was now bumming cigarettes on the streets and living in a cardboard box. When he didn't even call to see how his son was doing, Jensen lost all respect for him whatsoever, and didn't frankly care anymore what happened to him. He just tried to be the male role model Ace needed growing up. He'd take him to ball games, on boat rides, whatever, to show Ace he was important. He had also let him stay at his home with his wife and kids after the death of his mom for a few months and would have let him stay longer, but Ace wanted to be on his own and work out his own life without "leeching off" anyone. Jensen understood that, and he was thrilled how Ace had bounced back and had the vision to buy a pizza franchise down the road after he got off probation and even pursuing engineering in the future. Now . . . where was Ace?

Chapter 11

Later at Luigi's
Monday, May 19, 2003

When Robert Palmer opened the Luigi's glass door it was no longer the beehive he witnessed earlier. Dinner time had peeked and employees were either wiping down counters, putting the flat pizza boxes into a usable form in the back, standing near the phones for possible incoming orders, or throwing dough in the air. He walked to the office. This time the door was closed. He heard animated whispers and a phone settling back into its cradle. He knocked lightly and a voice asked testily, "Who is it?"

"Palmer. Tribune. Can I speak with you for a few minutes, Mr. Stanley?"

"Yeah. Sure. You can come in."

Palmer opened the door and faced the same man he had seen an hour and a half earlier. He looked like a man who had just finished the Boston Marathon in last place.

"Sorry to bother you, Mr. Stanley, but I was wondering if you have a public statement yet from the home office."

The man bowed his head slightly, put his hand on his forehead like he had a splitting headache, and then looked up at Palmer.

"Yes. All I can tell you is Ace Parks was our best driver. He was in training to be an Assistant Manager with the goal of co-running the new store opening in Delmar next fall. In fact, he normally doesn't even deliver much any more but someone called in sick today. Why he would leave the scene of an accident is beyond me. All the drivers are trained on how to respond to emergencies of this sort. There may have been circumstances that caused him to behave in that way, I don't know. That's the job of the local police. Other than that . . . I don't know what to say. I just hope they take into consideration that the kid's got no parents. His dad ran out on the family when he was small and his mom just died a couple of years ago." He let out a long sigh.

Palmer scribbled a few notes on his white pad of paper. Maybe he could work this into a human interest story.

"I understand how you feel, Mr. Stanley. How is the rest of the staff taking it?"

"Hard. Ace was very well respected. They are all as shocked as I am."

"Well, thank you, Mr. Stanley. If you hear of anything, please let me know."

"I will. But this isn't going to be a front page deal, is it? That would be horrible for business."

"That's the editor's decision. I just write the story."

As Palmer was putting the pad back into his back pocket, he heard Stanley mutter: "I should have listened to him. I should have listened to him."

Puzzled by these remarks, Palmer stopped writing and asked, "What's that, Mr. Stanley? You should have listened to whom?"

"Oh. Ace. He kept telling me it wasn't safe down there and we shouldn't be sending drivers in that area of town. Now he is in all this trouble and it's my fault."

"Why? Had there been some problems down there before?"

"Not exactly, with our guys anyway. Apparently Ace had heard about some incidents with drivers from other stores but I didn't think they were that serious—some pies taken, was all— so I didn't do anything. Now this . . ." He shielded his eyes with his hand and Palmer figured it was time to leave.

"All right. Thanks again." Palmer was hoping now he could get some of Ace's co-workers to talk. If he had asked, Stanley might have said no. Always easier to ask forgiveness than permission, as the saying goes. Instead, he just gave the manager the impression he was done. He left the threshold of the office door and came back into the main area of the store. He approached a girl with a Luigi's red cap and shirt with black pants who was wiping down the counters where drivers waited for the next order up.

"Excuse me. My name is Robert Palmer from the Albany Tribune. Could I ask you a few questions about Ace Parks?"

"I . . . I . . . don't know," she sputtered. "I don't think we're supposed to say anything."

"Oh, I just talked with your manager . . ." Although technically correct, Palmer said this to imply he had permission which he did not. Palmer was also used to this fear of the press. He did what he always did. He ignored her protests.

"How well do you know him?"

"Well, not very well. I've only been here two months." She sprayed the counter again a little nervously, averted her eyes, and continued wiping.

"From your contact with him, would you think he could run over a child and then leave the scene of the accident?"

"No. That I can tell you. He was a very diligent kind of person and was usually very careful. He was in training to be a manager and everything. Everybody can't believe what happened."

"Well, thank you for your helpfulness. I just needed to get some info on his character. One more thing. Is there anyone who works here who is closer to him than others?"

"I don't know. He's friendly with everybody. Maybe José. He should be back any minute. I think he had a short run a little while ago to Forest Avenue."

"Okay. Thanks again." Palmer figured it was best to wait in his car for the kid so as not to attract the manager's attention, should he come out of hibernation. It wasn't long before a bronzed-skinned boy driving a rusted-out blue Toyota Corolla pulled up next to him. Palmer jumped out of the car before the boy could go into the store and called his name, "Hey, José. Got a minute?"

José had just put the empty vinyl bag under his arm and was half running to the store's entrance. He was short and wearing the same apparel as the other Luigi employees but he had a small imitation diamond earring in the lobe of his right ear and a gold chained necklace swinging on his chest as he walked. He stopped at the cement stoop and blurted out, "Hey man. How come you know my name? I don't know you."

"Yeah, I know. But I work for the Tribune and I just got a few questions for you. Got a minute?"

"Well. If it's about my Ace man, I don't have much to say. He's a great guy. I wasn't there so I can't tell you what happened. Just hope he gets away and don't quote me on that."

"Don't worry. I won't. But how long have you known him?"

"Oh. I don't know. Maybe two years. He's the one who trained me. Never had such a good paying part-time job. Make ten to twelve dollars an hour but I gotta go . . ."

"Nice. One more question: Does Ace have a girlfriend?"

"Girlfriend? This guy could have almost anybody he wanted but he ain't that way. He even went out with Cindy Trola, the cheerleading queen. He just wants one girl he can settle down with. Don't ask me why. I say, 'When you're young have some fun,' kinda like a rap song, you know. But he has some old-fashioned ideas about romance. He's got some big ambitions too—wants to buy one of these Luigi franchises and maybe become an engineer some day. He even said he would hire me to work for him." José put his hand on the door to push it open.

Palmer fired off a parting shot: "But does he have a steady girl now?"

José hesitated, suddenly feeling he was betraying a friend to a complete stranger.

"Ah . . . no. He's waiting for the right one."

Then, looking at the camera around the reporter's neck, he tried to change the subject:

"Say, aren't you going to take my picture for the paper?"

"I'm sure you're very photogenic, José, but no . . . not this time. Thanks for answering some questions for me. I'll try to put a quote of yours in the article."

"Yeah, that's good. But don't put that in about me wanting him to get away, okay?"

"No. Promise. But, honestly, do you really think he will get away?"

"If anyone can, he can. He's a good thinker. He even beats that smart guy in the chess club. I won five dollars on that one!"

"José, this is not a game but a very serious crime. Driving away from the scene of an accident can get you in big trouble. I hope your friend gives himself up for his sake. And let's cross our fingers that the little girl lives."

"Yeah. Sure. I gotta go." José entered the store, flung his vinyl bag below the counter and checked the short strips of paper hanging down from the top counter about eye level, which indicated the next orders up. He then went to the refrigerator and pulled out a Mountain Dew. José liked it better than Coke because of the higher octane level. It kept him awake during the wee hours. He pondered the idea of calling Ace and giving him the name of a guy he knew who could keep him undercover for a while.

Palmer got back into his Volvo, set the camera down and leaned back on the brown leather seat reflecting on what he had just heard. The boy's character seemed exemplary to his boss and the co-workers—much different than the one presented by his friend at the police station. He was convinced, too, that José had lied. Ace had a girlfriend. That was certain. José was obviously withholding this information. Would Ace be foolish enough to ask the girl to run away with him, and would the girl be foolish enough to go?

Chapter 12

Montreal Airport
Monday, May 19, 2003

ooks like you got the go-ahead," Bradshaw said over his shoulder to Ace and Gabriella. "I'll just taxi over a little closer to the Customs Office and let you out. They'll let you know where to go from there."

The plane had made a smooth landing at Montreal Airport and they had only waited a few minutes before receiving the official word to debark. Ace grabbed two Cokes from the little fridge in the plane, if only to get the most out of this expensive flight, and handed one to Gabriella.

The pilot pushed the button to bring down the stairway, picked up their two suitcases, and went down before them. He handed them to Ace at the bottom and said, "Thanks for flying with Fast Flight. I hope you make that connection to Paris. If not, Montreal's not a bad city. I know of some good restaurants, if you're interested."

Ace shook the man's hand. "No. I don't think we'll be hanging around here tonight. Actually, we've been thinking of going to Switzerland instead of France. Thanks for taking us on such short notice, though, and have a nice flight back."

Bradshaw winked and said, "I understand. It's a nice place. Been there a few times myself when I worked for Delta. Well, have a good trip." He mounted the steps, made them disappear, and vanished from sight.

Ace looked at Gabriella and said, "Well, so far so good. Let's see how we do with Customs."

Gabby nodded and they walked toward the light coming through the door the pilot had indicated. As they entered the room, a woman at the counter said, "Bonsoir, Madame. Monsieur. Passeports, s'il vous plaît." Ace cast a smile over at Gabriella and said, "I think your French is better than mine. Wanna try responding?"

"Oui, bien sûr, chéri." But before Gabriella could get anything out, however, the woman said in a heavy French accent, "It iz okay. I speak Engleesh also."

Gabriella, however, took Ace's passport and her own and said confidently, "Voilà, nos passeports, Madame."

The woman smiled at the effort and examined the dark blue booklets carefully before handing them back.

Gabriella asked, "Où devons-nous aller pour un vol à Paris?"

"C'est simple, Madame. Vous suivez les panneaux qui indiquent les vols internationaux et vous verrez sur les moniteurs les prochains départs pour Paris. Mais, d'abord, vous devez nous laisser examiner vos baggages."

"Merci, Madame," Gabriella said, obviously pleased with herself for communicating for the first time with a bona fide French speaker. She turned to Ace: "She says just to look at the monitors for international flights and go to the gate indicated for Paris. She also wants to look through our suitcases." Ace complied and lifted both of them to the counter. A man opened them and looked through them in a perfunctory manner. Ace noticed the white wedding ensemble in Gabriella's suitcase and felt strangely excited and sad at the same time. He was glad she had decided to go with him, yet disappointed it had to be under such circumstances. He wondered if they could get legally married in France. He figured this country would probably be less strict about that than in the States. The Customs agent popped his daydream by saying, "You can go now," in perfect

English.

"Just follow me, Ace. I know where to go."

"Really? You understood all that she said. I'm impressed."

"Remember, I had the 92 and you only had an 85."

"Right. But Monsieur Malet always liked you better than me."

"Ace. We just follow the international signs. Did you understand that?"

"Well, kinda. I've been outa school for a year, you know," Ace winced.

"Point made. Let's go."

When they reached the right hall, they both stared at the screen hanging from the ceiling that said, "Départs." The next flight out was with Air France at 8:35. It was 7:52.

"Hey, Gabby. Looks like we are in luck. Air France leaves in less than an hour. Let's see if there are any seats left." They ran to the nearest Air France counter, which was less than 20 yards away.

Gabriella spoke boldly, but a little out of breath: "Excusez-moi, Madame. Pouvez-vous nous dire s'il y a deux places pour le vol à vingt heures trente-cinq pour Paris?"

Without looking at the screen the woman with a red, white, and blue scarf declared, "Non, Mademoiselle. C'est complet. Mais" (she then looked at her computer, tapped a few times and continued) "il y a un autre vol à vingt-deux heures vingt avec British Airways, si vous êtes interessée."

"What did she say, Gabby?" Ace asked nervously.

"She said there isn't any room on the Air France but there is another flight with British Airways at 9:20. Didn't you get anything she said?" She lowered her eyebrows and looked at him puzzled.

"Yeah. British Airways, Mademoiselle, and interessée. It's a lot different understanding French spoken at the normal speed than hearing it spoken slowly in a class."

"Well, you better let me do the talking when we get to France. You're terrible."

"Right. But I can do the talking at the next counter because I do believe, despite my accent, they will understand my English." Ace looked down the hall for British Airways." There it is. Let's hustle. I don't want to be in this airport longer than necessary." Again Ace and Gabriella raced to the next counter. Ace arrived first and spoke as he bumped into the counter: "Umm . . . Yeah. Are there two seats by any chance on the Paris flight at 9:20?"

The blonde woman chuckled and said, "I'll see." She looked at her flat computer screen.

"Sorry, it's full." Ace's face fell and the short-haired woman added: "You could wait around on stand-by and if someone doesn't show up you could take their place."

"Okay. We'll wait and see."

Gabriella let out a sigh, pursed her lips, and followed Ace to the vinyl seats closest to the British Airways counter. They both sat down and Ace pulled out the can of Coke. He snapped it open and took a long swig.

"Oh boy. I sure hope we can get on this one. I don't want to stay here tonight." Then he looked around and whispered, "The sooner we can get out of this country the better."

"Let's just hope for the best. If we don't make this one, we can figure something out," Gabriella said.

Ace smiled at her. He needed her optimism right now and he could tell in those words that she was committed—come what may. It was then he noticed in the corner of the waiting area that there was an all-news channel on. "Hey, Gabby. I'm gonna go to the men's room. Do you think maybe you could go watch the news over there and tell me what they reported when I come back?"

"Sure, Ace. I don't think we have anything to worry about.

You certainly won't make the national news."

"You never know. I won't be long." Ace got up and leisurely walked toward the rest rooms. He glanced up to the right at the talking head on the TV screen as he passed by. On the way to the toilets he spotted a store where they sold magazines and souvenirs and ducked in. He saw some red baseball hats with dark blue letters spelling *Montreal* on them and found one his size. He added a pair of top-of-the-line sunglasses when he saw them hanging on a rack near the cash register. The price was ridiculous but he didn't care. If it kept him anonymous, he'd be happy.

He also bought the same issue of *Glamour* for Gabriella, figuring she had not finished all the articles at the Fast Flight office, and a *Technology Today* for himself. Afterwards, he found the toilets. Apparently the cleaning person hadn't been by recently because crumpled paper towels were overflowing out of the metal garbage container and a few lay scattered on the tile floor. He entered a stall, closed the door, and sat down to flip through the TT for a while. He heard several footsteps scuffle into the outside room, urinals flushed, and the sound of paper towels being ripped from the roll as well as whooshing of air from the hand dryers. Hand dryers definitely were more popular. He finished reading the article, "Build Your Own Computer for Half the Price," and stepped out of the stall. He found Gabriella near the British Airways counter drinking her Coke. He plopped down beside her and asked, "So, anything interesting?"

"Nice glasses and hat. No. Nothing coming from Albany, anyway. Just another political scandal and more soldiers killed in Iraq. I don't think CNN does local stuff unless it is really unusual."

"No news is good news. Here's that Glamour issue you started back at Fast Flight." He threw the magazine on her lap.

"Thanks. What time is it?"

Ace looked at his sports watch and said, "It's 8:20. I wonder how close to takeoff they would take standbys."

"I asked the lady and she said up to fifteen minutes before."

"Great. That gives us about forty-five minutes. Let's hope they have two seats."

"What if they only have one?" Gabriella asked gingerly.

"We go together or not at all. This is a big city. We can find a hotel somewhere and maybe catch one tomorrow. I'm not leaving you."

"But isn't it more important for you to get out of the country than me?" Gabby pressed.

"Yeah. But I'm not leaving you here by yourself. If this is going to work, it will work for both of us."

"Thanks, Ace." With those words she interlaced her arm into his and grabbed his hand and gave him a warm appreciative smile. She then turned to the contents page of the magazine.

Instead of looking at his magazine, however, Ace used the cover of his sunglasses to keep a close watch on any official-looking people coming and going. He wondered if Mr. Bradshaw would hear anything about the accident on his radio on the way back. and if he would remember the name Ace Parks. It probably wasn't likely someone would be looking for him already in Montreal, but he couldn't be too sure. All it would take would be a call to security. Maybe he should dye his hair.

Chapter 13

A Pizza Run
Monday Evening, May 19, 2003
Loudonville, NY

José didn't expect what happened to him as he took the exit on Route 9 to Loudonville. He was thrilled to be the next man up for the delivery because this area was the most affluent in the city and with 10 pizzas to one house he was sure to clean up in tips. It was probably a teen party of some sort. He just hoped it was the parents who were paying, because kids weren't the best tippers and often gave him a pile of change.

He was optimistic, though, and was singing at the top of his lungs to a Fifty Cent CD and tapping the roof of his car with his left hand when a barrage of rocks the size of baseballs began to hit the side of his Toyota. One smashed the back windshield. He screamed and jammed the accelerator faster. Unfortunately, his '92 model was not big on speed and his actions yielded small gains. Another rock hit one of his back taillights. José cursed out loud and vowed to come back with his friends and have it out with whoever was trying to kill him.

After several seconds he was out of range of his attackers. He pulled the car to the side of the road and looked quickly to the top of the overpass he had just gone under. His enemies no doubt had thrown their arsenal from there. He saw several dark shapes running in the direction of Memorial Hospital. *Just wait,* he thought, breathing hard and shaking involuntarily from the shock of the attack. *I'll be back and I won't be alone. You cowards. No one does that to José Gonzales. No one.* He got out of the car and did a few karate moves just to get it out of his system.

He then checked out his car and saw the dents the rocks had made and cursed again. He had a $1000 deductible on his insurance. Finally, he got back into his car and drove to the delivery house. It was an old Victorian style house with the typical porch and pillars and a U-shaped driveway that allowed horse-drawn carriages in the 19th century to drop off passengers close to the front door. He shook off the glass particles from the top vinyl bag and carried the five of them, which held two pizzas apiece, to the entrance. He rang the doorbell and a man about 45 with dark hair on the sides and a balding strip down the middle answered. He was dressed in a black suit and tie, obviously just home from work. Avril Lavigne music blasted from the opening and a strobe light throbbed with a beat. Suddenly the smiling face of a girl of about 16 with long, perfectly combed blonde hair, squeezed past her father's side and grabbed the pies. "Thank yoooouuuu sooo much," she cooed and disappeared. The father asked, "How much is the damage?"

"Ahh . . . that's $99.90 please," José stammered, a little confused by the complete change of circumstances. The man pulled out a long brown leather wallet from his suit coat pocket, opened it and drew out a hundred dollar bill and a ten dollar bill and gave it to José.

"Keep the change, son," he said. He then closed the door without noticing the shattered back windshield. José had thought of maybe milking the whole incident for a bigger tip, but decided not to at the last minute. All he was thinking of at the moment was revenge. Ahh . . . sweet revenge. *Oh well,* he reasoned, *ten bucks isn't bad for one drop.* Then he thought he'd better get back to the store to warn others about what had happened.

Chapter 14

Montreal Airport
Monday Evening, May 19, 2003

It was 9:05 when the same young black-haired woman with the British Airways uniform signaled them to the counter. "We just had two cancellations, so you can take those seats if you wish," she said with a Queen's English accent. "Unfortunately, though, they are not together. Is that a problem?"

"Ahh . . . no," Ace said quickly. "We'll take them. We can always ask the person next to us to change. We'll just explain we're newlyweds."

"Oh, you are! How nice. Well, I'm glad we were able to get you aboard. Passports, please, and you can put your suitcases up here. We have to hurry a bit because it's so late."

Ace placed the suitcases on the conveyor belt and paid for the tickets with his credit card. He marveled at how the amount wasn't much more than what they had paid for their charter flight and this was across an ocean that took seven hours. The agent gave them their boarding passes and they hurried through the tunnel to get on the plane. They were greeted by the flight crew at the door and went in search of their seats. Being the last on board meant everyone stared at them walking down the aisle. Ace was happy he had bought the disguise. Who knows who might remember them and connect the dots if they saw his picture in the papers? When they reached Gabriella's seat, Ace leaned down to the elderly lady who was slightly dozing and whispered, "Excuse me, Madame. Do you think you could switch seats with me? We just got married and we'd like to be together."

The startled lady snapped awake and said, "Pardon, monsieur. Je ne parle pas un mot d'anglais."

This is when Gabriella jumped in and said, "Mon mari vient de dire que nouse nous venons de nous marier et nous préférons etre ensemble. Est-ce que c'est possible d 'échanger son siège pour le vôtre?"

"Son siège est où?" the woman asked.

"C'est là-bas," Gabriella pointed to the back of the plane.

"Absolutement pas. Je ne peux pas supporter le bruit. Desolée, Madame."

Ace looked at Gabriella with raised eyebrows, "Well?"

"She says that she cannot do that because she can't stand the noise from the engine at the back of the plane," Gabriella explained.

"Ask her if she minds if I sit on her lap," Ace retorted. A few English speakers chuckled nearby.

"I don't think so. She is liable to hit me with her umbrella."

They both looked over to the other passenger who was on the other side of Gabriella's seat but they saw it was useless to ask—the man was sound asleep already.

"Well, maybe we'll have better luck with my seatmates," Ace said hopefully.

A stewardess walked down the aisle and told them politely to take their seats.

"Okay. I'll ask them once we're up and the plane is leveling off," Ace said. Before leaving, he lightly put his hand on her shoulder and smiled. "I love you."

"I love you, too," Gabriella whispered.

Ace found his seat between a businessman hard at work on his laptop and a French man reading the French newspaper, *Le Monde*.

"Pardonnez-moi," Ace managed to say as he was squeezing himself into the middle seat. The Frenchman lifted his paper and let him in. The other man continued to look at his graphs. Once seated the same woman who had instructed them to find their seats began the demonstrations of the oxygen masks along with the pictures on the small screens in front of them. Ace wondered if there were any good films playing to help occupy the time. One thing he didn't want to do is think about the little girl he had run over just a few hours ago. He even said a mental prayer, *Lord, help her to be all right,* as he looked out the window. It was the first time he had prayed since his mom had died.

Chapter 15

Albany Tribune Office
Monday Evening, May 19, 2003

Palmer had just started typing his first lines on the hit and run story for May 20 when the voice of his editor, Norm Bascom, summoned him to his office on the intercom. *What does he want now?* Palmer wondered. He rose from his cubicle, grabbed a notepad and wound his way through a sea of desks to the editor's door. Before he could knock, he heard, "C'mon in, Palmer," and he entered. Bascom, smoking a cigarette, sat up in his stylish black leather swivel chair and motioned Palmer to sit down in the chair facing him.

Palmer hated Bascom's mini lectures on his writing and the fact he had to listen to him to keep his job. He couldn't wait to kiss this part of his job goodbye. He tried to look attentive. Bascom snubbed out the cigarette and looked directly at Palmer.

"We got a little problem here with that hit and run. I just got a call from Sergeant Pierce and he asked if we could avoid making a big deal out of it right now. Things are getting a little hot down in the projects because of it and he doesn't want anything to make things worse. We don't want to come down too hard on Luigi's either. They're regular advertisers and we can't afford to lose them. Can't bite the hand that feeds you, as they say."

"So, what are you saying, Norm? We let the police department tell us what to do? We report the news. If things are heating up down there, shouldn't we report it?"

"No. We don't let them tell us what to do. But we do have a certain civic responsibility. We don't want to report anything in a way that would get them angry. Apparently, Rev. Johnston is in town and he's trying to use this for his own agenda. You remember what happened with that Moore case." Bascom shook out another cigarette, put it rapidly in his mouth, and lit it with the silver lighter on the desk.

"Yeah, and I'd say it was more Johnston's meddling that sparked the problems here—not our paper."

"I'd agree with you but we don't want to be manipulated by him either. He had someone call and say he's speaking with the people at the Last Days Apostolic Pentecostal Revival Center tonight at 8:30. You might want to go and see what he says and how he's affecting the people. You can take some pictures, just in case, but we probably aren't going to print them. Just write a little article about the event afterwards and we'll . . ."

"Bury it in the back of the paper somewhere."

"Ahh . . . Right. But Bob, don't worry. I'll give you the next scoop. Stay with this one though. It may blow up into something big. Pierce said that they didn't get the driver yet and the girl is still alive."

"All right, Norm. I'll see what I can do." Palmer put his notepad in his back pocket and got up to leave.

"Thanks, Bob. I knew I could count on you." They shook hands.

Palmer shook his head on his way back to his computer. Money and politics always deciding what they did, or didn't, do. Why couldn't he just write the story and let the chips fall where they may for once? One thing he knew he had to do, however, was to give the boy a human face. He guessed that Johnston would demonize the boy and demand severe consequences and maybe even blame the white police chief for not doing all he could to bring the criminal to justice. Palmer felt he had to offset this negative picture of the boy. The public had to know he had lost his mom recently. They also had to know he was a responsible teen working at an honest job. What would spur him to leave the scene of an accident and then try to run away? Maybe, if he put that question in the article, someone who witnessed the accident might come forward. He got a tip, too, that the kid had an uncle who was a lawyer in town. Maybe he might have some answers.

Chapter 16

Flight Over The Atlantic
Monday Night, May 19, 2003

When the plane had leveled off and the *Fasten Seat Belts* signs went off, Ace turned to the young man reading *Le Monde* and tried, in his best French, "Pardon, Monsieur, mais ma femme . . ." Ace then pointed in Gabriella's direction where she was nodding and smiling. "Ahh . . . change . . . siège avec toi, I mean, vous?"

The man lowered his paper and laughed. "So, you want me to switch seats with your wife?"

Ace detected no accent and assumed he was an American. "Ah . . . yeah. If that's okay."

"No problem. I can't blame you for wanting to sit next to such a pretty girl." At that he folded up his paper and walked past the seat where Gabriella was sitting so she could get out. She thanked him, grabbed her purse, and came down the aisle and sat next to Ace.

"That man seemed nice."

"Yeah. I thought he was French because he was reading Le Monde but he spoke perfect English. He said he couldn't blame me for wanting to sit next to such a pretty girl."

"And you can't blame me for wanting to sit next to such a handsome man," Gabriella said, giving him a quick peck on the cheek.

"Right," Ace replied. He then picked up the program guide and said, "See any good movies?"

Gabriella grabbed her guide out of the pocket in front of

her and started looking as well.

"Yeah. On channel 11 they'll be showing *A Walk to Remember*. I wanted to see that one."

"Ah. No. Hey, there's a good one. *Bourne Identity* with Matt Damon! Channel 7."

"I'm not in the mood for an action movie. So, how about *A Walk to Remember*? You wanna watch it with me?"

"Well . . . umm. Actually, we both have our own screens so we can watch whatever we want."

"So, you don't really want to watch it?"

"I didn't say that. I just thought I'd like to see something with a little action in it."

"Aha. So now the truth comes out. You really don't like *chick flicks*. Or character movies?"

"C'mon, Gabby. I do like them. I don't know. I was just in the mood for something a little more fast moving."

"But we just got married. Shouldn't we watch a romance together?"

"All right, sweetheart. Let's watch *A Walk to Remember*." With that Ace put down the program guide and grabbed Gabriella's hand.

"That's more like it, Honey."

Despite her upbeat words, Gabriella began thinking, for the first time since they left, what they had done and the possible repercussions. She'd dropped out of school before graduating. She left a respected doctor high and dry. Ace left the scene of an accident while on probation. She also left her dad to visit her mom. Had she really done the right thing? But, she had a right to her own life, too, didn't she? Why was all the burden for her mom on her anyway? They'd come back eventually. She'd see her again. What about her dad? He'd be furious.

Meanwhile, Ace wondered if they would have a cold reception by "les gendarmes" in Paris.

Chapter 17

Driving Home
Monday Night, May 19, 2003

Jerry Jensen drove his dark green 2002 Prius in silence past the Delmar commercial plaza and the Bruegger's Bakery where he picked up his plain bagel with cream cheese and cup of black coffee every Thursday morning. He liked the area because it had a good library, public tennis courts (so he didn't have to pay high club fees), and the Five Rivers Educational Center where he could picnic and hike with the family. Not a bad place to live. The daily drive to the office wasn't bad either although with all the new houses going up it was going to get worse. Right now he clocked it at 25 minutes. Normally, he would be listening to an audio book or a seminar of some kind just so he wouldn't be wasting time in rush hour but today was different.

His only nephew had just committed a serious crime and he was powerless to contact him. Repeated attempts to reach his cell phone had failed. He even left a message for Ace at his home but he knew Ace probably wouldn't go back there—too risky. He guessed that the reason why Ace had not turned himself in was because of his probation, but still couldn't figure out why he had left the scene of the accident. He knew it was rough down in the projects so maybe someone had threatened Ace. He might even hear from the probation officer if Ace didn't turn himself in soon. Things didn't look too good for Ace. Poor kid. What else could go wrong in his life?

He turned left on Edgewood Avenue, went by the cemetery, and turned right on Horace Road to number 17. He got out of the car, picked up the bike lying on the lawn and walked it into the open two-car garage. On the right side was the grey 2000 Dodge Caravan. He set the bike against the wall and took the stairs leading into the house from the left corner of the garage. He could smell the aroma of spaghetti sauce coming from the kitchen even before he opened the door. He took off his suit coat jacket and pulled his tie through his collar and placed them both on the nearest chair at the dining room table.

His wife, Robin, emerged out of the pantry with some garlic in her hand and said, "Hi, darling. Welcome home." She threw her arms around him and kissed him on the mouth. She saw his things on the chair and said, "Oh. Jerry. Please put your things in the closet. We'll be eating in a few minutes."

"Sure, Dear. Where are the kids?"

"Oh, they're next door as usual."

He picked up the tie and the coat and put them in the closet. He came back to the table and added, "Robin, there is something I need to tell you about."

She finished cutting the garlic on the wooden cutting board and looked at him. "What is it? Did you lose that Bailey case?" She picked up a green onion and began to cut it on the board.

Her husband sat down in the chair at the head of the table but turned the chair so he could see his wife face to face. "Oh, no. That won't be decided for a week or two." He hesitated and then said, "Ace is in trouble."

"Trouble? What kind of trouble?" She stopped cutting the onion and waited.

"He ran over a kid on one of his pizza deliveries and left the scene of the accident. The girl is only seven and in critical condition at Albany Med." He shook his head despairingly.

"That's terrible. Just when things started looking up again

for him."

"I know." He put his hand to his forehead and began rubbing it.

"Have you been able to talk with him?"

"No. That's what makes it worse. He doesn't answer his cell phone."

"What can happen to him?"

"If he doesn't give himself up, the probation office could give him the time he would have got for cutting up that kid."

"That's awful, Jerry. Where would he go?"

"I don't know. But he could go almost anywhere with his inheritance money if he could make it to . . . an airport. Airport? I hadn't thought of that before." Jerry raced to the closet and grabbed his coat. He quickly put it on.

"You're not going to the airport now, are you? Have something to eat first."

"Sorry, Babe. If he's there I got to get to him before he takes off."

"All right. But the kids and I are going to eat. You can warm yours up when you get back in the microwave. Good luck."

Jerry kissed her on the cheek.

"I'll be back as soon as I can. Tell the kids I'll read them both a story before bed."

"Okay. I love you."

"You too."

Chapter 18

Capaldi Home
Monday Night, May 19, 2003

Steve Capaldi pushed his construction plans away from the table where they were spread out in the dining room, grabbed the remaining beer from the second six-pack and ambled over to his cream-colored leather armchair facing the television in the living room. He sat down comfortably and put his feet on the matching leather hassock. He picked up the remote control and flicked on the TV. Immediately, the screen materialized with a man talking about flooding somewhere in Vermont.

He wasn't interested in current events but the new ad for his business was scheduled to air during the news hour and he didn't want to miss it. He enjoyed seeing himself coming out of his Explorer, standing in front of the governor's mansion that he had renovated years ago, and talking like a movie star. He didn't like the expense, of course, but it did get him some lucrative contracts to pay for it and more. Not much gave him joy these days. There was his beautiful daughter, Gabriella, and his work. That was about it. His wife was admitted to Hudson Valley Psychiatric Hospital ten years ago suffering from what the doctors called "Manic Depression" and he didn't like to think about his inability to help her. During her manic stages she was impossible and embarrassed him constantly in front of his drinking buddies. As much as he hated to admit it, he preferred she stay at the hospital where she could be watched. He'd even caught her trying to kill herself in the bathroom one night with sleeping pills. He visited her now maybe once a month with Gabriella but that was about all he could stand. Gabby could go more often but he had a business to take care of. That's when he began the drinking in earnest. Who could blame him? The situation was almost intolerable. He couldn't get a divorce because that was against his Catholic beliefs and he felt guilty coming on to other women while his wife was still alive.

His eldest son, Joey, lived in Rochester and worked for Kodak. He didn't see him too often because of their mutually eruptive tempers. He would have liked to change his business name to Capaldi and Capaldi Construction but their personalities were too similar to work well together. He figured Joey would come around more often once he got settled in his career and got married. Still it was too bad. Joey was a hard worker and grasped construction principles immediately. After getting his degree in marketing at a big name school he was hired to help the photography giant go digital. They must have been impressed with him because he started at over $50,000. It took Steve 15 years to make that much.

After the flood segment the announcer said something about a hit and run accident by a Luigi driver down on Lincoln. Anyone knowing the whereabouts of the driver was to call the police. The girl was in critical condition at Albany Med still in a coma. The woman gave the description of the car, its license plate, and then flashed a photo of the boy. *What did he say the boy's name was? Ace Parks.* He'd seen that boy somewhere before. *Wait a minute. That's the boy Gabby was hooked on.* He wondered if Gabriella knew about it. *That should convince her he was right about this guy after all. Imagine. Running over a little kid and then leaving the scene of the accident. If she dies, he could even get some time in prison for vehicle manslaughter. Good thing I ended that little infatuation before it went too far,* he thought. He took the last gulp of his beer, carried all the bottles on the table to the recycling bag on the landing going to the cellar, and then went to bed. He'd give Gabriella a call tomorrow and see how she did on that Physics project and when she was coming home. Maybe he'd even invite Anthony, that Italian kid who did masonry projects for him, to dinner this weekend. Maybe Gabby and he would hit it off. Decent, stable kid with a good future. Not that he was in a hurry to get rid of her. She was only 17. Wouldn't hurt, though, getting her thinking in the right direction.

Chapter 19

Crossing The Atlantic
Early Tuesday Morning, May 20, 2003

A ce stopped the movie, took off his headphones, and leaned back into his seat. He looked over at Gabriella. She shook her head as if to say, "It's not working for me either" and also pushed the button to blacken the screen and removed the ear buds from her ears. She sighed and said, "Just can't get into it. Too many things on my mind. I want to talk with you about it but I don't think here is the best place, if you know what I mean."

"Yeah. You're right. Whatta we do then? That Coke, I think, is gonna keep me awake for a while. We've got plenty of time. The trip is gonna take another five hours."

"Why don't we try to remember everything we've learned about France."

"Well, you'll beat me on that. You always had the higher grades except on that geography test where I got the 95 and you only had . . ."

"90. That still wasn't bad, you know."

All right. Who starts? It was your idea so why don't you do the honors?"

The businessman made a low moaning sound and turned more toward the window. He was obviously an experienced plane sleeper. He had earplugs, a blindfold, and a small blanket covering him. His head was leaning at a sixty degree angle against the pillow on the window.

Both Ace and Gabriella chuckled at the unexpected noise.

Ace whispered, "We'll have to be quiet not to wake," he pointed, "le monsieur."

"Okay. Ahh . . . France is the fifth leading economic power in the world."

"Geographically, France is about the size of Texas." Ace winked at her.

"The Eiffel Tower was constructed by the same guy who did the framework of The Statue of Liberty."

"The Seine River runs through Paris."

"There are about 60 million people who live in France, around 10% Muslim immigrants."

"The Alps are also in France."

"C'mon, Ace. You know more than just the geography."

"Yeah, but it's the first thing that comes to mind."

"All right . . . ummm . . . 70 million tourists visit France every year."

"Really?" Ace retorted surprised. "That seems kind of a lot."

"Really. It was on that test where you didn't do too well. Your turn . . ."

"Okay. Here's one you won't know. Seventy percent of French people will say they are Catholic but only 12% go to Mass on Sunday."

"Oh, yeah. How do you know that?"

"My mom supported this Protestant missionary for years and it was in a book that broke down the different religions and denominations in every country. It's called *Operation World*."

"Well, you'll have to show that to me some day 'cause it sounds kind of low to me."

"Sure. Whenever we get back to the States, be glad too." At this comment, Gabriella's forehead furrowed and she winced involuntarily as if weighing the seriousness of what Ace had just said. Ace, seeing his mistake, blurted out quickly, "Napoleon was exiled to the island of Elba."

"Huh . . . What?" Gabriella woke from her revelry.

"I said, Madame French expert, that Napoleon was exiled to the island of Elba."

"That doesn't count. You got that from the movie, *The Count of Monte Cristo.*"

"Sorry. You didn't give any rules."

"All right. But, how about the Protestants? How many Protestants are there in France?"

"I think it was less than 1%."

"Beat ya." Gabriella smiled.

"Hey, I'm no Protestant. That was my mom." Ace knew Gabriella attended Mass every once in a while with her dad but also knew she wasn't too keen on all the ups and downs on the kneeling benches and the other rituals. Still, she considered herself Catholic.

"You gotta take into account, too, that the Catholics were in cahoots with the king and literally massacred the opposing side and forced them out of the country. Doesn't sound fair to me. During the Saint Barthomew's massacre alone they killed 30,000 Protestants in one day."

"That's terrible. But didn't the Protestants start killing, too?" Gabriella countered.

"Yeah, but that was much later when they were tired of being oppressed and ill-treated."

"Mmm . . . still it seems they should have reacted differently."

"Maybe. Hard to say. Even today we have people killing in the name of God, don't we?"

"Yeah, that's true. But is it really Christian?" Gabriella said thoughtfully.

"I don't know, you're the Christian, not me. To me, it doesn't matter if you're Christian or not. If somebody like Hitler comes along you have to stop him one way or another."

"I guess so. But we stopped the game. Who was the last one

to say something?"

"Me. Napoleon. Elba."

"Okay. The French hate capitalism and have socialized medicine."

"Not bad. Not bad. Ahh . . . let's try to go to sleep. All this school work is making me sleepy."

"Better wake up, Ace. Looks like some food is coming our way."

Down the aisle, a slender woman with short auburn hair and a British Airways uniform was pushing a cart with dinner trays—"Chicken or beef?"

Chapter 20

A Phone Call and a New Development
Tuesday, May 20, 2003

H ello, Yeah. Could I speak with Officer Pierce, please? This is the Albany Tribune."

Robert Palmer pushed the remaining butt of his cigarette into the ashtray on his desk and leaned back in his black vinyl office chair and waited. After several minutes a voice of authority barked into his receiver: "Hello. This is Officer Pierce. Can I help you?"

"Hey Phil. Bob from the Tribune. I was wondering if you got that Parks kid yet. All I've got so far is his mom died two years ago, his dad flew the coop when he was in diapers and he was ready to fork over his inheritance money to buy a Luigi's franchise in Delmar."

"No. We don't have him yet but we just got a good lead from a woman who works down at Adirondack Trailways. She got the whole story from a friend down in the projects about a half hour after it happened. Said she had just sold a ticket to a guy in a Luigi uniform and the guy paid with a check. She went and got it and told me it was Ace Parks. Obviously, he's panicking and not thinking, or, he's just plain desperate. The bus should be arriving in Kingston at 7:30. Let's put it this way —he'll have a nice reception committee waiting for him when he gets there. He's also on five years probation for hurting another kid pretty bad in a bar brawl. I've told the guys to expect anything. The guys who went to his mom's house didn't see anything unusual but did find a plastic hair clip on the wheelchair ramp and a girl's bike underneath the deck."

"What? Do you think he took a girlfriend with him or something?'

"No. I don't think so. The lady at Trailways said he just bought one ticket so I think he's alone. He didn't have time to go anywhere except straight to the bus station after the accident. Well, gotta go Bob. I'll let you know once we nab 'im."

"Thanks Phil. One more thing. Any word on the girl?"

"Last I heard she was still in a coma at Albany Med. Let's hope she lives. If not, it could be even worse for this kid."

"Right. Ciao."

"Ciao." Palmer put the receiver down and pursed his lips and lapsed into deep thought. Where should he go with this article?

Just at that moment Editor Bascom ducked his head from around the corner and yelled, "Oh Palmer. You're here. Want a piece of that pizza you brought me? I think there is one piece left if you decide fast. Ahh . . ." He turned his head to look down the hall and then faced Palmer again. "Sorry about that. Henson just took it. Hey, Henson, don't forget to drop the dollar twenty-five in the jar!"

Bascom then disappeared. Palmer decided to go back to the Luigi's. He wanted some more personal info that only Parks' friends could provide. They were certainly aware by now of what had happened. Maybe the manager was also authorized to give an official statement, or at least the name of someone who could. When he walked outside, it had stopped raining.

Chapter 21

Paris France
Tuesday Morning, May 20, 2003

The plane had made a smooth landing at Charles DeGaulle Airport in Paris and had come to a complete stop. Ace sighed and looked at Gabriella who looked travel-worn yet awake and ready to get out of her seat. "This is it," Ace said solemnly. He stood up and opened the luggage container above their heads and pulled out their jackets. He passed Gabriella her suede coat and put on his own black denim jean jacket.

The crowd moved slowly down the aisle. They finally got near the exit door where the flight crew stood smiling and thanking everyone for flying British Air. Ace muttered, "Thank you. Great flight." Gabriella just smiled slightly to them as she passed. Once on the ground they noticed the grey sky and the cool wind. An airport shuttle was waiting to take them to the terminal. The driver took as many passengers as he could squeeze in and took off. People were now a little more animated making small talk in a variety of languages, obviously happy to arrive at their destination. Ace and Gabriella stood near the back door ready to be the first people off. After five minutes they reached building 2. They descended with the crowd and followed the signs in the winding corridors to the luggage retrieval area.

Ace looked up to the fancy glass ceilings and said, "Hope the roof doesn't cave in. That could be messy."

"Nice thought, Ace," Gabriella said. "Remember the French are excellent inventors and engineers. I don't think we have to worry about that." Gabriella quickened her pace to stay abreast of him.

"Let's hope so. Let's just get out of here as fast as we can. I'm dying for a real croissant and a café au lait." What Ace didn't want to verbalize was his fear of "les gendarmes" with their funny tall hats and blue uniforms coming around each corner and arresting them before they could say, "Parlez-vous français?"

It was 10:27 a.m. French time, six hours ahead of New York, which made it 4:27 a.m. in Albany. If they could only get out of the airport, Ace thought, it would be the final hurdle before losing themselves among the millions of Parisians. Finally, they came to the moving conveyor belt that carried luggage of all shapes and sizes from their plane. Muslim women in headscarves and men in Arabic turbans and robe-like clothing waited at other luggage islands from other flights. After a half hour Ace and Gabriella grabbed their dark blue American Tourister suitcases and headed to the Customs check out stations. They saw some police officers with machine guns on the other side of Customs.

Ace turned to Gabriella, "They look serious here, don't they?"

"I guess they have their fair share of terrorists coming through," Gabriella whispered.

Both Ace and Gabriella tried their best to look nonchalant. Gabriella was the first to the counter. A grim-faced man in his thirties brightened up when he looked at the pretty young woman in front of him. "Mademoiselle, votre passeport s'il vous plaît."

"Madame, Monsieur," Gabriella said quickly. Then, nodding to Ace, "Nous venons de nous marier" (We just got married).

"C'est dommage. Tu sembles si jeune" (It's a pity. You seem so young).

Gabriella blushed, unused to such blatant flattery. The man closed her passport and handed it back to her. He turned to Ace and held out his hand.

"Monsieur."

Ace gave him the dark blue passeport and waited. The man scrutinized it, looked Ace dead in the eye, and handed it back slowly. After Ace had walked a few paces, the man behind the counter nodded to the man ahead passing the luggage, keys, and other metallic objects through the x-ray machine. The other agent returned his nod slightly. Gabriella put her suitcase and purse on the conveyor belt. She then walked slowly through the detector archway to the end of the conveyor belt to wait for her things. Ace did the same. However, when Ace went through the archway, a sound beeped. Another man on the other side motioned for Ace to step aside and to stand still. The man then ran a long flat object inches away from his body up and down and front and back. Again, a beeping sound was heard. Ace put his hand in his pocket and sheepishly pulled out a quarter. The man redid the procedure but this time there was no sound. Ace smiled and said, "Musta been the quarter." He went to the conveyor belt to retrieve his stuff but another agent commanded him, "Ouvrez-la s'il vous plait" in French and then said, "Opeen eet pleeze" when his suitcase came through the machine. Ace unzipped the suitcase and the man ruffled through the socks, shoes, shirts, sweaters, pants, underwear, and also the toiletry bag that Gabriella had hastily packed for him. Nothing captured his interest so he zipped it closed and said, "You can take eet," like he was disappointed for not finding anything interesting.

Ace picked it up and joined Gabriella who was watching. Ace put his left arm around her and they began to walk toward the main hall of the airport. When they were out of earshot he said, "Let's not stay here more than we need to. All these military guys make me nervous."

When they entered into the reception area they were met by people holding signs with names of companies for people just arriving as well as a throng of others to pick up family or friends.

Ace spied a table on the outside of a café in the large hall.

"Gabby, let's sit down and see where we're going."

They put their suitcases between their feet. Ace pulled his wallet out of his back pocket and took out a small card, which was a miniature map of the subway routes in Paris. His French teacher had given it to him in French class when she learned he wanted to visit Paris some day. Ace looked at the multicolored lines for a moment and said, "Gabby. It looks like we need to take the RER train into Châtelet and then take the métro in the direction of La Défense. It's only three stops to Champs-Elysées Clémenceau. We can get off there and get something to eat. Okay?"

"Sounds good to me," Gabriella said, "but let's find a place where we can talk. We need to talk about what we're doing. It was killing me not being able to say anything on the plane. I've got all kinds of questions."

"I know. I know. But let's get somewhere half-way private, first. Okay? I've got to change some U.S. money for some Euros. We'll hold onto the cash until we can find a place with a good rate. According to our French teacher, all we need to do is find an ATM machine and use my American bank card. They automatically give me Euros and I'm only charged about $1.00 for the transaction."

"But won't they be able to track your transaction?" she asked under her breath.

"Yeah, you're right, but the banks won't open for another five hours or so in New York and then we'll be long gone. I think it'll also take them some time to figure out where we are."

Ace put the card back into his wallet and then into his jeans. As they were surveying the area a thin man with a black vest, white shirt and black pants approached their table.

"Mademoiselle, Monsieur. Café?"

Ace said, "Non, Merci" and then slipped into English. "We were just looking for a ATM machine. Do you know where one is?"

"Ah. ATM macheen. Hmm. What izzz that, Monsieur?"

Gabriella came to the rescue. "C'est une machine pour retirer de l'argent."

"Ahh. Ca. Je comprends. Mais nous acceptons les cartes bleues. No problem" (I understand. But we accept credit cards). He smiled knowing Americans loved using this expression.

"Sorry. We were just trying to get our bearings," Ace said quickly.

"I am very sorry, then, sir. You must buy somezing to seet here."

"I gotcha. We'll go." Ace leaned over and put the map into his suitcase pocket and closed it. He straightened up and turned to Gabriella.

"Let's go, Gabby. We'll find an ATM on our own."

"But eet iz right over there, Monsieur," the waiter said pointing across the hall.

Ace looked and saw three machines attached to the wall next to a glass partitioned office for the bank Credit Agricole.

"Ah . . . merci. Au revoir."

"Au revoir," Gabriella repeated, wanting to practice her French.

"Au revoir, mes enfants," the man said in a patronizing kind of tone.

After they had walked a few steps, Ace shook his head and said, "Guy's got a lot of nerve. 'Mes enfants.' He can't be over twenty-five himself."

"Ace. Don't let it get to you. The French are not known for their politeness."

"Yeah, you're right. Can't afford to get into a fight here."

As they approached the ATM, Ace took out his bank card and inserted it into the appropriate slot. He tried to get 1,000 euros but it spit back his card with a message that he had to contact his bank. A cold wave of fear coursed through his body.

"No. They couldn't have blocked my account already. It's not possible."

"Whatsamatter, Ace?" Gabby leaned forward picking up on his anxiety.

"The machine wouldn't give me 1, 000 Euros."

"Wait. Ace. Isn't the Euro more valuable than the dollar?" Gabriella said hopefully.

"Whew, I was panicking," Ace said letting out a sigh of relief. "Thanks, Gabby. That's right. I think it's at $1.27 or something for one euro which would put me over the daily limit in dollars. I'll try again and only ask for 800 euros."

Ace put the card back in and tapped in the new number. Presto. Multi-colored bills appeared out of one slot and the card popped out another. He gave Gabriella a 20 euro bill and said, "Take this, Gab. Maybe you'll wanna get a souvenir somewhere."

"Thank you, Mr. Gates," Gabriella said smiling. "You're so generous. But you've kept 780 euros for you." She slid the bill into her pocket.

"Yes. Just for safekeeping. And it's for 'us' not me," Ace said. He put the rest of the cash into his wallet, and then slipped his wallet into his front pocket to make it more difficult for thieves to access.

"So far, so good," he whispered to Gabriella. "Let's find that train to the city."

Chapter 22

A Not So Romantic Experience
Tuesday, May 20, 2003

As Ace and Gabriella walked down the sidewalk of the Champs-Elysees they finally found a café with small round tables in front. Though it was a little cool, they decided to sit down at one of these instead of going inside. Several people were smoking and reading French newspapers or just drinking from little Espresso cups staring at the passersby. Ace found it funny that all the people were facing toward the sidewalk. Watching pedestrians was obviously a French hobby. They sat down at a small round table as far away from the others as possible. It took ten minutes for a woman to show up for their orders. She was thin as a pencil and wore black slacks and a red sweater.

"Mademoiselle, Monsieur?" she asked with the emotion of a bored cat.

"Ah, yeah. Could we have two Espressos and two croissants, please?" Ace blurted out before he realized he should have tried to speak in French.

"Yes. Are you Engleesh?" she probed.

"Ah. No. American."

"Good. I like Americans," she smiled demurely. They didn't know what she did: that Americans had the habit of tipping even when it was included in the total, while the English knew they weren't obligated to and were not known for excessive generosity.

"C'est bien," Ace ventured, "et nous aimons les Francais."

"That eese nice. We French don't like your president too much."

"No comment. Merci." Ace was not in the mood for a political discussion before lunch or after lunch for that matter.

After she left Gabriella said, "It's women like that who make me feel fat."

"Don't worry, Gabby, "Ace responded quickly, "I think you're just right. A little wind and she would probably fly away."

"Thanks, Ace, but can we talk about some things now?"

"Yeah. What's on your mind?" He buttoned his jean jacket to block out the cool air.

"Umm. Like what are we going to do after our breakfast?" She put her elbows on the table and framed her face between her two hands and stared straight at Ace.

"Well, we probably should get out of town and find a hotel or youth hostel somewhere in a different city—you know, after we have seen a few sights like the Eiffel Tower. If the police send someone after us they will probably check the major hotels here in Paris."

"You really think so? There must be hundreds and hundreds of them here. It would take them forever."

"Well, they could get lucky. You never know. If we hop the TGV train to the south of France, like Marseille, it would really throw them off. It's also a lot warmer down there this time of year."

Gabriella shivered and said, "That may not be a bad idea."

The waitress returned with the small white cups and saucers and two croissants.

"Voilà," she said and laid them on the table. "It eeese four euros twenty."

Ace fished his pocket, pulled his wallet and took out a ten euro bill.

"You can take two euros for yourself. I know tips are important."

The woman took the bill and said, "Zank you, Monsieur," and nodded her appreciation. After she left Gabriella said, "Ace, do you know you just gave her about a two-fifty tip for two coffees and two croissants? Normally, if I understand it right, the tip is included in the price."

"Did I? Is it? Oh. I guess I'll have to watch it in the future."

"Please. Your money won't last long if you spend it like that."

"Yes, Mrs. Parks. I will try not to spend our money so foolishly next time."

"Ace. I know I should be happy that we will be getting married but I'm nervous. This is nothing like I expected it to be. You've run over a little girl. I've lied to my father. My mother is alone in a psychiatric hospital . . ."

"Gabby. You're not sorry you came, are you?" Ace felt a gnawing in his stomach that didn't come from hunger.

Gabriella took out the elastic from her hair and shook her head. Her black long hair swung from side to side by her cheeks.

"No, Ace. I am not saying that. It's just scary. The police are looking for you. We don't know if this girl lived or not and we don't know when we can ever go back to our own country."

"Okay. You can go home, if you want. I'll buy you a ticket and you can go back this morning." Ace's anger was bubbling to the surface. Now he felt betrayed by his best friend. Gabriella started crying.

"No, Ace. I don't want to go home now. I made the decision to come with you. We're here. I'm just scared. That's all."

Ace scolded himself for being so quick to get angry and softened immediately seeing Gabriella's tears. He put his hand on Gabriella's.

"I'm sorry, Gabby. I'm scared too. I shouldn't have gotten you mixed up in all this." He picked up her hand with the ring on it and said, "This ring here says I'm committed to you no matter what. If you want to go back, you can. We can get married when all this is over in the States, if that's what you want."

Gabriella had her hand over her face to cover her tears and was inhaling deeply. After she shed a few more tears and stopped sobbing, she took her hand off her face. Wet streaks lined both her cheeks. With tired moist red eyes she said to Ace, "Ace. I love you. I want to marry you. I'm not going without you. If you think we should stay in France, I'm staying with you. If you want to go back, we go together, not alone. Okay?"

"Okay," Ace confirmed. "Thanks, Gabby. You're the best." To see her so vulnerable made her look even more beautiful to him. He marveled again how someone so good and attractive could be interested in him.

Gabriella laughed softly and looked down at her plate. "I think I got my croissant wet."

"That's okay. Take mine." He lifted it off the plate and gave it to Gabriella. He then took the one on Gabriella's plate and took a bite of it.

"Hey, it tastes even better," he exclaimed.

"C'mon, Ace. Don't be corny," she said, a smile curling up on the right side of her face. She took a bite of the croissant Ace had given to her.

"Hmm. Fresh. Sure beats the ones we get at the grocery store."

The waitress returned and gave Ace the change in coins. She said, "Merci, bonne journée" and walked over to another table where a new arrival had just sat down.

Ace and Gabriella grabbed their suitcases and continued down the sidewalk. They passed a magazine store with a sandwich board in front. On it was plastered a blown-up photo of a bare-breasted woman.

"Whoa," Ace yelped when his eyes landed on the poster. "That's a little different."

Gabriella was a little taken aback as well at the overt nudity right on the sidewalk.

"Just look the other way, Ace, please. I don't want you to want her more than me."

"Yes, Mrs. Parks. You don't have to worry about that. You know that you're all I want . . . which reminds me. Should we try to get married today? You know, so we can be together tonight . . ."

"How can you even think about that right now?" Gabriella said giving Ace a scolding sideward glance.

"Well, you're the one that brought up the subject and it is something practical we haven't really discussed yet. I mean we have been really good since we've been going out . . ." For some reason their pace had quickened, not to mention Ace's pulse.

"You are funny, Ace. One minute you're talking about escaping to the south of France and the next you're thinking about sleeping together."

"Well, we do need to think of our sleeping arrangements, don't we? It is logical."

"Well, Ace. We did make an agreement together last fall that we wouldn't do that until we were officially married. Remember?"

"Yeah, but . . ."

"But nothing, Ace. That was our agreement."

"You're right . . . Maybe we should just forget about the Eiffel Tower and everything and just get married right now. There must be a city hall around here where we can . . ."

"Ace. I doubt we can get married just like that. You probably need to make an appointment, fill out papers. You know, stuff like that. You're just like my dad, big on visions but short on details."

"So what do we do for tonight, then, Dear?" Ace said as sweetly as he could muster.

"Ace. Stop it. It's not funny. We made an agreement together and I intend to keep it." She hesitated briefly and continued, "We sleep in separate rooms."

"Wait a minute. That will be too strange if we say we are married and then sleep in different rooms. It would raise some suspicions. Maybe we could sleep in the same room in separate beds?" Ace offered.

"No. Ace. That would be too tempting. I suggest I take off the ring when we sign into a hotel and we register under different names in different rooms."

"But then they would have our real names."

"They are probably going to need identification anyway, Ace, to get the rooms so . . ."

"Okay. You're right. But still, it might be good to see what is involved to get officially married here."

"Let's get to our final destination for today, put all our stuff in the rooms and then check it out, okay? I want to get married and enjoy everything that goes with that, just like you do, you know."

"You do?" Ace stopped as well as Gabriella. Ace was looking intently at Gabriella. They were now in front of a take-out Chinese restaurant advertizing six different special platters.

"Of course I do. Don't be a dork. Now, where are we going?" She didn't want to look into his eyes for too long and weaken in her resolve. She thought a change of subject might help.

"It might be better to go to Marseille immediately rather than sightseeing," Ace suggested. "We can always come back to Paris." They were now standing in front of a department store called FNAC. Computers on shelves lined the store window along with other electronic equipment. A number of people were exiting and entering the building.

"Well, if we do that we will need to get back to the train station at Gare de Nord ou la Gare de L'Est, I think. Let me check the map." Ace pulled out his wallet. As he opened it to take out the little Metro card, a hand grabbed the wallet brusquely and pushed him hard onto the sidewalk. Gabriella screamed as the thief sped away into the bustling crowd. Gabriella reached down her hand to help Ace up. But Ace jumped up shaking his head, "No! No! He's not getting away with that!"

"Ace, please!" Gabriella grabbed his arm. "You'll never find him. Just let it go."

Ace, oblivious to her pleas, broke free of her grasp and bolted through the crowd in the direction where he had seen the culprit escape. He yelled as he ran, "Please. Please. Arretez-le! Arretez-le!" but people just shook their heads and kept walking. Ace saw the man run down an alley just after a florist shop and followed him. Before he had passed several apartment entrances, however, a foot appeared from a doorway. He tripped and fell, hitting the ancient street hard. Within seconds multiple fists were hitting him everywhere—the head, chest, arms. Shoes and sneakers were also kicking him from all directions. Automatically he put his hands on his head to try to cushion the blows but he had lost his equilibrium and thought he may pass out at any moment. He heard several boy voices probably cursing him in French and calling him an idiot. Suddenly he heard a hysterical familiar voice shouting, "Police! Police! La-bas! La-bas!" The kicking stopped and he heard the patter of many feet making a fast retreat. Suddenly, a soft hand caressed his face. "Ace. Ace," the voice said tenderly. "Are you okay?"

He opened his eyes and saw the compassionate green eyes of Gabriella, moist with tears, looking at him.

Ace looked behind her and to her left and right. "Ah. Where are the police?"

Gabriella smiled and said, "You're looking at them."

"You mean you just made that up?"

"Yeah." Gabriella stood up and took his hand and raised him to his feet. "Sometimes you have to be spontaneous."

Ace sighed and said, "Thank you, Gabby. You may have saved my life. I guess that was kind of rash to chase him like that. Sorry for leaving you alone."

"Forgiven. So what do we do now, brown cow?"

"Brown cow? You okay Gabby?" She took his hand and pulled him to a standing position. "You seem a little too chipper and upbeat for someone who just got all her money stolen and a boyfriend beat up."

"I'm sorry, Ace, you got hurt. I didn't think it would help for you to have a crying female on top of that. Neither will reporting this to the police for that matter. We want to stay as far away from 'les gendarmes' as we can."

"That's just great!" Ace said sarcastically as he brushed himself off.

"What a welcome to the romantic capital of the world!" Gabby said.

"Man. I just can't believe it. Why did I put all our money and the Travellers' Checks in my wallet? I am an idiot! I can't get any more money out of an ATM now because my bank card was in there!" Ace continued berating himself for a few more minutes while Gabriella looked on helplessly.

Finally, she summoned the courage to repeat her original question, "What are we going to do now, Ace?"

"I don't know, Gabby. I just don't know."

Chapter 23

The Jensen Home
Tuesday Morning, May 20, 2003

Robin Jensen, dressed in her turquoise silk bathrobe and slippers, dropped the two pieces of toast on her husband's plate to complete his breakfast meal of two fried eggs over easy, four sausage links, orange juice, and black coffee. He wore jeans and a blue cardigan sweater and his casual leather shoes from L.L. Bean. Their Siamese cat, Charley, was rubbing his side against Jerry's right calf. News from the NPR radio station acted as background filler.

"So, what are you going to do, honey?" Robin asked her husband and she watched him butter his toast.

"I don't know if there is much I can do but wait for a call from Ace. I was hoping I'd catch him at the airport, but like I said last night . . ."

"Sorry, I was half asleep when you came to bed."

"I know. But the Fast Flight lady said he took the charter to Montreal with the idea of taking a connecting flight somewhere. I checked with British Airways to see which major cities they were flying to. I saw there was a 9:20 with British Airways to Paris on the internet, but I wasn't able to get through on the phone. I know his mom knew someone in France. But I don't know. They could have gone to a number of large cities. I was able to leave an urgent message at Charles De Gaulle airport, though, at the information desk, but who knows if he is going to hear the announcement or if they are even going there. And did you process what else I said last night?" He took a quick sip of coffee.

"Oh . . . what was that?"

"Ace had a girl with him and told the Fast Flight people that they were married."

"What? Oh no . . . it wasn't that sweet girl who works at Dr. Glass's office, was it?"

"My guess is yes. Whenever Ace talked about any girl it was her and only her. He just said they were married to throw people off the trail. No way did they have time to do that officially. I found his mom's old Oldsmobile in the parking lot. His cell phone was in the back seat."

"That was how he was able to avoid the police I bet."

Robin sat down in the chair next to her husband, her elbows on the table.

"Yeah. He's a smart kid but I don't think he's acting very wise right now. He's running like a scared rabbit. I'm positive the probation office will be calling me soon about all this." He took another sip of his coffee.

"What will they want?"

"Probably just try and threaten Ace through me. Who knows? They may say if he doesn't give himself up he could be facing that time in jail that he could have received for that bar fight he got mixed up in."

"How about the girl? Will she get in trouble with the police, too?"

"Her problem will probably be more with her old man rather than the police. No doubt she went willingly. But, she could get nailed with being an accomplice to his escape, I don't know. If they have sex, he could be charged with having sex with a minor. I'd have to check the laws on that here in New York State. As far as I know she's not 18 yet."

"Shouldn't we call the police?"

"Not yet. They'll find his car eventually. I want to try and convince him to come back on his own first."

Chapter 24

The Eiffel Tower
Tuesday, May 20, 2003

Well, at least we can say we saw the Eiffel Tower," Ace said to Gabriella as they sat down on the concourse steps in full view of the famous metallic structure. They had just walked all the way from the Champs-Elysées and were worn out.

"Yeah. Impressive. But what are we going to do, Ace? We can't sleep outside tonight. Do you know anyone here we can call?"

"I don't, but my mom knew a missionary she supported for a bunch of years. Not sure, though, if he's still here. His name was Gary McKinley."

Gabriella looked confused. "A missionary to France? It's a Catholic nation. Why would they need missionaries?" Gabriella put her right hand in the middle of her back and stretched. "I thought all missionaries went to Africa."

"Yeah. I did, too, like Dr. Livingstone and Albert Schweitzer. But the way my mom explained it—although there are many confessing Catholics, few attend Mass and there are very few Protestants. I think the guy told us there was probably less than 1% Evangelicals. In fact, the guy said that you could consider Europe as a whole as post-Christian."

"Well, do you think he would help us if we could find him?"

"I think so. I've still got some change. Maybe we'll get lucky. Do you see a telephone booth somewhere?" They both looked in all directions. A few young boys with spiked hair and lip ornaments, wearing jeans and tee-shirts, were skateboarding down the concourse, even jumping down the concrete steps without falling.

"Let's ask that guy in the white truck over there by the Eiffel Tower. It says 'Frites' on the side. It must be a French fry stand. He might know."

Ace and Gabriella pulled out their suitcase handles and pulled their luggage to the truck. The truck, which opened up into an outdoor snack food store, featured French fries and crepes as well as other types of dough creations. A red-faced man with a white apron was throwing batter on a hot circular grill and spreading it with a special utensil.

"Excusez-moi Monsieur. Est-ce que vous savez où je peux trouver une cabine téléphonique?"

"Très bon français Mademoiselle. Anglaise ou américaine ?"

"Américaine."

"Bon... Tour Eiffel vous en trouverez une. Mais vous devez avoir une carte téléphonique pour l'utiliser" (If you go nearer to the Eiffel Tower you will find one but you will need a telephone card to use it).

"Oh. Comment puis-je obtenir une carte comme ça?"

The man pointed in the direction of the nearest street. "Là-bas dans un magasin où tu peux acheter des magazines et des journaux."

"Merci, Monsieur. Vos crêpes ont l'air vraiment bonnes" (Thank you, Sir. Your crepes look truly good).

"Merci. Pas chères non plus."

"Merci. Peutêtre un autre fois."

"Au revoir."

"Au revoir, Mademoiselle."

Gabriella led the way to the store as Ace followed. "What did he say?" Ace finally asked.

"There's one near the Eiffel Tower, but we need telephone cards to use it."

"Great. I wonder how much they cost." They passed a beggar sitting on a curb with a cigar box for an offering plate and Ace said, "You probably have more than we do today." The man smiled when he heard Ace say something, but it turned to a frown as they walked past.

When they reached the small store with the diamond-shaped yellow glass sign with a red feather and PRESSE in big black letters, Gabriella and Ace went in. Pornography covered the top three levels of the magazine racks while others featured periodicals with a variety of languages. Ace quickly turned his head from the onslaught of seduction and focused on the *New York Times* newspaper in English on the rack near the counter. An old man with a haggard look raised his eyebrows in anticipation of Gabriella's question.

"Oui. Avez-vous des cartes téléphoniques, Monsieur?"

"Certainement, Mademoiselle. Pour combien de temps? Une heure? Deux heures? Comme vous voulez" (One hour? Two hours? Whatever you want).

"Quelle est la plus petite carte?"

"Une demi-heure."

"D'accord. Une, s'il vous plaît." The man pulled out a packet and slid one card off for Gabriella. She gave him the 20 euro bill and he dropped the change in coins into her outstretched palm. They left the store and retraced their steps to the concourse near the Eiffel Tower.

A number of people were standing on line at the ticket window, including a group of Asians with big cameras hung around their necks. They were talking excitedly in their mother tongue when Ace and Gabriella arrived. To the left of the ticket booth they noticed three phone booths back to back. Before Ace went into one of them he said, "Gabby, watch the suitcases closely, okay? At this point, I trust no one in Paris." He pushed his way in but came out immediately. "Ah . . . Gabby. Could you tell me which numbers I need to call for information? I don't understand what's written next to the numbers." They exchanged places and Gabriella looked quickly and said, "Twelve."

"Twelve? That's it?" Ace asked incredulously.

"Yeah. That's it. Just twelve."

"Okay. Here goes." Ace pushed the card in the slot and waited for it to clear. Finally, the number of minutes he could talk appeared on the little screen and a request to punch in the telephone number. He punched in the numbers one and two. He heard a machine voice announcing France Telecom and the company theme music and then a request for a name and city. "Ahh . . . Ahh. Gabby . . . here, it's a recording . . ." They quickly changed places.

"Well?" Ace asked.

"I think the call is being transferred to an operator. What is the guy's name and where does he live?"

"Ahhh. Umm. His name is McKinley. M . . C . . K . . I . . N . . L . . E . . Y. Gary. I forget where he lived."

"Great," Gabriella said sarcastically. She waited a few more minutes and then gave the name McKinley, making sure to spell it with the French pronunciation of the letters instead of in English. She frowned and turned to Ace, "She says there's no one in Paris by that name. Should we have her expand the search to France in general?"

"Can't hurt, I guess. It is possible he moved."

Gabriella spoke a few more words in French and gave Ace a hopeful look. "She's checking . . ."

Gabriella turned her eyes again from Ace to concentrate on listening to whatever response she was given. "Oh . . . she says there's a person by that name in a city called Sézanne." She asked the operator, "Où est cette ville" (Where is this city)? She turned to Ace again and said, "She says it's east of Paris less than 200 kilometers . . ." She quickly pulled a pen out of her purse and began scribbling numbers on an old receipt. "Merci, Madame. Merci beaucoup." She hung up the phone. "Well, this could be him. I think you should be the one to call him. Here's his number." She handed Ace the phone and the slip of paper and they exchanged places again.

"It's kind of amazing that in all of France that there was only one McKinley. I guess that shows how few Americans actually live here. I just hope it's the right guy." He tapped off the numbers on the receipt and waited. A female voice answered, "Oui. Bonjour."

"Umm. I don't speak French too well. But do you understand English?"

The woman responded immediately, "Oh, yes. Are you American by any chance?"

"Umm, Yes. I am. I was wondering: is this the home of Gary McKinley?"

"Why yes it is. May I say who is calling?"

"Sure. My name is Ace Parks. He knew my mom."

"Ace Parks? Are you calling from the States?"

"No. Actually, I'm in France. In Paris. And I, rather we, have a problem."

"In France! That's wonderful. I'm sorry about your mom. We heard about what happened through some mutual friends. But wait just a minute. Gary will pick it up in his study." She then took the phone away from her mouth and yelled, "Gary! Gary! It's Ace Parks. He's in Paris. Pick up the phone, please."

Ace heard a faint "All right, dear" in the background and then a cheery welcoming voice: "Ace. What a pleasant surprise. Sorry to hear about your mom. What brings you to France? I thought you were still in school."

Ace hemmed and hawed a bit and then said, "Umm. Well. That's quite a complicated story. Right now, though, I am in kind of a mess."

"What's the matter, Ace?"

"Well, I'm here with my friend, Gabriella, and we just had all of our money stolen. Is there any way you could help us?"

"Gabriella. Oh. I think your mom might have mentioned her. She was quite impressed with her as I recall. But sure, we could help. Where are you now?"

"We're by the Eiffel Tower."

"Okay. It will take me some time to get there. We're about an hour and a half from you. But be at the entrance at two o'clock and I'll pick you up. Have you had any lunch?"

"Ahh . . . no."

"No problem. I'll bring some fruit and Wendy will prepare a nice meal when we get back."

"That's really nice of you, Mr. McKinley." He was smiling at Gabriella.

"Our pleasure. See you soon," McKinley said.

"Bye." Ace hung up after hearing the click on the other end and hugged Gabriella. They both exited the telephone booth still holding on to one another.

"Well. At least we won't be sleeping on the streets tonight," Ace said, taking his arm from around Gabriella. "We could get an earful of the Jesus rap though."

"I think I'll prefer that to sleeping on a park bench some-where," Gabriella confessed. "I was starting to get worried. When will they get here?"

"He said in about an hour and a half. Do you want to explore a little? "

"Sure. Why not? Only let's not go too far," Gabriella warned.

"Do you have a credit card or bank card by any chance?" Ace asked.

"No credit card. My dad hates them. Says he'd rather pay in cash or check with money he has, not with borrowed money . . . And no, I don't have a bank card either. Remember, I've been putting my money into a savings account."

"Oh yeah. Well, maybe we could find an internet café and see if there is any news about the girl."

"Good idea." They pulled the extended handles out of their suitcases and began rolling them noisily along the asphalt toward the business district. The sounds and smells of city life filled the air. Cars and buses were honking and moving. Pedestrians were clicking their heels on the sidewalk and also walking quickly to wherever they were going. Gabriella noticed that many women wore high heels, and black was definitely in vogue.

Chapter 25

Crepes in Paris
Tuesday, May 20, 2003

D id you find anything?" Gabriella asked, bending over to look at the flat computer screen that Ace was presently staring at intently. They found an internet café only three blocks away on the same street as the store with the telephone cards. Fortunately, the charge per hour at the café was only four euros. Ace had quickly gone to the *Albany Tribune* web page and found nothing. It was still early in the morning the day after the accident, so any article on the accident hadn't been posted yet. He tried Channel 10 News. Still nothing.

"I think it's still too early, Gabby, to get any news." He lowered his voice, "Maybe I should try Elijah, or somebody. What do you think?" Gabby looked down the table. The set-up was one long table with eight screens in front of the chairs and two computers piled on top of one another to the right of the screen. This arrangement helped create privacy for the users since your neighbor could not see your screen unless he rolled his chair backwards three feet.

"Is that safe?" she whispered, hoping no one spoke English. They had walked past a teenage boy of about 14 at the computer next to theirs, but he was completely absorbed in trying to shoot his man running down the corridor, so she doubted he could hear them. In fact, he had the sound on so high that she could hear the gunshots coming from his headphones.

"I really don't know, to tell you the truth," Ace said. "I could leave a message and we could check it later at the McKinleys."

"Okay," Gabriella agreed. "It would be good to know what happened to the girl."

Ace typed the following: *Hey, Bro, just checking in to see how you're doing. Sorry to have to fly but no choice. Tell me: how's the girl? Thanks. Be in touch. Ciao. Jack of Hearts.* Ace signed out and they both walked out of the café. The young Moroccan woman in modern dress behind the chest-high counter at the door said, "Thank you. Goodbye. Come again" in perfect English.

Ace and Gabriella found their way back to the Eiffel Tower and passed the truck stand selling crepes. The odors drew them near and they contemplated buying one.

"Do you think we should?" Gabriella asked, weakening every second they stood staring at the next crepe being made.

"Why don't we split one?" Ace suggested. His mouth watered watching the man in the white apron spread creamy chocolate from a Nutella jar over the crepe. The man then folded the crepe perfectly with his utensil, lifted it up gently, put it on a paper towel and gave it to a waiting customer.

Gabriella was the first to speak, "Une, s'il vous plait." The man went through the same process of spreading the batter on the round grill, turning it over, adding chocolate sauce, folding it length-wise and then folding it again to make it more manageable. He slid it on to a paper towel and gave it to Gabriella. She could feel the warmth of it through the paper. Ace dropped the few euro coins into the waiting palm of the man and they turned to look at the Eiffel Tower as Gabriella took the first bite.

"Hmm. Great. Try some." She pointed the crepe toward Ace and he bent down slightly to take a bite.

"C'mon, Ace, that's the size of three of my bites." She frowned and took another bite herself.

"Why did they build that thing anyway?" Ace said, looking

up at the metal erector-set-type construction. Gabriella finished swallowing, turned the crepe towards Ace and said, "There was a world exposition of some kind in 1889. It's 984 feet tall. "

"Very good, Mrs. Roden would be proud of you."

"They say it is very pretty at night when they turn the lights on," Gabriella said.

Ace took advantage of her reverie to take an extra bite of the crepe.

"Hey. That's not fair." She turned the crepe away. "When did your friend say he was coming?"

"Around two o'clock which should be in exactly . . ." he looked at his watch, "forty-five minutes."

"Well, there's a bench. Why don't we wait over there?"

Chapter 26

An Unplanned Escape
Tuesday, May 20, 2003

McKinley didn't really like big cities, especially Paris. He had lived there for 15 years when he first joined the missionary organization more than 20 years ago and found the spiritual oppression unbearable. The cost of living there was also phenomenal and eventually beyond his level of financial support with his growing family and the general cost of living. He was thrilled, therefore, when he was asked to direct a school about 100 miles east of the capital in a little village that had more sheep than people.

His job now was to line up teachers from around the world to teach on subjects as varied as The Father Heart of God, How to Read the Bible for All Its Worth, How to Spend Time With God, Spiritual Warfare, Relationships with the Opposite Sex, Intercessory Prayer, and Forgiveness, among many others. He loved the international flavor of his organization and the fact that young students came from around the world. He had learned so much just from interacting with the students from different cultures. He could also combine his own gifts of administration, teaching, and evangelism in the schools so he felt very fulfilled, despite some occasional challenges on teams because of the cultural clashes.

The school consisted of a teaching segment of three months, and then an outreach somewhere in the world for another three months, where the students would put the teachings into practice. In the beginning of his ministry, McKinley always chose one team to lead somewhere in the world, but now he just visited the team that stayed in France for the three months and kept in touch with the others through email or the telephone.

Overall, he was quite content with his present situation. His wife, Mary, loved to welcome the students into their home with special meals and fellowship and she was also involved with teaching in the school and counseling. His own kids, despite some minor tensions related to adolescence, were walking with God and finding direction for their lives. Soon his oldest, Monica, would be leaving for the States to go to the University of Albany to study Teaching English as a Second Language, which would be very helpful in her desire to go to China after she graduated. His twin boys, Joshua and Caleb, at 17, were finding their place in the music ministry at the Center and were talking about doing a Foundations School in another country. They thought it would be beneficial to change cultures and have someone else, other than their dad, oversee the school. They were hoping to go to New Zealand after a year or two and then possibly to Australia to attend a music school with Hillsong, the cutting edge, internationally known, leader in contemporary Christian music.

As he approached Paris he tried to gear himself psychologically for the experience. He had a Renault Espace, which was similar to an American Dodge Caravan, and it was not easy navigating the wide vehicle (wide by French standards, anyway) on the narrow streets of the big city with so many pedestrians and vehicles. He knew from experience that French drivers could explode into rages for even a slight nick in their car. In his early days, he had once received a severe tongue lashing in what he was sure was a stream of vulgarities for abruptly stopping in traffic. The man following him had rammed into the back of McKinley's car, which normally would mean it was the man's fault. Instead of admitting his mistake, however, the man jumped out of his car and started yelling wildly at McKinley, indicating that he should get out and fight. When McKinley wisely locked his doors and tried to give hand gestures that he just wanted his insurance policy number, the man ran back to his car and took off, never to be seen again.

As he put on his blinker to exit the highway to follow the signs to "Centre Ville," he wondered if Ace's position about God had changed. His mom had been a faithful supporter through the years and he had met Ace several times in their modest home, but it seemed Ace just couldn't get through the abandonment he felt from his dad. Any talk of God at those times were met with anger and distrust. Who knows what he was going through now after the loss of his mom? Was he still closed and harder than ever, or was he now open to hear about the Lord? McKinley knew he would just have to trust God to lead them in their conversations.

Maybe having a girl there would be an asset. It wasn't unusual for them to take in young travelers from time to time at the Center. As long as they understood that they could not do drugs or sleep together while on the premises, they were welcome to attend some of the teaching sessions and receive food and lodging for a limited time. He remembered his own search for the truth that led him to a Creative Global Outreach Center in Afghanistan many years ago. Although he wasn't particularly interested in Christianity at the time, the conversations he had with the director left a definite impact that bore fruit later.

In his schools he found, sometimes, that interactions with the students also helped the travelers to consider the claims of Christ more seriously. Other times it was obvious the young people had major rebellious attitudes and could not submit to any of the rules required of them. These types were kindly asked to move on with a picnic lunch.

McKinley quickly pulled the van into a rare vacant parking spot in front of a boarded-up storefront and lifted out his Paris map from the space in the driver's door to figure out the best way to the Eiffel Tower.

Chapter 27

A Ride East of Paris
Tuesday, May 20, 2003

When Ace and Gabriella saw the middle-aged man walking toward them with a New York Yankees baseball cap, red and black flannel shirt, and jeans they figured it was McKinley. He had a slight paunch, thinning brown hair and twinkling brown eyes. As he reached them he stretched out his hand and said, "Hello Ace. Glad to see you again." Ace shook his hand firmly. He didn't want to lie, though. He had no intention seeing this missionary if he hadn't been forced to. He was glad, however, that they would not be sleeping on the streets.

"Yeah. Good to see you, Mr. McKinley."

"And who is this pretty girl you have with you, Ace?" McKinley turned toward Gabriella and smiled.

"Ah . . . this is my . . . fiancée, Gabriella." Gabriella smiled shyly and said, "Hello, Mr. McKinley. It was very nice of you to come and get us so quickly. You're very kind." McKinley put his hand on her shoulder and replied, "Not a problem at all. Ace's mom was a great supporter of our work here, and anything I can do for her family is an honor. It wouldn't do to have you homeless on the streets of Paris. Congratulations on your engagement, by the way. I didn't know."

"Yeah. Well, it's kinda recent," Ace said, quickly looking at Gabriella, "but we've been thinking of it for a long time." Ace shifted his neck slightly in his collar. He knew his hopes of sleeping with Gabriella tonight were dashed. But maybe . . . he cleared his throat.

"Ah, Mr. McKinley. Speaking of our marriage. Is there ahh . . . ahh . . . a justice of the peace in your town?"

"So, you're not having your wedding in the States?"

"Umm . . . well, it's kind of complicated. We're kind of eloping."

"Oh. Well, as long as you're both 18, you could get married at a town hall somewhere, but you have to arrange that in advance."

"What?" Ace was flabbergasted. He just figured that a liberal country like France would have few restrictions in this area.

"Yeah. I know it's surprising, but that's the law." He paused and asked, "But you're both 18, aren't you?"

"I'm 19 actually," Ace said, "but Gabby's not 18 until the 29th of this month."

"You look much older, Gabriella," McKinley said. He suppressed a frown. Something seemed wrong to him about this whole scenario. *A seventeen-year-old girl in France with her boyfriend looking to get married?*

"Thanks, Mr. McKinley. People always tell me that at the doctor's office where I work," Gabriella said. She suddenly realized that she had to let the doctor know, somehow, that she would not be in to work this week or maybe ever . . .

McKinley didn't press the issue. *Let them get settled and everything before diving into the deep issues.* He decided to play along and turned to Ace. "But, nine days isn't long to wait. It's possible you could make the appointment beforehand."

"Yeah, you're right," Ace replied, but he was definitely bummed out. He gave a wistful look to Gabriella. Instead of frowning, however, she gave a little knowing smile as if to say, *See, it's not as easy as you think.*

Finally, McKinley put his hands on both of their shoulders and said, "Well, we better get moving. My car is down a few blocks. I couldn't find a parking place too close. Let me take one of the suitcases, Ace." Ace gave him Gabriella's and they started the walk across the concourse dragging the suitcases on their wheels behind them. When they got to the car they put the suitcases in the cargo area, Ace got in the front passenger seat and Gabriella got in the back. McKinley pointed to the paper bag on the floor next to Ace's feet and said, "There's some mangos and kiwi fruit in the bag there, Ace, if you want something to eat." Ace reached down, opened the bag and took two mangos out and passed one to Gabriella. They both bit into their fruit immediately.

"Wow. These are wonderful," Gabriella said. "So fresh."

"Yeah, we get ours at the local market. Nothing like it."

"French car, huh?" Ace commented, with a piece of mango in his mouth.

"Yeah. Most people here buy one of the top three—Peugeot, Renault, or Citroën—for the parts. If you buy a foreign car you usually pay up the nose for parts and repair. You're also better off getting a diesel rather than gas-powered car. Fuel prices here are about three or four times what they are in the States and with diesel you can pay a little less."

"Wow. That's ridiculous," Ace said incredulously.

"Yeah. They say, too, that every dollar you spend on fuel here, 74 cents of that goes to the government," McKinley added.

"There's socialized government for you," Ace said.

"I have to say, though, it's not as bad as it seems because the government also gives out a lot of money for families with children—even to foreigners like me. As long as we have kids in school, we receive thousands of dollars a year. It's even enough for a mortgage. It's quite a substantial help, to tell you the truth. We never could have afforded our house without it."

"That's different. An atheistic government supporting a Christian missionary," Ace said somewhat amused by the news.

"Oh, yeah. That is a bit ironic," isn't it?" McKinley said,

smiling as they rode down another narrow Parisian street. "But, if they took it away I'm sure God would provide another way to support us. They are not discriminatory though. Muslim families get the same benefit." Ace ignored the comment about God and looked out the window. Here it comes, he thought: the Jesus rap.

McKinley changed the subject, however, and asked Gabriella, "Are you from Albany too, Gabriella?" She didn't hear it, though, because she had fallen sound asleep. Her head was against the head rest and her eyes were closed.

After about half an hour weaving their way around the city, they were finally on the major highway going directly east of Paris. Soon they were traveling over long, straight roads going up and down rolling hills. McKinley mentioned that the roads were so straight because the Romans had built them centuries ago. Vast fields of green were on both sides of the road and more than once they noticed flocks of sheep grazing peacefully in the grass. Although Ace wasn't particularly sleepy, he told McKinley he needed to doze off a bit. He didn't want to get into any religious discussions and he thought that closing his eyes might be the best way to avoid it.

"No problem, Ace. Get some rest. We'll talk more later. Mary should have a nice meal waiting for you."

"Thanks, Mr. McKinley." Ace took off his jean jacket, folded it, and then placed it against the window to act as a pillow. He hoped this living arrangement would not last long. There must be some way to get his hands on some cash.

Chapter 28

Albany High School
Tuesday Morning, May 20, 2003

By the time the first bell rang at Albany High School, on Tuesday after the accident, many of the students had already heard that one of their former classmates had run over a little girl and was now on the lam. Officer Peter Farley stood in the front of the homeroom class with their teacher, Mr. Gambino. Farley didn't look the stereotype of a detective. He wore a gray turtleneck sweater with a white shirt, no tie, and black pants and shoes. His manner was relaxed yet serious.

"I appreciate your willingness to let me address the class, Mr. Gambino. I'll try not to take too much time."

"Please take all the time you want," Craig Barnes quipped from the back of the room and the class erupted in laughter. Farley smiled and glanced toward Mr. Gambino with a knowing look.

"That will be all, Mr. Barnes," Gambino said. "Detective Farley is a busy man and has something important to say to you." He waited for the class to calm down and continued. "Mr. Farley."

"Thank you. As I'm sure most of you know by now, Ace Parks, a former student here, was allegedly involved in a hit and run accident yesterday down on Lincoln Avenue."

A girl gasped and cried out, "Oh, I didn't know that."

"Well, most of you knew, right?" Farley opened his eyes wide in a questioning manner. "Who didn't know?" A few students raised their hands. "To make it short, he was delivering pizzas down there and backed up over a seven-year-old girl. She's in the hospital in a coma but so far she's alive, thank God. But this is our problem. So far we have not been able to locate him. I spoke to some of the people that work with him at Luigi's, but nobody's talking. Frankly, I need your help. Ace is in trouble and he needs to turn himself in for his own good. I know you've all seen the movies and may think it's not good to snitch on someone, but I'm telling you that would be a mistake. The longer Ace remains out of custody, the worse it could be for him and this city.

"Apparently, this girl who was hit has got some vindictive cousins who would love to get their hands on Ace before we find him. A Luigi's car has also already been stoned, probably because of what has happened. So, if any one of you know where he is, or you know somebody who might know, please stay after the bell and tell me. That's all I got, Mr. Gambino."

Three seconds later a piercing bell broke the silence. Farley searched the outgoing faces for one that might make his job easier. One skinny girl with glasses and a short pixie haircut stopped by a desk in the front row. Craig Barnes brushed by her and went straight to Farley. "Ah . . . the only person I could think of who might know anything is that big football player, Elijah Williams. I know they're friends." Barnes shrugged his shoulders.

"Thanks, I'll talk with him," Farley replied, grateful for at least one lead. He took out a pad of white paper and scribbled down the information as Barnes jogged out of the room. Judy Martin, however, didn't budge any further from the desk where she was standing. Her head was down and she appeared to be staring at her right shoe. Detective Farley approached her and said softly, "Do you have something to share?"

The girl nodded. "It's hard to say, though, because I might be wrong."

"Well, you could be right, too."

"I . . . I . . . took French class with Ace last year and it seemed like he was really good friends with Gabriella Capaldi. They might even have been boyfriend girlfriend, but that's really none of my business. One day I heard them talking about how they would like to go to France together some day. But . . . a lot of kids probably say that in French class."

"That's interesting. Was Gabriella in the room just a moment ago?"

"Oh no. I think she's in Mrs. Mergardt's homeroom down the hall in 202."

Farley could barely say a thank you before the girl bolted from the room. Farley looked over at Mr. Gambino, who was shuffling through some notes on his desk to prepare for the next incoming class.

"Do you know if Ace and Gabriella had a thing going?"

"Huh . . . ah . . . Ummm . . . I hadn't noticed any particular attachment, but then again, I'm not the one who keeps track of the students' love lives. I usually don't notice until they are hanging all over one another in class, and then I have to tell them to cut it out."

"Thank you, Mr. Gambino, for all your help. Would Mrs. Mergardt be having a class right now?"

"Actually, I think she is having a study hall. You'll find her two doors down on the left."

Chapter 29

A Surprise Phone Call
Tuesday Morning, May 20, 2003
Clifton Park, NY

Steve Capaldi was sipping his second cup of black coffee and chatting with the electricians in front of Pete's Chuck Wagon, the mobile coffee shop with sandwiches and drinks, when he got the call from Detective Farley down at the high school. After the caller identified himself, Capaldi told him to hold on while he found a quiet place to talk. He walked around the garage of the $500,000 home.

"Yeah, like I said. This is Detective Farley down at the high school and I was wondering if you know where your daughter Gabriella is at this moment."

"Gabby? She should be at school. What's the matter, Officer? She stayed with a friend last night and was supposed to go to school with her this morning."

"Could you verify that she did, indeed, stay with this friend, Mr. Capaldi, because . . ."

"What are you saying? That Gabriella is not at school? Why do you need to talk with Gabriella anyway?"

"Well, you've probably heard about that hit and run down in the projects. I've got a couple of kids here that say that Ace and Gabriella were a couple and I . . ."

"No, Officer. They were not a couple. I made sure of that. Maybe a year ago . . ."

"Mr. Capaldi, I've got a kid here saying she heard them talking about going to France together and others agreeing that they were very close. She is also not at school today. I'm calling you because it is very possible that she is with Parks."

Capaldi was speechless. This was a nightmare. He felt both fear and anger frothing to the surface at the same time, and a cold sweat on his forehead.

"Officer. Officer. I think I know my own daughter . . . I will call the family and call you right back. Then we can put an end to this nonsense."

The detective gave his cell phone number and hung up. Capaldi picked up a piece of sheetrock lying on the ground and threw it hard against the cinder block foundation of the garage, where it broke into several pieces on the brown soil. *No. Gabriella. No. You wouldn't do that to me.* He found the number in his cell phone address book and pushed the button so it dialed automatically.

"Hello." It was the voice of Mary's mom, Joan.

"Yeah. Joan. Sorry to bother you. This is Steve."

"Saw your new ad last night on TV. Classy. What's up?"

"Well, normally I wouldn't ask a question like this, knowing my daughter, but I think I need to . . ."

"Yes . . . ?"

"Did Gabby stay at your house last night to work on a Physics project with Mary?"

"Gabriella? Last night? No, Steve. Mary had gymnastics until late last night, came home, ate and crashed."

"Well . . . just pray, if you do that kind of thing, and keep it to yourself. Gabby may have just done a really dumb thing."

"Okay, Steve. If I can be of any other help, please let me know."

"I will. Thanks." Capaldi terminated the call, took a deep breath, and called Farley. They made an appointment to meet at Capaldi's house in half an hour.

Chapter 30

The McKinley Home
Tuesday, May 20, 2003

McKinley and the exhausted couple were unprepared for the dinner his wife had prepared for them. The spread on the table looked like it came right out of a Norman Rockwell painting—a beautiful roasted chicken, mashed potatoes, peas, and an apple tart. She even served cheese and a fresh baguette after the main course, like French people do.

Ace was famished, so he relished every phase of the meal. He especially liked the Brie cheese that he found creamy and not too strong like the blue cheese. He remembered a famous quote from Charles DeGaulle, a former president of France: "How can you rule a people that have 365 different kinds of cheeses?" Ace even forced down the dessert. He didn't realize how much a meal could lift your spirits. He had been starving and didn't even know it.

Mercifully, McKinley didn't get into any heavy discussions. He explained that his kids weren't around because they were at a youth conference in Paris. He kept the conversation light, and that suited Ace fine. Ace explained about their plans to go south and travel a bit before going back to the States. Ace also talked about his plans to buy the pizza shop and managed to sound enthusiastic despite the fact he didn't really believe this remained a viable option.

McKinley also talked about his daughter planning to go to Albany University soon to study Teaching English as a Second

Language. He asked Ace about the city and the church that his mom had belonged to. Ace admitted he didn't know much about the church but said there were numerous Christian groups on campus, so she shouldn't have a problem connecting with other believers. Only once did he detect McKinley bordering on a spiritual question of some sort. He had hesitated with a reflective look in his eye, but then apparently thought twice about it and asked a superficial one instead. Mrs. McKinley focused more on Gabriella and talked about what she thought of France so far.

"Well, so far I've enjoyed a croissant and a crepe, but getting robbed in Paris was not the best introduction to the culture," Gabriella said after swallowing her chicken and dabbing her mouth with a red cloth napkin.

"I understand," Mrs. McKinley replied. "There were a few things I really had trouble adjusting to when we first got here."

"Like what?" Ace blurted out, suddenly becoming more animated. He figured if he could keep the McKinleys talking they would ask fewer questions.

"Oh . . ." Mary McKinley said, a little taken aback by his sudden enthusiasm. "Like the schools, for example. The mentality is so different. They push the kids so hard academically and give so little encouragement. It's more of an elitist or sink-or-swim philosophy. If you are exceptional they work with you and if not . . . it's more like intimidation. I guess they really believe the evolutionists' motto: 'Only the strong survive.' My kids told me, on a number of occasions, that their teachers called them 'zeroes' and said they would never make it. I guess the teachers think reverse psychology will help them, but I think it has a more negative effect than they realize.

"It doesn't surprise me that their teenage suicide rate is so high. Most of the French kids I know hate school. We started homeschooling our children in their younger years after a few bad experiences in the French public system. After we felt they had a firm foundation in their faith we sent them back to high school. They were ready but it was tough. Caleb, being the more introverted of them, had a really difficult time with the philosophy classes because of the intellectual pride and arrogance he was exposed to, but eventually got through it all right. I was really proud of him the day he told them a little-known story about Voltaire, one of France's great philosophers."

"Oh, what story was that?" Ace said, baiting her, leaning forward on his chair, again diverting any possible personal questions.

"It's the one about him predicting that the Bible would be obsolete in a hundred years. Ironically, the Geneva Bible Society was printing Bibles in his house one hundred years later. Caleb was ridiculed for it, but it was good for his faith to say it. Later a student even came to him and said Caleb was right: he had looked it up to make sure."

"That's interesting," Gabriella said sincerely. She liked Mrs. McKinley almost immediately upon meeting her. She was straightforward and down-to-earth, not at all the holier-than-thou kind of person she expected. Gabriella gave Ace a reproachful glance. She could tell Ace was feigning interest and it bothered her.

McKinley broke the silence that came afterwards with, "Just so you know the sleeping arrangements: Gabriella will be staying in our home and Ace in a room in another Center house. I also think you should look over the sheet we normally give to young travelers. There are certain rules that we'd like you to respect. If you have any questions after you read it, let me know and we can talk about it."

Ace and Gabriella looked at each other. Both had assumed they would be sleeping at least in the same house. Gary McKinley, on the other hand, didn't want to risk any sexual misconduct.

He also thought it would be good to talk with them one-on-one. Ace's effort to disguise his lack of interest in what McKinley's wife was saying was so obvious, McKinley almost burst out laughing with a mouthful of peas and mashed potatoes. Fortunately, he was able to control himself and save his guests from a vegetable shower.

No. He'd put Ace in a room with one of his American staff workers, Brad Roberts. Brad was witty, fun, and in charge of a multimedia department that might interest Ace. He also had a dynamic conversion experience, which couldn't hurt Ace to hear about.

"Gabriella, I can show you to your room, if you'd like," Mrs. McKinley offered gently.

Gabriella looked over at Ace and said, "Okay. Thank you, Mrs. McKinley."

"Call me Mary. That's what all the students call me." She smiled warmly and took Gabriella's suitcase. Gabriella returned the smile and followed her down the large beige ceramic tile hallway.

Ace wasn't happy with this budding relationship. The best thing to do in his opinion would be to get some money quick and leave this place and never look back.

"Ace. You there?"

"Oh yeah. Just a little tired is all," Ace said, coming back to his present reality. "Do you have internet access by any chance? I need to find out what I can do about our money situation."

McKinley had begun to clear the table and put things away in the refrigerator. "Sure do. I'll show you where it's at when we do the tour."

"You mean you don't have it here at home?" Ace said surprised. He then got up, put his hands on his waist, and bent backwards to stretch. McKinley put the plates in the dishwasher, scraped off the various items in Tupperware-type containers and then put them in the Bosch refrigerator.

"No. I prefer to have it outside of the house. It prevents me from getting too dependent on it and also keeps away the temptations. Some studies have shown that over 80% of the photos on the internet are pornographic."

"Really? I didn't know that. I've received a few pop up ads here and there but that's about it."

Ace was surprised a leader in a Christian organization could be tempted. He'd only indulged a few times himself. He just didn't like to take the time to surf the net. He had too many other things to do. With school, the job, and tutoring—not to mention time with Gabriella—most of his time was accounted for. To get sucked into spending hours and hours playing games or passively looking at a computer screen was not his idea of fun. Plus, he didn't like the feeling he got in his gut looking at the nude pictures. It always seemed to pull him deeper, never really satisfying him. He remembered, too, the story of Ted Bundy, who started off with popular soft porn magazines and later kidnapped, raped, and killed many innocent girls. No. He'd stay away from that stuff. Another thing he especially hated were the mindless violent games becoming more popular with many of the students. To him it seemed more of an obsession than fun. Hard times had definitely matured him beyond his years.

After McKinley had finished clearing the table, he directed Ace into their living room. McKinley sat in a tan vinyl armchair and gestured for Ace to sit on the brown leather couch to his left. Ace looked around the room and noticed the antique furniture. He noticed that the walls were decorated with two kinds of wallpaper, with another colorful six-inch band with various fruits on it separating them about waist high. The bottom was dark maroon and the top more of a yellow gold with some lightly sketched wheat grains apparently blowing in the wind. The house was probably more than a hundred years old with some old dark wooden beams running parallel on the ceiling and large vertical windows that opened by a handle in the middle. A framed print of a woman praying in what looked like a prison cell was hung on the wall above another couch, opposite where Ace was sitting. When McKinley saw Ace looking at it he said, "That's an interesting story there. The woman's name is Constance and she was imprisoned for 40 years in a tower during the persecution of Protestants for believing in the Bible."

"Wow," Ace said. "That's a long time. Did she die there?" Ace turned his head to see if to see if Gabriella was coming down the hall any time soon. He sensed a personal question about his faith just on the horizon.

"Actually, France has a history of a lot of martyrs who were willing to die for their faith. You know at one time France was almost 40% Protestant?"

While the guys were discussing French history the ladies were chatting about French soap. Gabriella was pleasantly surprised to see a card on her pillow and a small clear plastic bag of little purple bars of soap scented with lavender and tied with a gold ribbon. The card had a miniature print of a painting by Monet and a handwritten welcome to their home. The single bed also had a beautiful quilt on it with blue and yellow squares. Two pink roses in a vase were on the bedside table.

It was a rare experience for Gabriella to be welcomed so warmly. Usually, she was the one who did all the welcoming when people came to their home. Nowadays it was pretty much limited to her dad's drinking buddies. To keep them happy all she had to do was keep the bottles of beer on the table and warm up a few pizzas. Eventually, she refused to do even that when they got too rowdy and demanding. Normally, she would just plan to go over to someone else's house the night they came. She and Ace had agreed that they wouldn't meet at his house.

One night they made the mistake and they went too far physically and she didn't want to repeat the mistake. They agreed together afterwards to keep to their original plan to wait until after their wedding to have sex.

"Umm . . . Gabriella," Mary McKinley began in a more quiet and serious tone. "I want to ask your forgiveness for being so negative about the French culture at the dinner table. There are really a lot of things I appreciate about the French culture."

"Oh. I didn't take it that way," Gabriella assured her, putting the plastic bag of soap on the bed and tilting her head slightly. "I thought you were just being honest. I would be interested, though, in what you like about France."

"Well, one thing I really like is how a lot of families take time in the middle of the day at lunch to eat the big meal together. I've noticed in America how rare that is becoming these days even in the evenings. It's actually healthier to have the big meal in the middle of the day, because then you burn off the calories instead of sleeping on them like we do in the States."

"That's interesting. I did notice how French women seem to be skinnier."

"You noticed that, too," Mary quipped with her eyes twinkling and they both broke out laughing spontaneously.

When Ace saw the womenfolk coming down the hallway he stood to his feet to show his zeal for a grounds tour. Instead, Mr. McKinley said, "Hold on now fella. We need to have our coffee now. You'll get a kick out of the little cups. Don't be fooled, though, it's strong stuff."

"Yeah, Espresso, right," Ace said knowingly.

"Right. Would you like some?"

"Ahh . . . naw. I mean no thanks. I had a cup this morning."

Gabriella sat down on the couch where Ace had just been sitting and nodded her head to encourage him to sit back down.

"Yeah, but I don't mind if you want some," he said, catching his faux pas and joining her on the couch.

Mrs. McKinley looked over to Gabriella. "Would you like some, Honey?"

"Yes, please," Gabriella said, leaning back into the leather couch, ready for more conversation. Ace, however, stayed on the front of the cushion, hoping for a rapid change of location. He was convinced that a God talk was coming and Gabriella was like a lamb waiting for the slaughter.

Chapter 31

The Capaldi Home
Tuesday, May 20, 2003

Would you like a beer, Officer?" Steve Capaldi said as he opened the small fridge behind the bar counter in the living room and grabbed himself a cold bottle.

"No thanks. Like to but I try not to indulge during business hours."

"I understand," Capaldi said as he popped the cap and took a swallow. He sat down on his lounge chair and tried to appear under complete control. His stomach felt otherwise.

"What can you tell me about my daughter?"

"Well, we're still working on it. We thought we had him in Kingston but he wasn't on the bus. The kid faked us out by buying a bus ticket to NYC and then driving off somewhere else."

"So, where do you think he is?"

"Not sure. One girl at the school said she heard this kid Parks and your daughter Gabriella talking about going to France together."

"How would they make it to France?"

"A plane."

"I know how you get to France, Officer. My question is: how could they possibly do that without the police stopping them? Isn't the airport one of the first places the police check out?"

"Ah . . . not necessarily. Since the kid was in a car the first thing we do is notify all the police on the major routes to be on the look out for his model car and license number. Most kids don't have access to that kind of cash on short notice, so we concentrate on the more likely means of escape."

"And if by some devil luck he did get the money and they got to the airport and there was a plane going in that direction?"

"That's yet to be seen, Mr. Capaldi. I will be checking that out this morning. I will let you know if we discover anything."

"This morning? The accident happened last night. They'd have plenty of time to do almost anything. I want this kid found, my daughter back, and I want him to pay for kidnapping my daughter."

"Well, ahhh . . . Mr. Capaldi. We don't believe this would be considered a kidnapping. It appears she went on her own volition."

"But she is a minor, only 17! She's a smart girl. Why would she drop everything and follow this idiot? It just doesn't make sense."

"Well, sir, kids get crushes on each other for different reasons. I had one on a girl back in high school because she wore black riding boots and long dresses to school."

"Black riding boots?"

"Yeah. I know. The point I'm trying to make is she could be infatuated with the guy for who knows what. Half the time it's being in love with love. He says "I need you" and bang, she's caught —hook, line, and sinker. It's called the Florence Nightingale phenomenon. The guy's hurt. She helps him. She feels needed. Bingo. It's love."

"The what?"

"I'm sorry, I didn't mean to get into all this. I took a psychology course in night school and . . ."

"Look, Detective Farley, I don't care what you have to do to get him. Just get him. I want my daughter back safe and sound. Do you understand?"

"Yes, sir. There are a number of people working on this case right now. I'll let you know as soon as we have something concrete." Farley got up to leave and walked around the glass coffee table.

"Detective. Just one more thing . . ." Capaldi got up from his chair and followed Farley to the front door. "What if by some stroke of coincidence, they were able to catch a flight to France or somewhere else? What would the police do in a case like that?"

"That would certainly complicate things. If they are still in the States we can work with the local police agencies. If the little girl stays in a coma and they make it to another country, there's not much we can do. I don't think France would extradite for a hit and run. If she dies, however, that could be a different story."

"Well, Officer, they must be stopped from leaving this country."

"We will do our best, Mr. Capaldi. Goodbye." Farley walked to his unmarked black Pontiac, got in and drove away. Capaldi finished his beer, gritted his teeth, and clenched the bottle tighter. If this Parks kid was in the room right now, he would not hesitate to strangle him with his own bare hands.

Chapter 32

Albany Police Department
Tuesday Afternoon, May 20, 2003

Hey, Sarge. Somebody named Reverend Johnston wants to talk with you."

Sergeant Pierce was not pleased with this information. He knew this guy was a nuisance and would do anything for political advantage. In his mind, this Johnston guy saw himself as the next Martin Luther King, but Pierce didn't buy it. To Pierce he was nothing more than a publicity hound who would do anything to get his face on the evening news. In fact, he was the one who got the blacks all riled up about the Howard Moore incident in Pennsylvania, which had repercussions in Albany. Already the call from the police in Kingston put him in a foul mood. He thought the hit and run was all sewed up and he could concentrate on something else. Now, what did this muckraker want?

"Tell him I'm busy. I'll talk with him another time."

"Ahh . . . he says he heard you and that you better listen to him. He's pretty insistent, Sarge. Says it has to do with that hit and run down on Lincoln. He wants to know if you've got that driver yet. He says things are liable to get pretty hot down there if he's not in custody soon."

Oh great, Pierce thought. *Who told this guy about the accident? He doesn't even live around here.* "All right. All right. I'll take it." Pierce shook his head and braced himself for what he was about to hear. He pushed the flashing plastic button on the phone and said, "Yes, Mr. Johnston. What's on your mind?"

A hoarse, forceful voice could be heard by the deputy three desks over from Pierce.

"My people up here in your town want to know if and when you are going to pick up that hit and run driver that ran over little Henrietta Wilson."

The "my people" routine really irked Pierce. The people in the projects might share the same skin color as him, but he doubted they ever saw him unless there was an accident that he could stoke for his advantage. To quote the name of the girl was vintage Johnston. Just the right personal touch to sway the masses. "Well, Mr. Johnston, I don't know how you got wind of this accident but I would advise you not to stir up the people down there. We have enough problems in that neighborhood."

"Hold on, sir. Hold on. They don't need me to get them stirred up. They're already stirred up. They called me this morning. They told me a little girl's been hit by a reckless pizza driver who didn't care enough to look behind himself as he was backing up. In fact, he didn't even stop to see what he had done, they told me. The momma's heartbroken and the girl is in a coma at Albany Med and they're not even sure if the girl is going to make it. No, sir. the peoples are already stirred up and they've asked me to see what I could do to bring this criminal to justice. I'm doing my best just to calm everybody down."

"Mr. Johnston." Pierce could not get himself to use the word *Reverend*. "Mr. Johnston, please tell the people down there that we are doing the best we can to apprehend this driver and we should have him in custody soon."

"I will do my best, sir, but I may not be able to control some of the rowdier ones. Some of Henrietta's cousins are pretty mad about what's happened and if the driver is not in jail soon I don't know what they'll do."

"Thank you, Mr. Johnston, for your concern. I just ask you

not to get the people worked up down there. It will only make matters worse."

"I will do what I can, sir, but I can't give you no guarantees. Please call me if you have any new info to give me. I gave my cell number to the first officer who answered the phone."

"Thank you. I will keep you abreast of any further developments."

Officer Pierce hung up the phone and gave some orders. "Peters. Have officers Harris and Bradley go over by Luigi's and be on the lookout for any suspicious characters coming from the projects. Tell them to advise the manager not to send any more drivers to Lincoln or anywhere near there for the time being. Have them interview some of the crew at Luigi's and see if this Parks kid has some close friends who could give us some leads. Also alert the guys down near the projects that there might be an impromptu rally by Mr. Johnston. If he gets too inflammatory, tell them to haul him in. Mary, you contact the local police in all the surrounding towns and the State Police and give them the license number of Parks' car and its description and tell them we need to find him fast. It could very well avoid a race riot."

Chapter 33

*The Apostolic Pentecostal Revival Church
Tuesday Early Evening, May 20, 2003
Albany, NY*

When Palmer arrived at the church it was already packed with black faces. He pushed his way in saying, "Press. Tribune. Thank you." A young black woman at the door gave him a smile and a song sheet. Reverend Johnston heard the magic words and bounded from his chair near the podium with a wide grin and shook his hand. "Glad to see you here, Mister . . . Mister . . ."

Palmer pulled out his business card and completed the sentence for him. "Palmer's the name." He bowed his head a little out of embarrassment for all the attention Johnston had bestowed on him. He felt guilty by association.

"Well, Mr. Palmer, I'm happy that the Tribune knows when something important is going on. Welcome. Please. We've reserved the first row for journalists. Just over here." The Reverend Johnston then led Palmer over to some folding chairs that had hand-written signs taped to the backs that read PRESS. A nervous young woman with long blonde hair and a grey raincoat sat on one of the seats. She was obviously relieved that there was at least one other white face in the crowd besides her own and the cop in the back.

"Howdy, Miss. Which paper you from?" Palmer said cordially as he sat down.

"Just the weekly Albany Standard. I applied for the Tribune when I first got out of college, but there were no openings." She frowned as if she worked in the minor leagues.

"It's a tough business but keep trying. You never know when something might pop up." Palmer hoped he was being prophetic for himself. She'd be welcome to take his job, but he wouldn't wish Editor Bascom on his worst enemy.

"Really? How long have you been with the Tribune?"

He wanted to say, "too long," but instead said, "Twelve years."

"Wow," she said, obviously impressed. He noticed that the TV stations were absent. That was probably why the reverend wasn't starting on time. On more than one occasion Palmer caught him casting furtive glances in the direction of the door as if expecting lights and cameras any minute. Palmer looked around at the crowd and remembered how he had felt one day at the capital concourse when it was filled with African Americans on Black Pride Day. He understood in a split second how a black person must feel in a sea of whites—uncomfortable and vulnerable. What if they suddenly turned on him because he was different? He felt no fear here, however. The Reverend Johnston would probably hurl his own body in front of any assailant just to protect the man who was going to print his words.

At 8:45 the silver-haired pastor of the church must have figured it was time to get the show on the road, because he nodded to the young man at the keyboards and then used his hands to indicate to everyone that they should stand up. There was a general shuffling of shoes and chairs and the young man began singing, "We will overcome." After a few more standard gospel songs, a young girl of about ten came to the microphone and sang, "His eye is on the sparrow." As soon as she finished the Reverend Johnston was properly introduced by the pastor and given the center stage.

His first words were, "My, my, my. That was one of the sweetest renditions I've ever heard of one of my favorite gospel songs. Thank you, dear child, for your lovely interpretation. 'His eye is on the sparrow and I know He watches me.' In fact, it is on behalf of a little sparrow that I have gathered you all here tonight. Henrietta Wilson. A little girl seven years old who just happened to be at the wrong place at the wrong time. At this moment she is unconscious in a coma at Albany Medical Center in critical condition. Why? Because a pizza driver was in too much of a hurry to look when he was backing up. A white pizza driver, I might add. I called the police station just a few minutes ago to see if the culprit was in custody. They said they don't have the driver yet. Brothers and sisters, tell me, if the girl was a little white girl from Loudonville from a rich family they'd have the guy before you could order a latte from Starbucks, wouldn't they?"

The crowd began to moan and make noises like "Hmm Hmm . . ." and "Amen." Palmer could tell they were getting stirred up.

"And if the driver was black he'd be behind bars already, wouldn't he?"

At this point someone yelled, "That's right. That's right."

Johnston continued, "But, because little Henrietta is from the 'projects,' is poor and is black, she don't rate the time. Do you call that equality, brothers and sisters? What we need is a black police chief who understands us and can give us justice. I'm not saying we need special favors. No. Just the same justice white folks get. I think we should go to the police department right now and let them know what we think. Little Henrietta is depending on us. She's looking to us to make sure the one who injured her is found and prosecuted to the full extent of the law. Isn't that right, Sister Wilson?" He looked hard to his right and two heavy black women with their arms around a gaunt, middle-aged black woman stood up. The woman's eyes were tired and teary. She wore black as if she were already in mourning. She nodded her head to the crowd, apparently too overwhelmed to speak.

"What do you say, brothers and sisters? We've got some signs here ready to go. Who will come with me?" A throng surged forward to grab the signs. The Reverend Johnston took the lead with the pastor and they charged out of the church.

Palmer and the young reporter sat stunned at how quickly Johnston had whipped up the people and led the charge. Only a few people resisted the frenzy and seemed opposed to the fiery preacher's parade. Palmer approached an elderly man who had begun to pick up the song sheets. "Excuse me, sir. Why didn't you go with them?"

The man stood up and said with a smile, "I think I would be more good here. People don't understand that it's in the little things we can make the most difference. My question is: why didn't we just pray for the girl and the boy who ran her over? This is a church, not a political convention. We're supposed to be a family, not a vigilante group."

"Thank you, sir. Can I quote you on that?"

The old man looked at Palmer straight in the eyes and said, "No. No. I'm already in enough trouble in this place for speaking my mind. It's better if I tells them face to face than them reading it in the newspapers." He resumed picking up the song sheets and Palmer left the church with the other reporter. They both said goodbye and got into their respective cars so they could get to the police station before the protesters. Palmer thought of giving Pierce a call to warn him, but he saw the cop already talking into his cell phone.

Chapter 34

A Protest in Albany
Tuesday Evening, May 20, 2003

E lijah Williams heard them before he actually saw anything. He was walking down Madison Avenue with a white towel around his neck after a grueling pickup game at the outdoor basketball courts in Washington Park when he heard voices singing, "We Shall Overcome." What was going on? He always thought they should find another song. These days he found more inspiration from Kirk Franklin's CDs. This dynamic gospel singer could give Elijah goose bumps just by saying, "Praise the Lord!" He respected deeply what they did in the Sixties but he loved the more contemporary gospel tunes.

He ached to see all the races, including whites and blacks, in the same churches worshipping together instead of according to skin color or country of origin. This was more of a reflection of the body of Christ, in his opinion. Yet, most churches he knew attracted people by race, culture, or the amount of money you made. He knew his church still had a ways to go in this regard, but at least they were trying.

He stopped and watched the long line of protesters walk past him until he saw someone he knew. Out of curiosity, he jogged up to the familiar face.

"Hey Elijah, whas zup, man?" said a tall thin boy with a shaved head and skulls tattooed on his biceps. He smacked Elijah's hand for 'five in the sky.'

"Just wonderin' what you're doing with that Reverend

Johnston?"

"Oh, him. Didn't you hear about it? Some Luigi driver ran over a little girl named Henrietta Wilson and looks like she's gonna die. We's jus' goin' to the police station to tell 'em to get that jerk and throw the book at 'im. That's all. Wanna come?" The rest of the protesters kept chanting and moving past them as they spoke. Elijah immediately thought of Ace.

"Do they know who did it by any chance?"

"Strange name. Think it was King or Ace or something. Last name was Parks. Like Rosa Parks. That's how I remembered it." He beamed, obviously proud that he knew a little of civil rights history. Elijah, however, felt someone had just punched him in the stomach.

"Oh. Is he in the city jail?"

"No. Don't got 'im yet. That's what we's going to talk with the Police Chief about. Seems they kinda slow to get that slime ball."

Elijah muttered something about needing to get home and walked down State Street. It was dark but the lights of the city lit his path on the sidewalk. He still heard the voices of the group although they were fading out as they went in the other direction. He turned right on Washington Avenue and passed the Dunkin' Donuts. He reached Washington Park and decided to walk to the lake. When he knew he could not be heard, he prayed out loud, "Lord, things are not looking too good for Ace right now. I know You know all the details even if I don't. I know I prayed for You to do whatever You needed to do so he would see his need for You, but this is terrible and I know it's not something from Your hand. Even this, though, I know You can turn into good for Your glory. Help him do the right thing and if there is anything I can do to help, please give me wisdom. Thank you, Lord."

Elijah then took out his cell phone from his gym bag and

tried Ace's number. He just got the automatic message with Beethoven's Fifth. After the beep he said, "Hey Ace man. What's happening? Give me a call ASAP. Ciao." He didn't want to take any chances by leaving his name. He needed to get home fast to tell his mom to organize a prayer chain with trusted intercessors to pray for Ace and who would not gossip. Time was of the essence—not only for Ace, but the city. Things could easily get out of control.

Chapter 35

ergeant Pierce slammed down the receiver and said, "That's just great! I got a little girl in the hospital in a coma, a hit and run driver on the loose, rocks being thrown at pizza delivery drivers, and now I got a crowd from the projects, led by this Johnston character, coming in a few minutes. Wonderful time for the police chief to be away." He stood up and began pacing in front of his desk, running his hands through his salt-and-pepper hair. He was a big man and had spent time in Viet Nam so little scared him, but he also didn't like being pushed around by anybody, especially this Johnston character.

People didn't understand that it took time to apprehend people and he couldn't just all of a sudden put all his men on one hit and run case. A deputy standing nearby looked concerned and asked, "What do we do, Sarge, to get ready for them? Tear gas?"

The sergeant reacted somewhat perturbed at being interrupted from his own private problem-solving session: "What? Tear gas? Are you out of your mind? No. No. That would definitely not be the answer. We will just go out there when they arrive and talk with them peacefully and then encourage them to go home. With luck, there'll be no TV cameras. I think I hear them now."

The singing was getting louder and someone, no doubt Johnston, was barking into a megaphone to keep them moving and in high spirits. When the crowd arrived at the police station, Pierce and four other officers were waiting on the steps. Pierce spoke first as Johnston strutted to the front of the group.

"Hello, Mr. Johnston. Seems you've been busy since the last time I heard from you."

"Reverend Johnston, sir. We're just here to make sure you police officers don't forget your job and you get that hit and run coward real quick like." The crowd moaned their approval.

"Well, Mr. Johnston, we are doing all we can do to locate the driver. Apparently, he has made the foolish decision to try and run away, which makes things a little more complicated. All the local and state police have been notified, so we hope to hear something soon. He can't get far."

At that moment a Channel 10 TV news truck screeched up close to where they were standing. A familiar face with long red hair immediately got out of the passenger side of the vehicle while two cameramen exited from the side door. The reverend gave a toothy smile and brightened at their approach. The redhead began her reporting: "Here we are outside of Albany Police Station. The Reverend Johnston is once more in Albany and is protesting something with a large group of followers. Reverend Johnston, can you tell me why you and your people are here tonight?"

"I certainly can, Ms. Shaw, and I especially appreciate your interest in our little demonstration here. We are here tonight to make sure justice is done in the case of a little girl named Henrietta Wilson who was callously run down right outside her home on Lincoln Avenue by a Luigi pizza driver. Isn't that right, people?"

At this the crowd cheered their support.

He continued, "Her mother is devastated and Henrietta is even now hanging on by a thread at Albany Medical Center in critical condition. We just want to make sure that just because she is poor and black this despicable, abominable, atrocious act will not be tolerated and the criminal will be penalized to the full extent of the law. We want to hear with our own ears that this case will not be neglected and this police force will do all in their power to apprehend this criminal, just like they would do for any white person, and bring him to justice for this shameful thing he has done." The people behind him again broke out into spontaneous shouts of "Amen" and "That's right."

"That is why," Johnston paused for dramatic effect, "we are here tonight." The crowd yelled their agreement.

"And Officer Pierce," Ms. Shaw said walking up a couple of steps and pointing her microphone into the face of the policeman, "Can you make that pledge to this crowd tonight?"

"Yes I can. Crimes committed anywhere in this city are treated exactly in the same way regardless of the neighborhood. We gather evidence and we do our best to find the criminal."

"Can we ask why the person has not been picked up more than 24 hours after the crime was committed? You know the identity of the driver, Ace Parks, and his car model, a black 2001 Eclipse. Why should he be so difficult to apprehend?"

Pierce knew there was something he didn't like about this woman, and now he remembered.

"Well, Ms. Shaw, sometimes people involved in these kinds of accidents don't always do the right thing. Sometimes they panic and they run and hide. In this case, we know who the driver is, so it is only a matter of time before he comes to his senses and turns himself in or he is stopped by the police. Anyone who has any knowledge of his whereabouts is strongly encouraged to call the police department and let us know where they have seen him."

"So, there you have it, ladies and gentlemen, the Reverend Johnston and his followers have demanded a commitment from the police department to fully investigate this hit and run on Lincoln Avenue and to bring the alleged culprit, Ace Parks, to justice. The police department has just given their solemn word to do just that. This is Jessica Shaw from Channel 10 News. More details on the condition of the little girl, Henrietta Wilson, later at 11:00. Back to you, Bill."

As soon as she finished, her assistant grabbed her microphone, the camera man shut down his equipment, and the trio walked briskly back to their van. They quickly got in and sped off in the direction of Albany Medical Center.

Chapter 36

The Williams' Home
Tuesday Evening, May 20, 2003

Usually the familiar smell of smoked turkey legs with collard greens and onions cooking on the stove and the warm welcome of his mom would be enough to lift Elijah's spirits, no matter how bad he felt, but today it didn't do the trick. When he saw the large form of his mom in her *For Him* apron stirring the pot in the kitchen, he just said, "Hey, Mom," gave her a peck on the cheek, and slumped down on a chair at the table with his athletic bag on his lap.

"Hey, babe," his mom said without turning around. Got an appetite after track practice, I imagine. Your dad couldn't wait to get out there and start doing some serious barbecuing." She turned to him smiling and wiping her hands on her apron. She knew he always had a big appetite after sports practices. In fact, once during his early teens, she was so shocked by his food intake she considered getting a second job and teased him about needing to take out another mortgage just to meet his basic needs. Her smile evaporated when she saw his sullen face.

"What's the matter, babe?" she said gently. "Bad practice today? Argument with Rhonda?" She walked over and stood in front of her son and put her hand on his shoulder. "What's up? It will do you no good too keep it inside. You know you gotta tell your mama."

"No. Mom. It's not practice. And Rhonda and me are fine. Something else. Something more serious." He looked up at his mother who was staring at his face intently, waiting for his response.

"Well, Mom. You heard about that accident with that little girl right?"

"Yes. That poor mother. She is overwhelmed with grief and expecting her daughter to die any time now. The ladies from the church have been visiting her, providing meals, and taking her to see her baby at the hospital. Why?"

"Well, there was a protest today and a guy told me Ace was the driver involved."

"Oh, no! Not that friend of yours you've been witnessing to? That's horrible. What would make him want to leave the scene of the accident?"

"I don't know why he'd do that. There must have been a reason. There must have been." He looked straight into his mother's brown eyes. "I know Ace, Mom. Something is not right about this."

She suddenly remembered her cooking duties and stepped lively to the stove and lowered the heat. She turned back to her son.

"He wanted to know where I thought Ace might be. He also said that maybe Ace's girlfriend, Gabriella, may even have gone with him. The thing is, I think they probably went to France." Elijah looked down, put his hand to his forehead, and sighed heavily.

"France? You mean, France, the country in Europe!"

"Yeah, Mom. They were planning to go there for their honeymoon after she graduated so they had everything ready. Money. Passports. Everything."

"You don't say. That is unbelievable. Did you tell the detective that?"

"No, I didn't, but I think some of the other kids did. I wanted to wait and see if he was going to contact me first."

"Well, did he?"

"No. Nothing yet. I called him and left a message but so far . . ." Elijah stopped speaking at the last word and shook his head. Both were silent for a moment. Then Elijah raised his head, his eyes clear with conviction. He took the sports bag from his lap and put it on the floor.

"Mom. I got an idea and I think maybe the Lord gave it to me."

"What is it, babe?"

"I would like to go to France and convince him to come back."

"You do? What about school and everything? Track. College preparations, and all that. It'll also cost you big money. How could you even find him if you did go?"

"Mom, take it easy. I don't plan on going any more than two weeks if I go. I was thinking maybe Ace's lawyer uncle might want to go with me. This far along your senior year things are pretty much over and I have plenty saved up so . . ."

At that moment a big heavyset man in his 50s entered the room with a big grin and a platter of barbequed meat. As he set it on the counter he said, "Hey, mister track star. Got something special from the grill tonight. Prime ribs. Yes sir, I might even share a few with you." He washed his huge hands in the sink and then grabbed the dish towel off the fridge handle to dry them. He then faced his wife and son. His bantering stopped. "Something wrong? Why the glum faces?"

"Your son, I think, has to something he wants to tell you."

"Don't tell me you went and got Rhonda pregnant, now," he blurted out.

"Arthur! What a thing to say to your son!" his wife said reproachfully.

"No. Dad. You know me and her took the pledge and we ain't gonna break it."

"Sorry. Son," he replied sheepishly. "It's the first thing that popped into my mind seeing your serious faces." He then looked first to his son's face and then to his wife's. "Well, then. Somebody gonna tell me what's going down?"

Mrs. Williams looked at Elijah. He sighed heavily and said, "Dad. You heard about that accident, right? Down on South Lincoln where a little girl got hit by a pizza driver?"

"Yeah, but what's that got to do with you, son? I don't understand."

"Well . . . the pizza driver is my friend, Ace, and . . ."

"Ace? You mean that white guy you had over one time? That went on that retreat with you?"

"Yeah."

"You mean you know where he is? That boy is in a tub of hot water. Even at church there's some people that want his hide."

"I know, Dad. The thing is, I was just telling Mom, I think he took off to France and . . ."

"France! Why would he go there? They speak another language. And, from what I hear, they don't like Americans all that much."

"It's kind of a long story, Dad, but I'd like to go there and try to bring him back. I am sure there is something more to this because Ace wouldn't just hit a girl and run away without a reason."

"That's a noble thing to do, son, but number one, how would you find him in a big place like that? And number two, is this the best thing to do right now? You have to think about your future, son. You got football practice in a couple of months at UM and you're not even finished with school yet."

"Yeah I know, Dad. But he's my friend and if it was me I'd want someone to set me straight if I was making some bad choices. In terms of finishing this year, it's really over. Only a few tests left. I've got good grades. The full scholarship to UM really helps financially, and I've got some money saved . . ."

Arthur J. Williams listened to his son's heart and his eyes suddenly teared. He said quietly. "You're a good friend, son. I admire your commitment to Ace. But how are you going to find him? It will be like trying to find a needle in a haystack."

Elijah, seeing this as an opened door, said excitedly," Well. The first thing I wanted to do is go see Ace's Uncle Jerry. He's a lawyer and has been kind of a father to Ace all his life. Maybe he would go with me. He might know where Ace might go. Plus, let's not forget God. Mom's always said that our God majors in the impossible. If He put it on my heart, He'll lead us."

Elijah's father looked over to his wife who was shaking her head up and down in her agreement with Elijah's plan. He looked back to his son. "Well, it looks like you've been thinking about this and the Lord can't direct a boat when it ain't moving nowhere. Why don't you start going in that direction and see if He opens the doors. We'll keep you covered in prayer and your mom can contact some prayer warriors from church who know how to keep their mouths shut."

"Thanks, Dad, for your support. It means a lot to me."

"I'm proud of you, son. You've grown up to be a real man of God." He put his arms around his son and his wife embraced them both.

She smiled and said, "And I am grateful I have such tender-hearted men who can hear God's voice. Now that's settled, could one of you set the table? I think those collard greens are ready if I didn't burn 'em with all our jabbering!"

Chapter 37

The Missionary Base
Wednesday, May 21, 2003
East of Paris

T he light coming in through the window and the sounds of birds finally roused Ace despite his desire to hug the covers for another hour or so. With his eyes half shut, he pulled his left arm out from under the quilt and looked at his watch. Ten thirty-five European time. His roommate, Brad something, had shown him the internet room in the Center after the official tour by McKinley. Fortunately, no one else was there and Brad had left him in peace.

Ace quickly found the *Albany Herald* article about the accident and was relieved that the little girl was still alive and that the police didn't know where he and Gabby were. There was no mention of Gabriella in the article so, hopefully, her father would not find out that she went with him right away. Who knows what Mr. Capaldi would say or do when he found out? Ace thought that perhaps they should at least figure out a way to let him know that she was safe without giving away where they were. Maybe they could leave a little message from Gabby on his business website like: *Dad, sorry to leave so suddenly. Just wanted you to know I'm ok and I will be contacting you soon with more details. Love, Gabby.*

He smiled at the quote the reporter used from José in the article, "Ace is my man. No way he did anything like that on purpose." He could see José in his Luigi uniform, the obligatory red hat and his cocky manner. Deep down, though, he knew

José was a loyal friend and one you'd want on your side in a fight. Although he was small he fought with all he had, knew martial arts, and wouldn't hesitate to tear an antenna off a car to whip an opponent if things got too intense.

He looked over to the other bed and saw that it was empty and made to perfection. Brad apparently had gotten up a while ago. He had mentioned something about picking up a guy from New Zealand at the airport. He was going to speak that evening.

Brad had showed Ace the multimedia studio where he worked and some of the music videos he had done with a local youth group. Although Ace was impressed with his creativity, the six hours difference in the time zone was finally catching up to him. When they got into their beds and Brad started sharing about his life "before Christ," Ace drifted into dreamland just after the part in the story where Brad said his friend got stabbed at a party for not giving a guy a cigarette or something. It was quite a dramatic story, but he already knew the punch line . . . he got saved by Jesus and now everything was wonderful.

Ace thought about Gabriella and wondered if she was up and talking with the McKinleys. He just hoped she wouldn't let anything slip about the accident. He got up out of the bed and went to the sink near the right corner of the room. He splashed cold water on his face and then flattened down his messed-up hair with a generous dose of H_2O. He then saw the tray with the plate of French bread slices, butter and strawberry jam and the mug of hot chocolate on the desk.

Sticking out from under the plate was a note by Brad. It explained his trip to the airport and instructions to heat up the hot chocolate in the pot on the hot plate. The room had several movie posters and some enlarged photos of Steven Spielberg. Ace recognized one poster of the movie *The Matrix*. He picked up the mug and poured the contents into the pot and turned the hot plate on. He then went to the window, turned the handle to open the window and flung it open. It was a little cool but refreshing. He looked out over the field next to the house and could see the McKinleys. He could also smell some livestock excretions mixed in with the spring air wafting up to his window and saw some young people reading on a bench underneath a tree.

To the left he saw the main road running through the village, a building that looked like a town hall or school, and the gray stone edifice of an old Catholic church. Seconds later the bell at the Catholic Church began to ring. He closed the window to dull the sound and went over to the end of his bed to pick up his clothes from the previous night. He took off the black shorts he wore to bed and slipped on his jeans and shirt. He then sat down to butter his bread and spread the jelly on it. He rubbed his eyes and tried to think of some goals for the day. He definitely didn't want to stay in the room too long. Gabriella was in a vulnerable state and he didn't want her pouring her heart out to Mrs. McKinley. They were getting a little too chummy for his comfort. If she told them anything they might even have her on the next flight back to New York.

He got up suddenly and went over to the hot plate and poured the cold chocolate back into his mug. He couldn't wait for it to heat up. He chugged it down, finished off the first piece of bread and then took the other in his hand so he could eat it on his way to the McKinleys' house. He grabbed his black jean jacket and put it on as he descended the wide wooden staircase two steps at a time. He passed the kitchen where he saw a young guy mopping the floor, said "hello" and then "bonjour" when the guy replied in French, and kept on going to the huge front doors, which opened with a strange metal contraption. He fumbled with it briefly before figuring it out and then bolted into the cool spring air and pungent cow manure.

Chapter 38

The Missionary Base
Wednesday Evening, May 21, 2003
East of Paris

ce fidgeted uncomfortably in his metal and vinyl-cushioned folding chair in the back row with Gabriella on his left and Mary McKinley next to her. About twenty-five young people were seated already and talking in animated French. The spacious room was wood-paneled with sound equipment up front and guitars were leaning against the wall. McKinley had explained that he had to sit up front to start the meeting and introduce the guest speaker. Ace could see him talking with a tall lanky dark-haired man next to him in the front row. Several students came forward to introduce themselves to Ace and Gabriella in French. Gabriella gladly responded in French with several phrases, but Ace just offered his hand and said, "Enchante" and hoped they would move on. Most of them seemed French, but a couple of them came from South Korea, the U.S. and other European countries.

Although Ace had tried to convince everyone he was too tired to go to the meeting after spending the afternoon with the McKinleys, which included a sumptuous lunch and a leisurely walk in the country, Gabriella had insisted on his attendance and the McKinleys, of course, would not take no for an answer. They said the speaker from New Zealand, Peter Bury, was a wonderful teacher and that Ace would love him. He was very down to earth, funny, and incredibly gifted in teaching. They also said the music was very contemporary and upbeat.

Ace felt trapped. His mind wandered back to a conversation he had with Gabriella on the way to the main house.

They had dropped back behind the McKinleys a few paces and Ace told her about the *Tribune* article. Gabriella was thrilled with the report and even muttered, "Maybe we could ask the McKinleys to pray for her," which shocked Ace. He immediately grabbed her arm and they both stopped walking.

"No way, Gabriella. You haven't told them anything, have you?" The McKinleys were now 20 feet in front of them.

"Of course not, silly. We don't have to say how the girl got injured. Just say we know about a little girl who got hurt in an accident. It can't hurt, can it?"

"You never know. They could read about the accident on the internet and connect the dots." Ace glanced at the McKinleys and back at Gabriella. "Let's just say as little as possible and think of a way we can get hold of some money so we can get out of this place." He nodded to her to continue walking.

"I don't mind staying here a few days. I like the McKinleys. They seem like really nice people. Do you have any ideas on how to get some money somewhere?"

"Please, Gabby, don't get too comfortable here. We need to keep moving. If I can get through to my Uncle Jerry, maybe he could wire us some money somewhere. I can't think of anyone else who might help. I'll send him an email tonight if I have time."

Suddenly, the band began playing and Ace's mind snapped back to the present. He thought it was cool that the young people led the worship. The music was more his style and the lyrics seemed more personal without a lot of "thees" and "thous." He had to admit as well that the tall guy with the loose fitting multicolored island shirt was hilarious as he told them some story about traveling in New York City for the first time. Apparently, he'd heard footsteps following him one night and he just turned around and yelled at the top of his lungs, "Glory to God!" and the would-be attackers fled into the night, probably convinced he was a mad man.

The more serious part of his message, however, Ace found hard to swallow and too close to home. Peter Bury zeroed in on the story of the fall of man from Genesis. "After Adam and Eve had sinned they tried to hide from God. Imagine trying to hide from an all-knowing omnipotent God. Anyway, they not only tried to hide from God but they tried to conceal their nakedness with fig leaves." At this point a few people laughed.

"Now, when God asked Adam, 'Adam, where are you,' do you really think He didn't know, or was it more for Adam's sake?"

Someone responded, "Yeah. Adam's sake."

"Right," Bury said, looking squarely into the eyes of the people sitting in the front row, "God is looking for us to acknowledge our sin before Him and be honest and transparent —not try to find a fig leaf to hide behind. You see, you can't hide from God, no matter how hard you try. It's better to admit it and receive His forgiveness and start again."

What Bury said next really surprised Ace. He told them about a time when the Holy Spirit convicted him of lying to someone. He had been talking with a pastor of another church about why he didn't go to a certain conference in town. Many Christian leaders had attended, but Bury had given a lame excuse for missing it. After he had hung up the phone he felt the Holy Spirit say to him, "You know that is not why you didn't go to the conference. You just didn't want to go. Call him back and confess to him you had lied and tell him the truth." Bury explained after he had obeyed the Holy Spirit he felt the presence of God in a wonderful way. The problem wasn't that he should have gone to the conference. The problem was he didn't tell the truth why he hadn't gone.

Bury continued, "What God is looking for are people who

are real with Him. And when the Holy Spirit convicts us of something we should be quick to acknowledge it, confess it, and repent—or in other words 'go in the opposite direction' and not do it again. If we find ourselves stuck in something we know is not right we get help—we don't deny it's there and put on a pious face to keep up an image. King David did some horrendous things including committing adultery with Bathsheba, which was punishable by death at that time, but he even went further and also arranged for the death of her husband.

"Yet, God calls David 'a man after his own heart' because after Nathan the prophet confronts him he doesn't try to justify his sin or blame someone else. He could have blamed Bathsheba, right? What was she doing taking a bath within sight of his palace terrace? But no, he doesn't do that, he says, 'I have sinned.' That's it and he doesn't do that again. Yes. There were some terrible consequences to that sin—the child conceived died and Nathan prophesied that there would be troubles in his family as a result—but he was forgiven by God and God established his kingdom and used him mightily to the point where it says this in Acts 13:36: 'For when David had served God's purpose in his own generation, he fell asleep.' In other words, he did not die until he accomplished all that God had for him."

Ace was amazed at the teacher's honesty. Bury wasn't pretending to be some spiritual giant who never made any mistakes—here he was, humbly telling them where he had blown it. But it seemed too much of a coincidence for Ace to believe that Gabriella didn't tell the McKinleys something and they, in turn, said something to Bury. It was an obvious set up.

Bury then talked about the importance of "bringing things into the light to see if they are really of God" and the danger of a "lone ranger" mentality in our Christian walk, but Ace had stopped listening. He stood up quickly and moved past Gabriella and Mrs. McKinley without looking at them. He felt betrayed and just wanted to get out of there. How else could Bury have known about their "hiding?" He saw Brad videotaping the session at the back of the room and motioned to him like he wanted to ask him something. Brad tapped the guy next to him on the shoulder, pointed him to the camera, and walked over to Ace. He put his finger to his lips when Ace started to speak and ushered him out of the room into the little hallway outside the room.

"What's going on, Ace?"

"Ahh . . . two things actually. One, I wondered where the bathroom was located."

"Oh . . . just two doors down on the right."

"Yeah. Thanks. Hard to listen when you gotta go." Ace hoped he bought that line.

"I understand."

"The other thing is . . . I was wondering if I could use the internet now. I have a really urgent message I need to get out to someone and it's important that I do it now."

"Sorry, Ace, we close down the internet room during meetings. You can go on it tomorrow morning if you want."

"How about after the meeting? Is that okay?"

"No. It's closed every Wednesday night."

"Great. What time does it open?"

"Nine o'clock. But you need to remember if you are sending it to the U.S.A it will be six hours behind us or three o'clock in the morning."

"Oh well. Thanks anyway." Ace then walked toward the bathroom as Brad watched. Ace looked at him and smiled as he pushed open the door.

"Ace, come back to the service after, okay? We all eat together when it's over and you can meet some people."

"Thanks."

Brad said a prayer under his breath and went back into the big room and resumed his filming. Ace took his time in the bathroom trying to plan his next step. He looked out of the large vertical window at the French countryside. He saw fields with oil rigs going up and down methodically, and a few cows. Brad had told him the government had done the exploratory work in the fields and had found the resource a couple of years ago. Although the state took most of the money, the owner received a little and so did the town. The town ended up using the extra funds to build a modern community center just down the road, and they even let the mission use it for the larger conferences when needed. He had said it took years to win the favor of the local officials, but after they renovated several buildings and showed that they were not a strange religious sect, things got a lot better.

What bugged Ace at the moment was Gabriella's betrayal and the prohibition of internet use on Wednesday nights. This meant that Uncle Jerry wouldn't receive his message before some time on Thursday. *Who knows how long it will take to get the money,* Ace thought. He went back to his seat in the meeting room. He gave Gabriella a suspicious look as he squeezed past her chair. As he sat down he whispered in her ear, "I need to talk with you right after this guy's done, okay?" Gabriella nodded her consent and lowered her eyebrows as if to say, "What's the big problem?"

As Bury concluded his talk, Ace grabbed Gabriella's arm and led her out of the row to the aisle. He explained to Mrs. McKinley that they would be right back. When they finally got outside the house, Ace let his frustrations fly.

"You told Mrs. McKinley something, didn't you?"

"No, I didn't, Ace, and I don't like you accusing me like that—and stop squeezing my elbow."

Ace released his grip but added, "Oh yeah. Then why did

that guy start talking about 'hiding from God' and stuff like that? It seems somebody must have told him something."

"Well, I didn't say a thing to the McKinleys about anything. Have you ever thought that maybe God knows about what we've done?"

"Very funny. C'mon, Gabby. Don't you give me that God stuff, too. You're starting to sound like my mother."

"I'm not your mother, Ace, but I do believe in God and I have been talking with the McKinleys about a personal faith in God and I am interested in what they have to say. Although I have gone to Mass a lot in my life, I can't say that I've had a real personal relationship with God. Yes, I've prayed to Him when I'm having problems and said the rosary sometimes, but I can't say I really experienced His love for me. I want to learn more. The guy tonight really helped me to understand some things."

"So what are you saying? You want to stay here?" Ace was getting more ticked off by the second, and panic was now creeping into his voice.

"Ace, it might not be such a bad thing to stay around a little longer and see what they have to say. I don't think the police will find us here, do you?"

"I don't know, but it probably isn't wise to stay anywhere for a long time. They could talk to people at my mom's church and discover she supported the McKinleys and who knows? They could track us here."

"But where are we going to go without any money or credit cards?"

"I don't know. I was hoping to send an email to Uncle Jerry tonight, but they close the internet room on Wednesday nights. I'll have to do it tomorrow, I guess. I don't want to risk calling him. With that new wiretapping law in effect I don't know if that means that the police can listen to anybody's line or not. But he won't look at it before probably three in the afternoon French time, and that is if he looks at it first thing in the morning."

"Well, it looks like we're stuck here for the time being, so why don't we try and just make the best of it?" Gabriella moved the strands of hair that had fallen in her face back behind her ear and waited for Ace's answer. Ace was quiet for a second or two and then said, "Yeah. I guess you're right. Just don't expect me to get all that excited about God talk. I've heard it before from my mom and others. Just look at my life. Isn't it obvious God isn't around? My dad leaves when I'm a kid. Mom dies young."

"Is that so? How about me, Ace? Don't I count? What if God is the one who brought me into your life?"

"Ahh . . . umm . . . in that case, I would be very grateful to Him but so far, I'm not convinced He had anything to do with it."

"Okay, Ace. Can we go in now? I'm getting cold out here." Gabriella closed her jacket tighter around her and brought her feet closer together.

"Okay, Gabby. I'm sorry I accused you of . . . you know . . . and being a little rough with you . . ."

Gabriella smiled and said, "Forgiven. Apology accepted." They hugged and went back upstairs for the meal.

Chapter 39

The Missionary Base
Thursday, May 22, 2003

"'mon, Brad, don't tell me nobody here can figure out this problem!" Ace said in unbelief to his roommate when he had found him in his office after returning from the internet room. A note had been posted on the door that said there were some difficulties with the server and that internet access was not possible until a guy named Bjorn came back from the youth conference on Friday.

"Afraid not, Ace. He is the one who knows about these things. Internet is pretty new to these little towns."

"Well, is there a bigger town we could go to where they would have an internet place?"

"Maybe they might have something at Châteaux Thierry. It's about forty-five minutes from here, but I don't think anybody is going out there today. You might be able to go with me when I drop Peter Bury off at the train station on Friday, if you want. I'd have to get permission first, though."

"All right. I guess I don't have much of a choice."

"No. You don't. Sorry. I know this was important to you."

"Yeah. I'm trying to contact my uncle so he can maybe wire me some money somewhere. Do you know where he could send it to around here?"

"I've had money sent to a town called Montmirail about ten minutes from here. They have a Western Union."

"Great. Thanks. Sorry to bother you here at work."

"No problem. I'll ask if it's okay if you go with us to the train station."

"Thanks Brad. I'd appreciate that."

Chapter 40

The Jensens' Home
Thursday, May 22, 2003
Delmar, NY

Would you like some coffee, Mr. Farley?" Robin Jensen asked the detective who just sat down at their breakfast table. He wore a thin brown leather jacket, a black turtleneck and ironed blue jeans.

"No thanks, ma'am. I'd best get to the point."

Her husband, Jerry, sat across from Farley in his navy blue business suit on a matching oak chair. He had cancelled all his morning appointments to meet with the detective who had called the night before. He knew what was coming, but that didn't lessen the blow or the sadness he felt at what he was going to hear.

"Well, you both know why I am here." They both nodded and he continued.

"As family members closest to Ace Parks we thought you might know where he might be hiding. Somebody called in about his Eclipse hidden down by the Hudson yesterday. He faked out the department by buying a ticket to the city. We now believe he may have gone to France with a girlfriend. She is probably the one who picked him up and drove him to the airport. Have you heard anything from him since the accident?"

"No, Officer," Jensen replied. "I wish we had."

"Do you have any idea where he might have gone in France?"

Jerry looked his wife and said, "No, sir. I know he was interested in visiting the country someday, but where he would go, I really don't know."

Farley sat up straighter in his seat and cleared his throat. "Well, this is the situation. If Ace and the girl are indeed in France as we presume . . ."

"Excuse me, Officer Farley, but what makes you so sure he is in France?"

"A pilot from the charter service Fast Flight called the station yesterday and said he took a young couple to Montreal the night of the accident and that they were planning on going to Paris. I have a man right now checking with the airlines to confirm that they were on the flight to Paris. He saw Ace's photo on the news and confirmed it was him. The girl, we believe, was Gabriella Capaldi. She has been missing since the night of the accident and other students have confirmed that they were very close.

"Okay. This is our dilemma, folks. If they are in France, as we suspect, we obviously are not going to send anyone overseas to look for them for a hit and run crime. If the girl dies, Lord forbid, who knows if the French government would cooperate? I personally doubt it with the way our relations are with the French right now. Plus it is highly unlikely that they would sacrifice the time of their own limited police force to hunt down fugitives from our country when they have enough of their own problems to worry about."

"So where do we come in, Mr. Farley?" Robin asked politely.

"You can help if he contacts you by persuading him that it is in his best interests to come home and turn himself in. We understand that he has quite an inheritance and we are going through the legalities right now to block his account. We've already talked with his probation officer and he tells us the probation board is ready to send him to prison for at least a year if he does not give himself up soon."

Robin gasped, "Oh, no."

"Oh yes, ma'am. This is serious stuff. We also have our old friend, Reverend Johnston, back in town stirring up the people in the little girl's neighborhood demanding justice. That's not to mention the Luigi driver who had his car stoned out of retaliation. I can't emphasize it enough, Mr. and Mrs. Jensen—Ace needs to give himself up soon for his sake as well as for our city's sake."

"Thank you, Officer. We'll do our best to convince him if he gets in contact with us."

"Please let us know if you hear anything. The police chief would be very happy to put this case behind him as quickly as possible."

After Jerry Jensen walked the detective to his car and returned to his living room, his wife asked him the obvious, "What are you going to do, Jerry?"

"Well, sit tight for now and hope he calls. If he doesn't soon, I may have to go to France and try to find him."

Chapter 41

Denny's
Thursday, May 22, 2003
Albany, NY

The black Explorer turned into the parking lot of the Denny's on Western Avenue. It had been two days and two sleepless nights before Steve Capaldi finally received the confirmation that his daughter, Gabriella Capaldi, had very likely run away with the pizza delivery boy Ace Parks and gone to France. The detective had called and confirmed that a pilot from the Fast Flight charter service had called the police station after seeing the photo of Ace Parks on the news and said he had flown a young couple to Montreal looking for a connection to Paris.

Normally, this restaurant was the place for pleasant business meetings with clients over coffee or breakfast combinations rather than a clandestine rendezvous to discuss unusual or even illegal ways to track and find a runaway teenage daughter. But Capaldi was convinced the police were powerless to do anything and he was sick of hearing from the police chief that they were still "working on the case." An associate in the construction business had given him the name of Joe Peterson, who had been with Special Forces in the Army and now ran his own private detective agency. Apparently he excelled in locating missing people and came with an impressive resumé of out-of-the-ordinary feats. The one that especially attracted Capaldi was his involvement in locating a top-ranking Nazi officer who had been hiding in Peru since the end of WWII. On that mission he had worked with a highly trained Israeli team whose goal was to find Nazi war criminals and bring them back to Israel for trial. Their target was eventually executed for his role in exterminating innocent Jews in gas ovens. Capaldi's friend said Peterson also was a martial arts expert, had a Masters in Criminology and had spent ten years as a street detective in New York City. Capaldi knew he wouldn't come cheap, but money was no object at this point. He had to get his daughter away from that loser as soon as possible. Who knows what could happen to them in France? Maybe the kid was into drugs. What did he know, really? Speed was what counted now.

Capaldi closed the door of the car and walked briskly to the front of the restaurant. Without turning around he waved the key fob in his hand with a backward flick of the wrist to lock the doors. Peterson had said on the phone that he would be sitting in the corner booth at the far right of the restaurant. The man Capaldi saw was not exactly what he had expected. The man looked to be in his early forties, balding, medium build, a colorful red and dark blue wool sweater, brown corduroy pants, and small gold-rimmed glasses. A briefcase was opened on the table and he was reading the daily paper. To Capaldi, he looked more like a Sociology college professor than a private detective. He folded the paper and stood up from his seat at Capaldi's approach. He stretched out his hand, "Glad to meet you, Mr. Capaldi. Please sit down."

The handshake showed some strength which encouraged Capaldi. He noticed, too, the man had no midriff bulge like he did but had the figure of a college wrestler. The man motioned with his right hand toward the seat across from him and sat down himself.

Peterson smiled and looked Capaldi in the eyes, "Not exactly what you expected, eh, Mr. Capaldi? Long black leather coat, sunglasses, tattoos, scars more in line with your imagination, or was the Chuck Norris style more to your liking?"

"Well, not exactly but . . ."

"I work for myself so I like keeping things casual. I could show you some scars from some close calls but fortunately they are not where they can be seen. Remember you want to hire the guy with less injuries, not the guy who lost. If you look like the stereotype of a detective everybody is on their guard. But, I don't think your case will be a particularly dangerous one. We just have to track this guy down and convince your daughter that it is in her best interests to come home with me. It appears more of a diplomatic mission than anything else. You should be grateful Gabriella wasn't kidnapped by a stranger. Many times these girls are never found."

"Thank you, Mr. Peterson, but I can't say that I am grateful for what has happened. I don't really know this kid, so I have no idea what he is capable of. Just the fact he took Gabriella away from her job, her family, and her school shows me he is more interested in himself than my daughter's future."

"I understand your feelings completely, Mr. Capaldi."

A waitress appeared, took a pencil out of her hair that was tied back in a pony tail and faced them with eyebrows raised and pencil poised to write on a white pad. "Good morning, Mr. Capaldi. Would you gentlemen like to order?"

"Ahh . . . yeah. Just coffee and a donut for me, Pam," Capaldi said. "And you, Mr. Peterson? Would you like something? It's on me. Anything you want."

"Black coffee is fine, thank you." The waitress scratched on her pad and scurried back down the aisle and behind the counter where the coffee machines were percolating. After she left, Peterson leaned forward and lowered his voice. "I understand how you feel about this kid. However, in my profession and in my experience, some cases offer more hope than others. I just want you to know that after your call yesterday I took the liberty of going down to some of the teen hot spots and talking with some of them about Ace Parks. Most of them see him as kind of a loner but also kind of strange in that he doesn't party like most kids his age or go out much with girls. Through the eyes of his teachers, he was somewhat of a genius in math and computers and even tutors other students, even though he graduated last year. He also worked instead of playing in school sports when he was a senior. That's not your normal kind of teenager, which could be good news."

"The only good news I am looking for right now, Mr. Peterson, is the news that you found my daughter and you are bringing her home." The waitress came back, deposited their orders with the bill and left immediately.

"All right, Mr. Capaldi. Let's cut to the chase. I charge $300 an hour and I expect to get paid weekly. With the amount of travelling I'll be doing I'll require $5,000 in advance which will be credited toward the expenses. This includes all transportation costs whether by car, airplane tickets, trains, rental cars, meals, etc. I will supply you with all receipts. I will also keep you abreast of all my activities but . . ." He stopped and then continued in a more serious tone, "I do not tolerate people trying to tell me my business. I understand the emotional element in cases like this, but I know what I am doing and my track record proves it. Do you have any questions, Mr. Capaldi?"

"Ah yeah. How would you go about bringing her back if she doesn't want to come with you?"

"I will just reason with her to make the smart decision. She needs to finish school. The guy is a fugitive from the law. I don't anticipate any great problems once I find her, but that will be the greatest challenge—finding them in a nation of 60 million people. But I will find them, Mr. Capaldi, that you can be sure. It is just a question of when. Of course, I will encourage Ace Parks to make the right decision as well."

"I'm not paying his way back," Capaldi said adamantly.

"Right. One more thing, Mr. Capaldi. Do you have any problem if we have to do something a little unethical or illegal?"

"What exactly are we talking about, Mr. Peterson? Drugging my daughter? Taking her by force?"

"No. I don't think that will be necessary. That would only complicate things at the airport. No. I am thinking more about maybe having to lie to get her to come with me or sending someone to break into the Parks' house to look for clues as to where in France they might be heading."

"With lying, I don't have a problem. She lied to me. With the other, you're on your own. I will not testify that I gave you permission to break the law. What kind of lie were you thinking of?" Capaldi's eyebrows lowered and his eyes locked directly onto Peterson's.

"Well, I will want some good arguments just in case she resists. You might be able to help me there. Her weaknesses. The things she is most concerned about. You know Gabriella much better than I do."

"I don't know about that now. I thought I knew her, but after this . . . I'm not so sure."

"I'm confident you can think of something. So, Mr. Capaldi, shall I start today?"

Capaldi wasn't one to take a lot of time making decisions. He was an entrepreneur and he was used to making snap judgments daily, sometimes decisions costing thousands of dollars. If he felt someone was legit, his word was his bond. He pulled out his checkbook, wrote out a check for $5,000 and handed it to Peterson. "You're hired. So when do you fly to France?"

"Not so fast. We need to do what we can here first. It could save us a lot of time once I'm over there. Remember, I don't speak French."

"You don't?"

"No, but the clues are here in the States. Once I am over

there I can hire an interpreter if I need to."

"Actually, I may be able to help you in that department. I have a mason named Anthony who grew up in an Italian French home. Maybe he could go with you."

"That may be a possibility. We'll talk more about that later. Before you go, Mr. Capaldi, just one more question. Did you remember to bring a recent photo of Gabriella with you?"

Capaldi reached into his inside coat pocket and pulled out a white envelope and handed it to the detective. Peterson took it, said, "Pretty girl" and put it in his briefcase. He clicked it closed and said, "Thank you. I'll be in touch."

"One more thing. You'll get a $5,000 bonus if you can bring her back before her 18th birthday. I don't want her to do anything more foolish like marry this guy."

"And when is that?"

"May 28th."

"So that gives me about a week. I'll do my best."

Chapter 42

Law Office of Gerald Jensen
Thursday Afternoon, May 22, 2003
Albany, NY

Jerry Jensen's eyes shifted from the computer screen and the web site of Easy Trip to his Swiss wristwatch. "Almost time," he said to himself. A few minutes later one of the plastic squares on the bottom of his telephone lit up, indicating an inter-office call. He pressed the button and lifted the receiver.

"Yes, Sue. What's up?"

A raspy middle-aged woman's voice responded, "Excuse me Mr. Jensen, but Elijah Williams is here to see you. His name isn't on the list for today, but he says you told him to come . . ."

"I'm sorry, Sue, I didn't tell you. Please send him in. I'll see him right away." He hung up the phone and the light disappeared. He sat up in his chair and straightened the piles of papers on his desk.

Jensen had never been up close to the football player, but he watched as many home games as he could. He had read Williams got a scholarship to the University of Michigan and he was sure he would do well in college ball and probably make the NFL draft. The boy was just unstoppable. Jensen was amazed when Ace said they were friends. He respected Williams even more when he called to say he wanted to talk about Ace.

Ace needed friends right now and a popular black one just might help save his hide. He also might know where Ace is in France. He heard a slight knock on the door.

"C'mon in," Jensen said warmly. He didn't expect the mountain of a man who came through the doorway. His chest muscles and shoulders filled out the Albany High varsity jacket and his thighs were like tree trunks in the Lee jeans. He had a white and blue striped sweat band on his right wrist and Nike sneakers.

Despite his impressive appearance, his manner was gentle and confident. Jensen came around his desk to shake his hand.

"Hello, Mr. Jensen. Thanks for seeing me on such short notice."

"No problem," he said. He motioned to the set of brown leather chairs and couch on the other side of the room. "Why don't we sit over here where it's more comfortable?"

Williams sat down on one of the chairs and Jensen on the other. *The Wall Street Journal, Forbes,* and *Newsweek* were lying on the coffee table between them.

"Nice to meet you finally. I've seen many of your games. Congrats, by the way, on the University of Michigan scholarship."

"Thank you, sir. Ace told me you liked to watch the games."

"You'll probably start training with the team during the summer, I'd imagine," Jensen said.

"Yeah, gotta be there sometime in July. Cuts the summer vacation short but I'm looking forward to it."

"I'm sure you are. It's not everybody who gets such an opportunity," Jensen confirmed.

"Yeah, I'm really thankful to the Lord for the blessing," Williams said softly.

"I forgot. You're a religious man, aren't you?"

"Yes, sir. But I don't like the word 'religious' much."

"Why's that?" Jensen's eyebrows lowered and he tilted his head to the side in bewilderment. Elijah moved more toward the edge of the chair. He clasped his hands and looked at Jensen like he was going to give a pep talk in a football huddle.

"Well, I prefer to call my faith a personal relationship with God rather than just a belief in a set of creeds or doctrines. God is a person and we can get to know Him and He can direct us in our lives in a very detailed way if we listen to His voice. It is possible to have religion, but not have God."

"That's interesting . . . ah . . . do you have any idea where Ace might be in France? Did he ever talk with you about going there?"

Elijah wasn't surprised at the change of subject. Some people got nervous talking too much about God. He sat back in his chair, a little disappointed but flexible. *Must not be the right time to talk about the Lord,* he thought.

"He told me he wanted to go there on his honeymoon with Gabriella after graduation but he didn't really say exactly where he wanted to go. I would think Paris, but I could be wrong."

"You know that she is probably with him, don't you?"

"Yeah. Not surprised. I think he really loves her and I believe it's mutual. I just hope he doesn't get into a lot of trouble for running away. I was wondering if there was anything I could do."

"Truth be told, he could get in a lot of trouble. I heard from the parole board, and if he doesn't turn himself in soon he will get the year for cutting that kid in the bar fight." Jensen pursed his lips.

"Yeah. I remember Ace telling me about that. Said you were a super lawyer to get him on probation," Elijah said.

"I don't know about that but it did help that he didn't have a record at the time. Now, things are different. I really have to get in touch with him to convince him to come home. I left a message for him at Charles DeGaulle, but it's a big airport and he probably didn't get it. I was just looking on the internet for a flight to France tomorrow to see if I can find him."

"Really, Mr. Jensen . . . Umm . . . Do you think I could go with you? I'd really like to try and talk some sense into Ace. That is, if you think that would help?"

Jensen seemed taken aback by the bold offer. "It could, but

do you think you can take off like that with school and all? It's not cheap either, you know."

"Now that I have the scholarship it takes a lot of the pressure off. My grades are good, even in computer science, thanks to Ace, so I don't think it would be a problem. I've got some money saved up for college I could use. And I went on that trip to Spain last year so my passport's good."

"You'd use your own money to go with me to Europe? You know, it could take some time to find him."

"I'd like to come, sir, if you don't mind. With the full scholarship I won't need as much as I thought. I've already talked to my parents and they are behind me if I think God wants me to go. I think God will help us. I know a lot of people are praying for Ace right now."

"That's great. We'll need all the help we can get—even from God if we can get it."

"We'll get it. I believe that. God has got a plan for Ace. I'm convinced of that. He just doesn't see it yet. Unfortunately, sometimes it gets worse before it gets better. You know that old expression 'it's the darkest just before the dawn.'"

"Well, I don't think it can get much worse than this except, of course, he has to spend time in jail, and that I will fight with everything I've got. First, though, we have to find him and convince him to come back with us. If you are determined to go, I wouldn't mind your company. Just give me your number and I'll let you know once I get the tickets. I really can't leave until tomorrow night. I have some court cases I can't postpone. I figure we can take a late flight and arrive in Paris early Saturday, if that works for you." Jensen got up and ripped off a sticky sheet from the little yellow pad on his desk and gave it to Williams. He quickly wrote down the numbers and gave it back to Jensen.

"That's fine with me, sir. Just let me know where and when you want me to meet you, and I'll be there."

"Thanks. I'll be in touch. It's nice to know that Ace has got some good friends."

"Thank you, sir. I know we'll find him. I just know it."

"Well, I like your confidence." Jensen's eyes then unexpectedly filled with tears and he sighed. "He's a good kid, really. I just don't want anything else to go wrong for him. He's had some tough breaks so far."

"I understand, sir. Have a good day."

"Oh, by the way, Elijah, do you know any French?"

"Pardononez-moi."

"Really. You know French?"

"Just kidding. I only know a few words like "bonjour," "au revoir," "Comment ca va?"

"Well, we'll just have to get by with an English-French dictionary, I guess."

They shook hands and Williams went out the door while Jensen headed back to the computer screen.

Chapter 43

Breaking and Entering
Late Thursday Evening, May 22, 2003
Albany, NY

L anny Tompkins had been watching the house with the wheelchair ramp from a safe distance behind a clump of trees. He wore black sweats, black sneakers, and skin-tight black leather driving gloves. He also had strapped to his back a knapsack that contained a flashlight and tools to help him break into the house as quickly and quietly as possible. He brought these only in case his normal method of just ramming his shoulder against the door didn't succeed. He was a big kid at six foot four and 240 pounds who had played varsity football until he was kicked off the team for drinking, so most door frames folded like the defensive linebackers he had played against. Yet, for the money he was offered by the dude on the phone, he wanted to be sure he was ready for anything. He knew the guy was on the level because he had paid him well before and knew his friend Willy.

It was 2:00 a.m. with little moonlight and the neighborhood was quiet. His job was to look for any papers that had a French address, which meant looking for a personal address book of any kind. He hoped the house did not have a security system. Judging by the unpainted exterior, and the low-middle-class neighborhood, he doubted it. Usually only the upper-scale homes like in Loudonville or Delmar installed them. This kind of residential area was prime for the picking. The people didn't have enough money for the high-priced security systems, but they did buy things that he could sell—computers, televisions, DVD players, and jewelry. The only thing he would have to worry about would be the dogs. The man assured him, though, that at least at this house there were no pets. One time after he had broken into a house he opened a bedroom door and a Doberman bolted out. Fortunately, this dog was just looking for daylight and ran right by him out the front door. It had been a close call, however, and one he didn't want to repeat.

Looking in several directions he drew in his breath and lightly sprinted across the dewy, ankle-high grass lawn. He leaped over the wheelchair ramp railing where it turned to the front door and huddled close to the extended part of the house that was perpendicular to the front entrance. He was glad for the large shrub next to the ramp that shielded him somewhat from the view from down the street. It took only two shoulder hits to loosen the door frame and allow him to push his way into the foyer. He closed the door quickly, took off his knapsack and drew out his flashlight. He pointed it to the right and the beam highlighted a couch, a stereo system and then a television. He was tempted to take the TV but reminded himself of his mission and the big bucks he could rake in with the right information.

He turned left and walked into another room. He waved the stream of white to the left again and saw a mahogany china cabinet that featured fancy porcelain plates on wooden stands and a matching dining room table with six chairs. He continued walking into what seemed to be a breakfast room that had a bay window looking out into the backyard. He quickly pointed the flashlight to the floor when he saw the reflection in the glass. He didn't want the light to be seen from a house from the parallel street. The flashlight still gave a circular glow from the floor and as he moved it up the wall to the left he saw the wooden legs of a small piece of furniture, a drawer with a brass knob and then a telephone resting on a small flat piece of white and blue marble.

He pulled open the drawer and saw a thin red book with "Addresses" printed in black on top of the regular yellow telephone book. He pulled the address book out and went into the adjoining kitchen. He sat down on the linoleum tile with his back to the door leading outside and began flipping through the pages looking for something, anything with a French address. When he came to the letter M he noticed that the name McKinley included a Parisian address in a place called Belleville. It had a name of an organization called Creative Global Outreach.

He smiled, took off his knapsack and placed the book inside and zipped it up. He looked around the kitchen and decided to check what was in the fridge. After all, why not reward himself for a job well done? This was easier than he thought. The address book in itself was going to pay big dividends. He opened the door and saw a plastic bottle of peach ice tea and a square cardboard box with Luigi's printed in big letters on the outside. That's all he needed. He smiled and pulled them both out and sat again with his back to the door. He opened the box and discovered there were two pieces left. "Oooh . . . mushrooms," he muttered to himself with a frown. He gently lifted off the offending fungi with his gloved thumb and index finger and placed them in the empty part of the box and began to take large mouthfuls of the now more acceptable slices while slugging down the rest of the ice tea.

After he finished them both he wiped his mouth with the back of his hand. He then crumpled up the pizza box and put it and the plastic bottle into the garbage container that he found behind the cupboard door underneath the sink.

Tompkins retraced his steps to the front door. Directly opposite the door were stairs leading to the second floor. He bounded up the stairs two at a time to the top. Immediately to the right there was a door. He opened it and walked in. It was a bedroom but to the left there was a computer desk with a monitor and a keyboard on a sliding shelf under the desk. The desk also contained a collection of reference books, including a dictionary, a book titled *Operation World*, a thesaurus, a French-English dictionary, and a Strong's Concordance standing between two bronze Arch of Triumph book ends. Straight ahead was a tall mirror with a vanity table and bench in front of it. To the right was a queen-size bed perfectly made up with a multi-colored bedspread.

Tompkins pointed his flashlight at the wall and saw a framed picture of a castle and a purple field of lavender on one side and a field of yellow sunflowers on the other. On the bottom it had the words La Provence. He thought the computer might have some valuable info, but it might need a code to open it and he didn't want to take the time. The more he thought about it the more he thought he should just get out of there before the cops decided to stop by. He had a French address and that's what the guy wanted. He heard the sound of a car and quickly clicked off his flashlight. He waited for it to pass and then said to himself, "I'm outta here." He clicked it back on and descended the stairs. He let himself out the front door, leaped over the ramp railing and ran to the trees that concealed him earlier. He picked up his ten-speed and rode down Fowler Avenue to New Scotland. He pedaled past the junior college and the hospital to Western Avenue, took a right over to Delaware and over to the 24 hour Price Chopper. He stopped in the parking lot that looked like it only had workers' vehicles, took his cell phone out of his pocket and called the number the man had given him. He looked into the store as he waited for the ringing to stop. A tired voice answered, "Yeah. Do you have anything?"

"Yes, sir. I'm at the Price Chopper on Delaware. Got it."

"Good job. Let's have a coffee together at the Dunkin' Donuts down the street in about five minutes."

"Sounds good to me. Whatta ya look like?"

"Don't worry about it. I know what you look like. I'll be driving a red BMW."

"Right."

The line went dead and Lanny rode his bike down the vacant street through the traffic light at the corner of Delaware and Western Avenue and rolled to a stop in front of Dunkin' Donuts. He walked it to the multiple iron bike stands for customers, unwound the chain lock from around his seat and slipped it through the spokes of his bike and the metal frame. He pushed his way through the glass entrance and went to the counter to order. The place was empty except for a thin young man with a five o'clock shadow and a white apron. He met Tompkins with an apprehensive manner.

"Can I help you?"

"A Boston Crème, please, and a medium hazelnut black coffee."

The man grabbed a piece of waxed paper and retrieved the donut and placed it on the counter in front of the big man. Tompkins picked it up and began eating immediately. The salesman then grabbed the appropriate cup size from the stack and filled it from the coffee maker to the left of the donut display shelves and also put it on the counter.

"That's $2.20 please," he said without emotion.

Tompkins paid him and shuffled over to the table overlooking the parking lot. By the time he got to the table only one bite was left to finish the donut. He popped it into his mouth and sat down. He yelled over to the counter man, "Hey, got another Boston Crème? Looks like I need another one to go with my coffee."

The man scooped up the donut and brought it to the counter. Tompkins dug his hand into his pocket and paid him in exact change. He returned to his seat and continued the vigil of watching the parking lot. Not more than five minutes after he had popped the last morsel of the second donut into his mouth a red BMW swerved between the two parking lines directly in front of him. A medium-build man with small gold-rimmed glasses and a brown corduroy suit jumped out. He walked rapidly to the entrance and opened the glass door. He walked confidently to the counter and ordered a large black coffee. Only after he had received his order did he turn to Tompkins and walk to his table. He pulled out a chair and sat down facing the big boy.

"Hey, Lanny. What did you find?"

Tompkins smiled and took off his knapsack. He opened it and started to go through the insides.

The man looked straight in his eyes and said softly with authority, "Don't give it to me now. You can give it to me in the car after we leave. Just tell me."

"Yeah. Sure. I found an address book that has a French address."

"Great. Good work. Any cops come by?" The man took a sip from his Dunkin' Donuts paper cup.

"No. Maybe they were here," Tompkins whispered back with a smile, chuckling at his quick wit. "Even found some cold pizza in the fridge," Tompkins boasted.

The man made no expression but quickly dismissed him as an amateur and someone he would never deal with again.

"All right. Let's go." They both got up. The man threw his half-full cup into the white cylinder-shaped garbage can on the way out. Tompkins did the same, though his was empty, and followed the shorter man out the glass doors. The man got in the driver's side while Tompkins got in the passenger side. Tompkins slid into the comfortable white leather seat and said, "Nice." He ran his hands over the smooth soft leather. He then put his knapsack on the black floor rug and took out the address book and handed it to the man.

"Well, here it is. Letter M."

The man took the little book and turned to the right page. "Great. Did you see anything else?"

"Ah . . . there was a poster in one of the bedrooms that said, "La Provence." Tompkins smiled expecting good things to follow. "I think that's French."

"It is. The south of France," the man said. "Here. You've earned it." He reached into his inside jacket pocket and handed his accomplice a white envelope.

Tompkins took it and opened it on his lap. He pulled out five one hundred dollar bills.

"Thank you. If you need any help in the future, just give me a call." He stuffed the envelope into his knapsack.

"Don't spend it all in one place," the man cautioned with a slight turn of the corner of his mouth.

"I won't." Tompkins smiled. He opened the door and reached back for his knapsack. He strapped it on his back and went to the bicycle rack. At that moment, three young black men appeared from behind the store wearing baggy jeans and dark jerseys. They ran to Tompkins. The taller kid, about the same height as Tompkins but not as wide, did the talking. "Hey, dude. What's the hurry?" He pulled a knife out of his back pocket. The others did the same. Tompkins stopped dead in his tracks. Three against one was not good odds if they had knives. If it weren't for the blades, he would have given it a try.

"We won't hurt you if you just hand over your little knapsack there."

The man in the BMW opened the door and pointed a Tech 9 with suppressor in the direction of the leader.

"Police. Detective Hamilton. If you would just put down your knives . . ."

At the split second when all eyes jerked toward the man, Tompkins swung both fists up into the faces of the unsuspecting thieves standing next to him. They both fell backward dropping their knives. Tompkins scooped one knife off the ground and kicked the other away from the sprawling bodies. He backed away from the leader, whose cockiness was now replaced with agitation at the sudden change of power. The man walked around the BMW's open door to move closer to the attackers. The two boys on the ground were stirring; one was sitting up and rubbing his jaw with his right hand, obviously still dazed by the blow, while the other was shaking his head.

"If you will drop your knife I think you will be better off," the man said with the barrel of his gun directed at the boy's chest.

"Yeah. It looks that way," the tall boy admitted dryly. He let the switchblade roll off his palm to the asphalt.

"Pick up the knives, Lanny, and bring them to me." Tompkins obeyed, retrieving the weapons and putting them in the man's outstretched palm.

"You can go now, gentlemen," the man said.

"C'mon guys. Let's get outta here. That guy's no cop. Silencers are illegal." The two on the ground swiftly jumped to their feet and followed the leader around the store, disappearing into the night.

"Not bad, Mr . . . Mr. Hamilton?" Lanny said nodding his head and raising his eyebrows, obviously impressed.

"Yeah. You didn't do so bad yourself," the man answered, smiling for the first time since their meeting, "but we better get outta here before the police arrive. I believe our friend in the store called them a few minutes ago."

They both left hurriedly in their chosen mode of transportation. The man burned rubber as he turned sharply on Western Avenue while Lanny pedaled wildly on his way back to the Price Chopper.

The man in the BMW sang heartily with the Jimi Hendrix song playing on his CD player: "Foxy Lady." Tomorrow, he'd be flying to France with Capaldi's mason, who spoke fluent French and Italian. Who knows, maybe in Paris he'd have some time to give Nicole a call. He hadn't seen her in years.

Chapter 44

Albany Tribune Office
Thursday, May 22, 2003

Palmer reviewed his latest article for on the Parks hit and run case. He liked the title, "Hit and Run Driver Flees to France; Girl still in Critical Condition." *Always nice to have alliteration or two if you can. Makes it sound kind of poetic.* Although the article itself still wasn't on the front page, Bascom approved of a reference to the article at the top with the page number, which showed the growing community interest.

When the boy turned himself in, or was caught, it would certainly get top recognition, Palmer was sure. He liked the slow-building drama. He had already painted a sympathetic picture of Ace Parks as a parentless teen who had gone through a lot with the abandonment of his father at a young age and the death of his mother. He wrote too about his strong work ethic and his ambitions to manage a Luigi's store. He also mentioned the girl who was still in a coma. She was apparently a very vivacious girl with a bubbly personality according to neighbors, and loved sports and music. He also hinted in his article that it was possible there may have been other factors that led to Ace leaving the scene of the accident, and if anyone had anything to report they should call the police. So far, no one had come forward to confirm that suspicion and subsequent interviews in the neighborhood turned up nothing.

Palmer was amused when he received an irate phone call from Reverend Johnston for not "reporting the facts." *He might be a charismatic orator but the pen is mightier than the sword—or the mouth,* Palmer thought. *Let him get mad. Maybe a vein will burst in his forehead.*

Henrietta Wilson was also still hanging on. *If she died,* Palmer thought, *perhaps the French police would get involved and try to locate Parks and extradite him, but for now, fat chance.* Palmer felt sorry for the Albany police chief who wanted to put the case behind him, but slightly envious of Parks, who outsmarted the police and flew the coop to France with a beautiful girl. Since his divorce a few years ago he had trouble getting a woman to have a cup of coffee with him at the local greasy spoon, let alone going overseas.

Unfortunately, the girl's father was not saying anything to the press. Rumor had it he had hired a private detective to go after them. It was possible. From what he heard, Capaldi was rolling in the dough. Although he still couldn't print her name in the paper, it was pretty much all over town that Gabriella Capaldi went with the kid. Unsummoned, an image surfaced in his mind of Vickie, the first girl he had ever kissed when he was 16. He smiled and snorted in amusement. He hadn't thought of her in decades.

Chapter 45

Missionary Base
Thursday Afternoon, May 22, 2003
East of Paris, France

When Ace walked into the McKinley's living room he knew something was up. Mrs. McKinley and Gabriella both had cups of tea in their hands. A wooden platter was also on the coffee table with a tea pot, honey jar and a plate of cookies and chocolates, which to him meant a long conversation. Mrs. McKinley was sitting in the armchair across from Gabriella on the couch and smiled warmly as Ace entered the room. Ace quickly looked over at Gabriella who was nestled comfortably into the back cushion with a peaceful and gentle, though sheepish, kind of smile. She looked like she was beaming with joy. Something was wrong.

"What's going on?" Ace blurted, obviously dismayed by what he saw.

"We were just having a nice little chat, Ace, woman to woman," Mrs. McKinley said matter-of-factly, taking a sip from her cup.

"What kind of little chat—if you don't mind me asking?" Ace said, looking from Mrs. McKinley to Gabriella as if his stare could pry out a response.

"Why don't you tell him, Gabriella?"

"Why don't you relax and sit down, Ace?" Gabriella said.

"Why? Is it something serious?"

"Yeah. I guess you could say that."

"Don't tell me. You accepted Jesus. I knew it." He turned to

Mrs. McKinley. "I knew it. I knew that once I was gone, you or Mr. McKinley would pull her aside and give her all that Jesus stuff and talk her into it."

"Ace. Listen. She didn't talk me into it. It's just that I understand now. I can have a personal relationship with Jesus. It doesn't have to be based on rituals and laws but on love. Look at me, Ace. I feel a peace I have never known before. It's wonderful. Finally I feel God is with me. It's awesome and . . ."

"That's just great. Whatta ya gonna do now? Join the mission and go to Africa? What about me? We're supposed to get married next week, if possible."

"Ace, I love you. You know I do. But if it is of God why do we have to rush it? Why do we have to do it in secret away from our family and friends?"

"Well. You know one reason. Your dad hates me and thinks I'm a jerk. Another reason . . . you didn't tell her . . . *that*, did you?"

"Ace. Please. We need help. We have to tell somebody."

"Great, and you probably told the police, too. I thought I could trust you. You said you wouldn't tell."

"Ace. Of course I didn't tell the police. Don't. They just want to help us."

At this Ace punched the door and ran out of the house. Gabriella burst into tears while Mrs. McKinley got up and put her arms around her.

Chapter 46

Monkey in the Middle
Friday Afternoon, May 23, 2003
Châteaux Thierry, France

A ce opened the passenger sliding side door of the grey Peugeot and got in. It wasn't too different from the mini-vans at home except it had a small stick shift just right of the steering wheel near the dashboard instead of on the floor. He chuckled to himself at the novelty of it and leaned back in the cloth seat. Maybe if he pretended he was asleep the two evangelists wouldn't bother him. He wasn't in the mood for being preached at, and his body had not yet adapted to the time change in France.

Brad and Bury were talking at the back of the van. They put Bury's suitcase in and shut the rear door with a gush of fresh air, which hurt Ace's ears slightly. They both got in their respective doors at the same time. Bury turned around in his seat and looked at Ace and said: "How's it going, mate? You look like you just ate a sour kiwi for breakfast."

"The fruit or the bird?" Ace retorted with an attempt at humor.

"Aha. Very good. Not all Americans know that much about New Zealand. How did you know that?"

"Gabby and I were considering going to New Zealand for our honeymoon, so we looked it up on the internet and got some books from the library. We finally decided on France."

"Well, if you ever get the chance, you're welcome to stop by my place. Here's my card. Be glad to show you around." He reached into his inside jacket pocket and handed Ace a card.

"Thanks. Could be awhile though before we get there." Ace hardly gave it a glance as he shoved it into his front right jeans pocket.

"No worries. You never know."

"Yeah." Ace turned to look out his window and saw some oil drills going up and down automatically in the fields they were passing. Somehow the scene seemed out of place in the rural country setting. A few minutes later he noticed a flock of sheep within a fenced-in area near a small old stone house. An older woman with a black wool scarf was putting clothes on a line in the back of the house. A few chickens scurried to and fro searching for seeds on the ground. The thought of the little girl he had run over came to his mind and he wondered if she was still alive. He didn't want to dwell on it, though. There was absolutely nothing he could do to help her anyway.

"Ah. Brad. Did you have any problems adjusting to the culture here? They say the French don't like Americans much."

Brad smiled and nodded. "Well, it was sort of tough at the beginning, but I'd say it's more a problem with our country's foreign policy—like in Iraq and our President Bush—than with us individual Americans. Whenever I would talk to people they would insist it was not the people but the government. They abhor capitalism and feel our country imposes itself too much on other countries. It also doesn't help that many American tourists don't make a big effort to learn French and expect the French to speak in English all the time.

"What made it really hard for me at the beginning was the fact I had studied the death penalty before coming over and came to the conclusion I am for it under certain situations. Here in Europe they don't even think you can be a Christian and believe in that. Did you know the European Union won't even let a country join if they have the death penalty?"

"No. I didn't know that. So, how did you deal with that?"

"At first, it bothered me that most French Christians have not examined all the verses in the Bible on the issue and can't really articulate their reasons for being against it, so it left me frustrated because I had. Finally, I just gave up trying to debate the issue.

"I discovered that some of my frustrations were that I just wanted to be right and prove that I was. In praying about it, I felt God was saying to let it go because it was my pride that was saying I had to be right about the issue. I needed to just let it go and agree to disagree."

"In what cases do you think a person should be executed?" Ace's voice came out a little more dry and crackly than he intended.

"Definitely in cases where a killer has abused sexually and murdered—child or adult. Some cases are so horrendous that the only fair thing to do for society, the victim and the families of the deceased is to kill them. What is more merciful? Killing them through lethal injection or letting the prisoners do it? Jeffrey Dahmer—you know that guy who killed children and cut them up and put them in his freezer? He should have died publicly, not at the hands of inmates. Generally though, I'd say that anyone who premeditates murder and then commits it should be executed, but I think there may be other factors to consider in some cases like when a murderer has abused the victim over and over."

Ace leaned back in his seat and said, "What if someone accidentally killed someone? You don't think they should die, do you?"

"No, of course not. But the sentence would depend on the circumstances. If it involves repeated negligence or carelessness on the part of the killer I think the punishment should be greater."

Ace didn't dare go any further. Too many details and Brad

might put two and two together. At least this guy didn't think he should be executed for his crime if the girl died. He let the subject drop.

"Any other things you found to be different in France?" Ace asked after a few minutes of silence.

"Well there was something I found to be a little funny. In the United States we have the habit of greeting people often if we see them several times during the day—sort of as a way of acknowledging them. I started by saying "Bonjour" several times during the day at the base and a Swiss guy pulled me aside and said: "Brad, you know you only have to say 'Bonjour' once and it is good for the whole day. You don't have to keep repeating it." I thanked him and became very economical with my *bonjours*. Then I get back to the States for furlough and I am working with this guy at a retreat center, painting or something, and he must've said hello five times during the day. It was kind of funny, the difference in culture.

"I think, generally speaking, our personality as a nation is more outgoing and gregarious, while France tends to be more introspective and melancholic. For example, in America we are usually very forward when we meet people. 'How are you?' 'What's your name?' 'Where do you work?' In France it is not uncommon to introduce yourself in a social setting, put out your hand and have the other person not even give you their name. They may shake your hand but that's about it. Which brings me to another vast difference—in France they kiss on the cheeks if they know you. Depending on where you are from determines the times you kiss, and how well you know the person—twice, or even three or four times can be the norm. Rarely do the people actually kiss though. Most of the time they just brush cheeks and kiss the air. Once in a while, though, you will get the passionate kisser who will plant a big wet one on you, but like I said, these events are rare. As a guy it is quite an adjustment to let guys give you pecks and to give them in return but that is part of the package in coming to another country. You have to do certain things so as not offend people. Here again you have to make sure you do this only once during the day. I once kissed a woman twice in the same day and she quipped that she had already kissed me for the day and pulled back in dismay. It was a little embarrassing to say the least."

"I can imagine," Ace said with his mouth, but his mind was beginning to wander. The fate of the little girl wouldn't let him alone. He could forget about it for hours at a time, but like an unpaid bill it kept coming back in the mailbox. At this point, he would have preferred to just look out the window at the French countryside, but Peter Bury began asking him pointed questions about his objections to God. After a few exchanges he thought he had shared too much about his personal life and he was getting uncomfortable. The only reason he agreed to go with Brad and Bury was so he could find an internet café and make contact with Uncle Jerry and possibly get some money sent to the other city closer to the missionary base. He should have known that this New Zealand evangelist would see it as a golden opportunity to drill him on his beliefs.

"So Ace, if I hear you correctly, the big obstacle you have right now from accepting Christ as your Savior is your mum's passing away and the fact your dad left your family when you were young? Is that right?"

Ace didn't want to revisit his mom's death just then and the way this stranger talked about it so easily bugged him, even though he might be right in his assessment. Her death was a life-changing event for him. His use of "mum" instead of "mom" also sounded weird and infantile.

"Yeah. How do you factor in a loving God into that equation?"

"I don't have all the answers, Ace, even though I'd like to.

Tragedies often do surprise and shock me. I don't know why God allowed your mum—or your mom, as you Americans say, sorry—to die, or your dad to leave. However, I do believe that God can turn anything the devil or whatever life throws at us into something good. You said that your mom was a devoted Christian. Maybe the good thing that can come out of her death is you meeting her Savior."

"I don't know about that. But do you think we can give it a rest? This whole subject brings up a lot of emotional issues for me and I'd rather not go there right now, if that is okay with you."

"Absolutely, Ace. Sorry if I pushed you a bit there. It's just that it is oftentimes in our darkest times and deepest needs that we pull away from God instead of drawing near to Him. I had a rough time a number of years back when my wife had a miscarriage. We had prayed for so long for a child and when Jenny did get pregnant we couldn't understand why God would take our girl. It was devastating but God helped us through it—mainly by showing His love through the community of believers we belong to. It took some time to come out of that one, but we did, and today we have two lovely children."

"Okay. Thanks, Mr. Bury but . . . I'm just not there yet."

"I understand Ace. I'll be praying for you."

"Thank you."

They passed the remaining time in silence until the van pulled into the train station. Brad got Bury's luggage from the back of the van and they all walked into the facility.

"Don't forget to punch your ticket before getting on the train, Peter," Brad said. "There will be a place on the platform to do that."

"Thanks Brad. I would have forgotten that," Bury replied.

"Things are a little different here, aren't they?"

After dropping Bury off at the station and asking the man at the information desk where the internet café was downtown,

Ace and Brad drove to the address given and parked the car in a small parking lot nearby. They passed a group of elderly men playing bocci ball at a level dirt area near the parking lot.

"Hey. Look at that!" Ace said. "I guess they really play that game here, huh?

"Oh, yeah. Everywhere. I imagine they wager some too on the matches."

"You try it yet?"

"Sure. Usually you try to be on a team where you have a guy who can knock the other balls away. You'd be amazed how accurate some of these guys are. You know how to play?"

"Yeah. We talked about it in French class. You throw out a little ball called the 'cochonnet,' which literally means piglet, and then you try to get as near to it as possible with the bigger metal balls. The ones nearest get the points. Kind of like horseshoes."

"You got it. The only thing is sometimes you get these players that can knock your ball away with their balls every time you get it close." As they passed the playing area, speaking in English, they got a few suspicious stares from the men. Brad said, "Bonjour" to be polite, but the men did not feel obligated to return the greeting so they just ignored him. The group stared at them as they rounded the corner at the boulangerie. An old man with grey sideburns and blue overalls merely muttered, "Les Anglais," and they all shook their heads and resumed their play. Ace took a special interest in the pastries in the window but said nothing, knowing that he had to borrow money from Brad for the internet usage.

Brad arrived at the little internet café in the alley first and read the store hours.

"Sorry Ace," he said as Ace joined him at the door. "It says they close from Midi to 14:00."

"But what's the problem? It's 11:45."

"Maybe the person had to pick up their child at school or

something. You know families usually eat the midday meal together in these smaller towns."

"Oh no. You mean we're gonna have to wait two hours before they open up again?"

"Sorry, Ace. Can't wait. Gotta get the van back. And like Peter said, 'Things are done a little differently here.'"

Chapter 47

Parks' Home
Friday Morning, May 23, 2003

Jerry Jensen was surprised to see the front door of Ace's house obviously forced open. Even though the door was placed back in position, Jensen noticed the broken door-frame. He used the key anyway and entered the house through the door. He wondered what the robbers were after. The house was warm, which made sense since Ace didn't turn it off in his haste to beat it out of the country. He wondered if the intruder was still in the house.

He turned on the light in the living room and called out: "If you're still here come on out. I just called the police so you better give yourself up."

His gut feeling told him, however, that no one was there or had been for a while. He listened for a few moments for any noises and then went into the dining room and turned on the light. He figured some local delinquents or addicts just broke in looking for something to sell for hard cash or drugs. In that case, it could be dangerous. He looked around and saw nothing amiss in the dining room and then continued into the breakfast room and did the same. Nothing except the drawer of the telephone stand was a little open. He pulled on the knob. Just a telephone book. Odd, he thought. Wasn't that where Ace's mom kept the address book? Maybe Ace had moved it upstairs somewhere or put it in the kitchen. Jensen entered the kitchen, turned the light on, and began checking all the drawers. After finishing to no avail, he stopped and stroked his chin.

Absentmindedly, his eyes went to the refrigerator and he noticed a wide variety of photographs, notes, and cards attached to it by small magnets. He saw a card with an image of the country of France and, on the freezer door above the refrigerator, was a photo of a family. At the top of the card was *The McKinleys serving in France* in large white letters. He took it off the freezer and turned it over. On the back was a French mailing address, an email address, and a web site. Also written on the card was the name Creative Global Outreach. Jensen took the card and put it in his windbreaker. At least now he had a lead to bring with him tomorrow when he and Elijah Williams took a Delta flight to Paris. He'd try to make contact via the internet back at home. He had his doubts that Ace would visit a missionary unless he absolutely had to. But there's no telling what someone might do when they are running from the law.

Chapter 48

Albany Medical Center
Friday Morning, May 23, 2003

T
he elevator door opened at the pediatric floor of Albany Medical Center and an entourage of three well-dressed black men in suits and ties and a few white men in casual apparel with cameras burst out like a team going for a touchdown. The barrel-chested black man in the lead had his lower lip pushed into his upper lip in a stiff determined fashion and his eyes were narrowed in a mission-focused mode. He walked fast and the others had to hurry to keep up. The white men peppered him with questions, which he ignored. The sounds of their leather shoes and voices echoed down the hallway and the head nurse, Margaret Hall, stopped talking to the receptionist at the nurses' station and was instantly annoyed. She straightened up to confront the intruders to her sacred domain as they rounded the corner.

Reverend Johnston came into view first, followed by the rest. He stopped at the desk directly in front of Margaret Hall.

"Good evening, Ma'am," he said politely. "We would like to see the little girl Henrietta Wilson. Please. She's in Room 403. We are close friends of the family."

"First of all, gentlemen. I would appreciate it if you keep your voices down. This is a hospital and there are sick children here that need their rest."

"Please forgive us, Ma'am. You are absolutely correct." He looked at his followers. "We apologize deeply for our transgressions."

"As for your request, the right to see Henrietta is reserved for her mother and immediate relatives."

Johnston reached into his inside coat pocket and produced a piece of paper and a laminated card. "This is a legal letter from the mother and her lawyer giving me permission as a minister of the gospel to see the child and to pray for her. And this is my minister's license."

Head Nurse Hall took the material and scrutinized it at length. She handed it back to Johnston.

"Very well. You can see the child but no one else. The reporters and the cameras and everyone else stay here. Do you understand, Mr. Johnston? The child is still in a coma."

"Reverend Johnston, Ma'am, if you please."

"Reverend Johnston. Do you understand?"

"Yes. I understand, Ms. Hall, but may I please bring my assistant Mr. Miles. You see, we pray as a team. We feel there is more power whenever two or three are gathered together like Jesus said . . ."

"No, Mister—or rather Reverend—Johnston. You will go alone." She turned to the young woman that just came behind the desk from another hallway. "Nurse Barrington. Will you please escort Reverend Johnston to Room 403 to pray for Henrietta Wilson?

"Certainly, Mrs. Hall." She looked at the smiling Johnston.

"This way, sir." Johnston nodded to his associates and followed the nurse. He noticed a young couple talking to a little boy in Room 401. The boy was giggling as he hugged a stuffed bear he had evidently just received.

They entered the noiseless room of 403 and immediately saw the small form of a little girl in pig tails lying motionless on the bed with an IV connected to her right arm. The blue blanket and sheets were folded over at the level of her armpits and neatly tucked into the bed while her arms lay at her sides. Her eyes were closed and she breathed lightly.

Johnston put his hands together and approached the girl slowly. "How is she doing, nurse? Any signs of improvement?"

"She has stayed pretty much the same since she came to us. We had a close call a couple of days ago when she had some breathing problems, but she's been fairly stable since then. You never know with cases like this. She's had a head trauma and if she has a convulsion we could lose her at any time. You just never know. Some children can come out of a coma in a week, a month, a year. Others may never come out of it and just stay like that perpetually. Some die."

"I see. So she is still in the valley of the shadow for now."

"I'm sorry?" said the nurse.

"I mean 'the valley of the shadow of death,' like David spoke about in Psalm 23."

"Yes. I guess you could say that."

"Well, if you will excuse me. I will just say a prayer for the child." Johnston then placed his hand on the girl's shoulder and prayed earnestly for her healing in a sing song kind of way, with frequent 'hallelujahs,' elongating the 'loo' and punctuating the prayer like a period, with a short 'yah' at the end. 'Amens' and 'my Fathers' also were repeated between phrases like quotation marks. During the long petition, Nurse Barrington stepped back out of the entrance and looked both ways down the hall for any red lights flashing above the doors. She saw one above Room 410, looked at Reverend Johnston and decided she had time to attend to the call.

When Johnston no longer sensed the nurse's presence in the room, he went to the doorway, looked both ways and then returned to the bedside. He thought about asking the parents of the boy in room 401 to take a picture of him praying for the girl but vetoed it because of limited time. He went back to the bedside of the girl. Quickly he took out his cell phone, flipped it open and took several pictures of the girl and himself praying for her—his left hand holding the small object and his right hand on her head. He also made sure the IV in her arm was clearly visible in the frame. He clicked it shut, slipping it back into the little leather case on his belt, and walked back to the nurses' station.

He thanked Nurse Hall for her kindness in letting him pray for the child and led his group back to the elevator. Once all were aboard and descending he said: "Well, gentlemen. Now I will answer any question you have. And, I think I have a photo or two that might be of interest you."

Chapter 49

Ibis Hotel, CDG Airport
Saturday Evening, May 24, 2003
Paris, France

So what do we do now, Mr. Peterson?" Anthony Scalafoni said as he wearily pulled off one of his Nike's while sitting on the hotel bed. Peterson was standing staring out the sliding glass doors that opened onto their small outside terrace.

"We'll just have to go back to the neighborhood tomorrow and ask around," he said nonchalantly. They had finally found a taxi to take them to the Belleville area and had spent all day trying to find someone who knew the missionary, McKinley, to no avail. A Chinese family now lived in the apartment at the address that Lanny had supplied to him, and they had no idea where McKinley had gone. Unfortunately, the only Chinese Peterson and Scalafoni knew was limited to food items they ordered at the local Chinese buffet back in the U.S. They then knocked on other doors of the apartment complex but few people were home and those that were hadn't lived there for very long and were reticent to divulge any information to strangers.

Peterson was impressed with his younger colleague's attempts at speaking in French but they still had no leads. They had tried the ancient-looking, stone Protestant church nearest to the apartment complex to see if anyone there knew anything but the pastor was away at a conference in London and the woman at the church, although bilingual, was new and hadn't heard of McKinley. She said the pastor would return on Sunday night and they could call him then if they wanted, or they could just come to church on Sunday and talk with him there. She smiled and said, "We have a very contemporary service and there are people from many different nations. I'm sure you would like it." The detective took the piece of paper the church secretary gave him with the telephone number and said, "Merci for the invitation. We'll try calling him Saturday night and, who knows, maybe we will see you Sunday." As an afterthought he added, "Oh, here's our phone number at the Ibis Hotel by the airport. If you think of someone who might know him, please have them give us a call." He would have liked her number (he found French accents intoxicating) but figured she wouldn't be interested in a pagan like himself; plus, she was probably half his age, though that did not bother him.

Peterson turned from the window to look at his associate on the bed and said with a slight smile, "As you can see, Anthony, this detective life isn't as exciting as they portray it on TV, is it? A lot of times, it's just plain tedious and boring." He looked back to his view of parking lots, garages, and lighted moving vehicles wondering what Nicole was doing at that moment. Bringing this kid along did have its disadvantages.

"It's interesting, though, being in another country," Scalafoni said pulling off his second sneaker. He then scooted back on the bed with his back against the bed board and ripped open a package of peanuts. He began popping them into his mouth.

"Yeah, I guess," Peterson admitted. "We'll find 'em. Don't worry about that. It just might take some time."

"Oh boss," Scalafoni said suddenly, "I thought you might find this interesting. I saw that Elijah Williams dude at the registration desk with another guy when I went down to the lobby for snacks."

At this Peterson jerked his head around. "What? You don't mean that black football player who's a friend of Ace Parks, do you? Here, in Paris?"

"Yep. The same."

"Well, isn't that interesting. Does he know you?"

"Not from a hole in the wall."

"Good. I've got an assignment for you."

Chapter 50

Ibis Hotel
Saturday Evening, May 24, 2003
Paris, France

Anthony Scalafoni smiled to himself at how easy it was to obtain Williams' room number. All he had to say in French was: "I am a friend of Mr. ElijahWilliams who checked in today. Can I have his room number, please?" He even had the right response when the French guy said no one had registered under that name. He just said he was a big black guy who was with another man. The French guy immediately responded: "Ah oui. Il était avec Monsieur Jensen, je crois" (He was with Mr. Jensen, I believe).

Now all he had to do is act casual, find the room and listen outside the door to see if he could pick up anything that could lead them to Ace and Gabriella. This definitely was better than lugging cement blocks around all day. And who knows, maybe Gabriella would fall for him. She was hot, and from what Mr. Capaldi said he would be rescuing her from a crummy life with this idiot Parks. Mr. Capaldi even offered him a bonus if he roughed him up a bit. No problem. It would probably only take one punch to put him down.

Scalafoni just hoped neither Williams, nor the other guy, would come out of their room while he was listening. The carpeted hall floors were perfect to muffle the sounds of footsteps and no one was in sight. He came to Room 334 and stopped. Carefully looking around, he took out the listening device that Peterson had given him, pressed the adhesive pads to the door and the attached plugs into his ears. The amplifier was attached to his belt unseen. If he heard someone coming down the hall or opening the door to their room, he would just have to yank the pads off the door, shove them into his pocket and start walking. He could keep the plugs in his ears since they looked exactly like the ones used for listening to music.

Mr. Jensen and Elijah had the TV on and were watching the news in French. It suddenly stopped, and he thought for a moment that he was caught. Instead he heard: "No sense watching French news . . . can't pick up a word they're saying," a man said.

"I'm in the same boat with you, Mr. Jensen. I took Spanish."

"Might be good to hit the sack early so we'll be fresh in the morning. I'm feeling that jet lag myself. Sure hope the strike is over by tomorrow. It's a lot easier, not to mention cheaper, to take the train to Châteaux Thierry instead of renting a car or taking a taxi from Paris."

"How far is it?"

"By the map it looks about 100 miles east of us which is about two hours by train with all the stops and then somebody from that missionary group will pick us up at the station. I think their base is about 45 minutes from Châteaux Thierry."

"Does Ace know we are coming?"

"No. Our contact McKinley thought it might be better if we surprised him so he doesn't bolt. He thought together we all might be able to talk some sense into him."

Scalafoni listened for a few more minutes but when he heard someone go into the bathroom and turn on the tap water he figured it was time to vacate. That was all right. He had the goods.

Chapter 51

Ibis Hotel
Saturday Evening, May 24, 2003

Y ou must have beginner's luck, Tony. Maybe you're in the wrong profession," Peterson said. He had his map of France laid out on the small table by the window and was using his index finger to locate all the cities and towns to the right of Paris.

"Let's see . . . what did you say the name of the town was about two hours east of Paris?"

"Chatow Teery is what it sounded like. It's spelled c . . . h . . . a . . . t . . . e . . . a . . . u . . . x with an inverted "v" over the the first "a." It's the word for castle in French." Scalafoni bent over to look at the towns with the detective.

"Excuse me, Tony. But those peanuts you've been eating have given you some wicked breath. How about using the mint spray in the bathroom?"

"Oh. Sure. Sorry. What mint spray?"

"It's mine. Don't worry. Just don't put the sprayer in your mouth. All right? Keep it at a safe distance."

"No problem, Boss."

"Where was I? Château-Thierry. Oh. There it is. Got it, Tony. And you said the place they were going was 45 minutes from there?"

Scalafoni came out of the bathroom and walked back to the small table where the detective was scrutinizing the map.

"Yeah. That's what I heard," he said, coming alongside

Peterson, yet making sure he didn't get too close to him. He eyed the map without bending down.

All of a sudden Peterson hit his right hand to his forehead and stood up and looked at Scalafoni.

"We don't have to guess on this. In France they have this thing called the "minitel." It's even quicker than the internet. They should have one at the front desk. We just have to type in Creative Global Outreach and, bingo, we got the address and the telephone number."

Chapter 52

Closing In
Monday Morning, May 26, 2003
Montmirail, France
(Five miles from the Mission Base)

Man, the French really like their coffee cups small," Scalafoni said looking over the Espresso-sized cups, which were just deposited on their small round table with two fresh pastries called "milles feuilles" by a slender young waitress with dyed pitch black hair cut short with the sides curving behind her ears.

"What?" Peterson said quickly as he turned his attention from watching the waitress retracing her steps back to the kitchen.

"The cups. Look how small they are."

"Yeah. I thought you'd know about that growing up with Italian and French parents."

"I guess by the time I came along they'd pretty much adapted to the American way of doing things."

"Well as a warning I'd say they probably pack as much caffeine in that little cup there as you get in those big mugs from Dunkin' Donuts. Take my advice and sip it like this." Peterson lifted the little cup with his thumb and index finger daintily holding out his other three fingers in an exaggerated way and brought it slowly to his lips.

"Ahhh . . . C'est bon, mon ami."

Scalafoni tried to do the same but his big fingers made the job difficult on the small porcelain handles so he put it down and grabbed the whole cup with his hand and drank it that way.

"Whoah! I guess you're right about that! That is strong!"
He put the cup down and turned his attention to the delicacy
with the marble vanilla and chocolate icing on top and the finely
layered structure with custard-like filling. He stuffed a quarter
of it into his mouth. Some flakes of the pastry fell off onto the
maroon table cloth and shot out of his mouth as he spoke:.

"That's great!"

"Yeah. You can get them in the States but there we call them
Napoleons. Not sure what "milles feuilles" means."

"I think it means a 'thousand sheets' like sheets of paper,"
Scalafoni said shoving another mouthful into his mouth with
more flakes falling on the table.

Irritated with Scalafoni's lack of manners, Peterson just
shook his head. He was tempted to reprove the mason but
decided to let it slide; there were more important things to talk
about. He edged closer to the table and leaned forward to the
table to speak more quietly.

"All right. I think we need a plan here. We got a jump on
the other two by leaving last night in that rental car. It looks like
they'll be able to take the train into that Teery place you heard
them say last night. The guy at the hotel said they expected the
trains to start up again today. Then they will have to wait for
someone from the missionary place to go and get them." The
detective looked at his Rollex. "It's 7:30 now. I doubt they'll take
the earliest train so I'd say they would get here around 11:00 or
12:00. That doesn't leave us much time to find the girl and
convince her to come back with us. Actually, the fact that she
knows you may make that simpler. It probably would be best
to talk to her without Parks around."

"I can take care of him, sir," Scalafoni suggested.

"I'm sure you can, Tony, but let's not complicate things here
or make trouble when diplomacy will accomplish the same
goals. Does he know who you are?"

"Yeah. I guess you could say we had a run-in."

"Whatta ya mean run-in? A fight?"

"I wish. I just saw him once at the Napa Auto Parts store after Mr. Capaldi told Gabriella to stay away from him. I just stood in front of his car door when he came out and made sure he understood what Mr. C. had said."

"And how did he receive your encouragement?"

"Not too well. Seemed a little irritated by my intervention and told me it was none of my business and that I should just stay out of it. Tell you the truth I almost popped him one right there."

"What happened?"

"Just told him that he better listen to Mr. C. or there might be some consequences. He just said, 'Are you threatening me?' and I said, 'No, I'm telling you so you know' and then I let him go."

"Okay, Scalafoni, let's get something straight," Peterson said drawing closer to the mason's face and staring directly into his eyes. "You may have something to gain by Parks being out of the picture, I understand. I'm not blind. She's a cute girl. But let me make myself very clear. I do not want you to start a fight with this guy under any circumstances. All we need is for some-one to call the French police and we are screwed and stuck here for who knows how long. This government invented red tape. That's one of the consequences of socialism—administrative nightmares. And I know that from experience."

"But Mr. C. said . . ."

"Mr. C. is not here and you will listen to what I say. Got it?"

"Err . . . yeah. I understand." Scalafoni said this softly but the fingers of his right hand automatically formed into a fist underneath the table.

"Okay. When we get to the missionary place you will stay in the car unless I come and get you or I bring Gabriella to the car. Neither she nor he will recognize me. I will go to the person in charge and find out where she is. I will explain the serious situation they are in and my job to bring the girl back home with me. I will then ask if I can speak with Gabriella alone with the leader present, of course. I believe I can convince her to come with us. If she doubts who I am I have something that may convince her, and if not, I may come and get you or bring her out to you. Okay? Is that clear?"

"Yeah."

"Good. Let's go." They both stood up. Peterson pulled a 10-euro coin from his pocket and placed it on the table. Scalafoni quickly picked up what was left of the pastry and took another huge bite and followed Peterson to the black BMW sedan, eating as he went. The detective clicked the doors open with his remote and was about to get in the driver's side when he saw Scalafoni with the food. He frowned and said, "Finish it off first, please. I don't want crumbs in the car."

Chapter 53

Missionary Base, East of Paris
Monday, May 26, 2003
Montelimar, France
(Five miles from the Mission Base)

Peterson put on his left signal and pulled the BMW between the two stone pillars with the number that matched the address he had obtained through the minitel at the hotel. He immediately saw an older model 15-passenger grey Renault van and a small white Deux Chevaux to the right and parked next to the van.

He turned to his passenger and said, "Remember, I do not want you getting out of the car and letting Parks or the girl see you. Is that understood?"

"Yeah. I think I can understand that."

"If I need you, I will come and get you. Maybe you can listen to the radio and test your French. I'll leave the keys."

The detective got out of the car, opened the rear passenger door on his side and took out a brown leather briefcase. He could smell and hear the presence of chickens. They were located under the stone overhang in a row of cages in front of the cars next to an enclosed stone structure. As he walked a few steps he suddenly heard some loud grunting of a pig echoing from the enclosed area, which made him jump a little. He looked around to see if Scalafoni had seen him twitch like that and smiled in the direction of the car but the boy was too busy playing with the radio dials to take notice.

He looked at the house as he walked up to the entrance and was impressed. It was probably built during the 19th century and had recently been painted with a light yellow-colored stucco. There were bricks pointing outward around the doors and windows, which gave it an added decorative look. He went up the few stone steps to the two huge oak doors with iron rings and black iron levers to open them. He noticed, too, a small raised iron rectangle attached to the stoop off to the right, and figured it was probably meant for removing mud from boots and may have been there for centuries.

Peterson knocked on the door but when no one came he pushed down on the lever and entered. He immediately heard the din of the sound of many people talking and saw to his right some stairs leading down, probably to the basement. In front of him were a few tiled stairs leading to the main floor or the "rez-de-chaussée." He went up the few steps and entered the foyer. He saw, through an open door on his right, several young people sitting at what looked like a long table eating breakfast and talking amicably. They did not notice his entry.

The foyer was in the shape of a rectangle that ran the length of the house, about thirty feet, with huge doors, similar to the ones he entered at the other end. To the left was the entrance to the kitchen and he could smell the wonderful odor of baking bread. Between it and the next door, which was closed, was a large oak credenza with a long flat top and different piles of papers in rows on top of it. On the wall above it were photos of missionaries from around the world, including Africa, Asia, Europe and America. Below their pictures were brief descriptions of their ministries. He quickly located his man McKinley with his family and read the description underneath: International Director and Base Counselors.

On the wall to the right was a large map of the world just past the open door, and on the other side of the map was another open door. Judging by the sounds Peterson figured it was probably one large room with two entrances. He scanned the map and saw blue-headed pins stuck out at various locations indicating the many Centers of the organization.

Before Peterson could decide what to do, a short, stocky woman with an apron and short blonde hair came out of the kitchen and asked, "Bonjour, Monsieur. Est-ce que je peux vous aider?" She had tired eyes and ruddy face from the stove but her smile was genuine and her light blue eyes sparkled.

"Ah . . . Madame . . ."

"Mademoiselle."

"Ah oui . . . mademoiselle. Pardon."

The woman raised her eyebrows expectantly waiting and, before he could reply, said: "Don't tell me. You speek Engleesh. You can speek in Engleesh. I understand better than I talk."

"Oh. Thank you. Yes. I am looking for a man by the name of McKinley. You know this man here." He pointed to the photo on the wall. "Do you know where I might be able to find him?"

"Gary. Yes. He leeves at another place. Stay here and I can call heem." She ducked back into the kitchen doorway and disappeared to the left of his view. A second later she popped back out into the doorway with a phone to her ear and a cord leading horizontally to the left. She cradled it with her head and shoulder on her left ear while she wiped her hands in her apron. She then lifted her right index finger, nodding her head and smiling like it would only take a second. Her eyes locked on his.

"Oui. Monsieur Gary. Il y a un home qui parle anglais ici qui te cherche. Oui." At this she turned to Peterson and asked:

"Ah. Yes. What ees your name? Meester Jensen?"

"No. My name is Joe Peterson from the USA. It is an urgent personal matter that I need to speak to him about privately as soon as possible."

"Il dit qu'il doit parler avec toi le plus vite possible et c'est urgent . . . Oui. D'accord. Je peux demander à Brad s'il peut amener Monsieur Peterson chez toi. D'accord Gary." She went back into the kitchen and reappeared phoneless.

"Monsieur, eef you can stay here for a few minutes, I can find someone to take you to hees house. Okay?"

At that moment Peterson saw two young men come out of the door to the right of the world map. They were speaking English and one was tall with blond hair wearing jeans and a jean jacket and the other was shorter with dark hair. The blond-haired boy seemed upset about something and the other boy was trying to console him.

Peterson turned towards them and the blond-haired boy and his eyes met for a second.

"Excellent . . . he ees there now. Brad . . . est-ce que je peux te demander quelque chose?"

The dark-haired boy said,"Sure. Just a second, Ace." Yet, while he turned toward the woman the blond-haired boy quickened his pace, descended the stairs to the left and went out the door. Peterson followed him with his eyes. The dark-haired boy shook his head slightly and sighed looking in the direction of the boy who left. He turned to the cook.

"Yes, Sophie. What would you like me to do?"

"This man . . . Monsieur Peterson would like to see Gary. Can you take heem to his house, pleeese?"

"Yeah. Sure. I just have to do it quick because I have to go to Château-Thierry to pick up some Americans that are coming by train from Paris. My name's Brad Roberts. Glad to meet you."

"Pleasure. We can take my car. No problem."

"Won't be necessary really. It's just a couple houses down. We just go out the door here," he pointed to the double doors to his right, which were on the opposite side of the house where Peterson had come in. The detective hesitated trying to decide if he could trust that kid to stay in the car or not. He then said curtly, "Yes. Let's go quickly."

Chapter 54

Missionary Base
Monday, May 26, 2003
Sezanne, France

Ace Parks descended the concrete steps rapidly. His lips were pressed together, teeth clenched and his eyebrows lowered in intense concentration. His face changed significantly from one of meditation to alarm to decisiveness when he saw the new BMW and the back of the head of someone in the passenger seat. He picked up speed and went out between the two stone pillars and onto the sidewalk to the right. He stopped and waited.

Within a few minutes he saw Brad and the man who was in the foyer appear on the sidewalk further down. Fortunately they did not look back. He leaned close to the six foot wall in front of the house and some overhanging branches just in case they did. He stared at the two figures for a few seconds and then suddenly sprinted in their direction and quickly turned right on the little pathway the two had just taken from the house. He stopped, bent down and grabbed some gravel pebbles from the walkway and resumed running. He jumped the stone wall separating the next house and ran past a tethered goat chewing something, ducked a clothesline that had several blue overalls hanging on it and some pairs of black socks. He jumped the next stone wall and hid behind the corner of the house and peeked out. He could see the two men walking into view on the sidewalk.

Ace crossed the backyard of the next house and looked around the corner again. When the two men passed the area between the houses and walked up the path to the stone house and out of view, Ace ran to the back of the same house until he was just below a large vertical window. He threw several pebbles at it, making pinging noises off the glass and muttering to himself, "C'mon Gabby. Open the window. Open the window."

Chapter 55

McKinley House
Monday, May 26, 2003

"C ome right in gentlemen," McKinley said as he opened the door to a man in a dark blue turtleneck and brown corduroy jacket and a young man in a grey hoodie and jeans.

"Thank you, Mr. McKinley. I am very sorry for the inconvenience. I hope I am not interrupting your breakfast."

"No. Not at all. We've already eaten. To be honest, I'm expecting someone else from the States and they are supposed to be arriving this morning as well. What did you say your name was?"

"Joe Peterson." The men shook hands in greeting.

"Excuse me, Gary," Brad interjected, "but I gotta go to get those guys at the station. Don't want to be late. Nice to meet you Mr. Peterson."

"Same here. Thanks for showing me to the house."

"No problem." With that Brad began a speedy walk back to the base Center. McKinley escorted Peterson into the living room and motioned for him to sit on the couch. At this point Mary McKinley entered the room and her husband introduced her to their guest.

"Would you like some coffee, Mr. Peterson? It's real fresh."

"Ah, no thanks, Mrs. McKinley. I just had some a little while ago. Perhaps you'd like to join us. The reason for my visit might be of interest to you; also, you both may be able to help me."

"Surely." She then sat down on the edge of the other living

room chair to the right of her husband and waited for him to go on.

Turning to one and then the other he said, "Sir. Ma'am. I am a private detective under the employ of a Steve Capaldi from Albany, New York, and we have reason to believe that his daughter Gabriella Capaldi is here at this Center. Is that right?"

McKinley hesitated and then leaned back into his lounge chair. "Why would Mr. Capaldi need to hire a detective to come all the way to France?"

"Unfortunately, there have been some crimes committed by her boy friend, Ace Parks, and Capaldi thinks it would be in her best interests to come back to the States with me rather than be implicated with him for these offenses. She is also 17 and considered a minor."

"What crimes are we talking about here, Mr. Peterson?"

"The boy backed over a seven-year-old black girl, who is still in a coma in critical care, and left the scene of the accident." Peterson picked up his briefcase, opened it, and handed McKinley some newspaper clippings. "Here are some articles from the local paper about the whole thing."

McKinley scanned the articles briefly and then passed them to his wife.

"What makes it worse is Parks is on probation from having a serious altercation at a bar, which complicates things somewhat."

"I see. What do you propose to do?"

"Actually, I only want a chance to speak with Gabriella. I think I can convince her of the wisdom of coming back to the States with me. I'm sure she does not want to be charged with being an accomplice in helping Parks get away. With your help I may succeed."

"How do we know you are who you say you are?"

"Here is my card and driver's license." Peterson pulled out

his wallet and slid two cards out of the leather compartments and handed them to McKinley.

"Thank you." McKinley looked them over and handed them back. The detective put them back and added:

"I also have a short video I could show you on my laptop which will prove beyond any doubts that I was sent by Mr. Capaldi. It's a plea from her dad. I also have Mr. Capaldi's telephone number and we could just give him a call if you want. I checked in with him this morning and he's aware that we are now at the Center."

"And if she does not want to go back with you?" Mrs. McKinley asked.

"Personally, I think when she understands that she could be charged as an accomplice in this case if she does not come back, she will see the wisdom in it. If not, that's her choice and I will go back to the States without her. From what I've learned about her, through her father and friends, is that she is a bright kid—so I don't anticipate a problem."

"And what about the boy?" McKinley interjected.

"That is really none of my concern. I am not a police officer and I do not have jurisdiction to coerce him to do anything here in France or anywhere else for that matter. If he is open to it I will try to explain to him the gravity of his crime. Other than that he is free to do whatever he wants. If he sees the light and wants to come back I would prefer that he takes another flight. Let's just say he won't get a very warm welcome from Mr. Capaldi."

McKinley turned to his wife. "What do you think, Mary?"

"Personally, I would like to talk with Gabriella alone when she gets out of the bathroom and break it to her gently. I think that would be better than . . . oh Gabriella. We were just talking about you."

Gabriella had just entered into the living room from the

hallway. She was brushing her wet, long, black hair and wearing jeans and a loose-fitting white linen blouse which descended to about the middle of her thighs. She was also barefoot. She immediately smiled at Mrs. McKinley but suddenly became alarmed at the presence of the stranger.

"Oh. What's going on?"

"Well . . . let me introduce you to Joe Peterson. Mr. Peterson, this is Gabriella Capaldi. Gabriella, this is Mr. Peterson."

"Nice to meet you, Ms. Capaldi."

Gabriella just nodded her head and lowered her eyes.

"Well Gabriella. Would you like to sit down and join us?" Mary McKinley asked as she got up and moved a cushioned antique chair from against the wall to the place between she and her husband.

"I guess," Gabriella said as she walked over to the chair and sat down. "What's this all about?"

"Gabriella. Mr. Peterson has something he wants to say to you."

"But I have never met you before."

Peterson moved his neck a few times like he had to work out a stiffness and said: "That's right, Gabriella. You haven't and I am sorry I have to meet you like this. I am a private detective hired by your father . . ."

"Oh no," Gabriella gasped, bringing her hand to her mouth.

"I know it is probably a shock to you, and like I said, I'm sorry. Just so you know, I am not here to take you by force back to the States. I am here to just talk with you and let you know of some things that you may not be aware of."

"How did you find us . . . me . . . so fast?"

"That's my job, Ms. Capaldi. I'm a professional but that is beside the point. What I wanted to ask you is if you are cognizant that you may be formally charged with assisting a fugitive from the law?"

"It wasn't his fault! Someone tried to drag him out of the car. That's why he took off. It was an accident. Really."

"That may be the case—but why, then, didn't he contact the police to explain what had happened, instead of fleeing the country with a minor? It sounds like he was only thinking of himself."

Gabriella shifted uncomfortably in her seat. "It happened so fast. He was afraid that being on probation and all . . . that he would have to go to jail."

"And he may, Ms. Capaldi, he may. The little girl is still in a coma and if she dies, it could get worse. My question to you is, are you ready to be charged with him?"

At this point Gabriella began to cry. Tears ran freely down both of her cheeks as she spoke.

"It was not the way it was supposed to happen. We were going to wait until after I graduated and then get married."

Mary McKinley got up from her chair and went to Gabriella and put her hand on her shoulder. "I know, Honey. I know."

Peterson let her cry a bit before he continued. "I understand, Ms. Capaldi, this is a messy situation—but you can make things a lot better for yourself and your family by coming back with me. Here, let me show you a little clip your father gave me to show you." He lifted the laptop from his briefcase and put it on the coffee table between them with the screen facing Gabriella and pushed the on button. He slid the CD into the side tray and used his finger on the front section to make the selections. The picture showed her mother in the psychiatric hospital, sitting on a rocking chair going back and forth. She nodding her head as she rocked. Her father then appeared on camera and went to the side of his wife and said, "Gabriella, your mom has something to say to you. Go ahead, Jane. Tell Gabriella what you've been telling me. Go on."

"Hi. Gabriella. Where have you been? I've missed you. When are you coming back? I need you." She then looked up to her husband for approval to see if she had done her job. The camera then focused on the white-haired man who looked directly at the camera. "That's the question I'm asking too, Gabby. When are you coming back home? That's not the way to leave home—pretending to be somewhere else with a guy who is wanted by the police. Please Gabby. Think of your Mom. Think of your future. You haven't even finished school. I sent Mr. Peterson to bring you home. We can work things out. I've already spoken to the police. They are ready to drop any charges if you give yourself up. Please think, Gabby. The doctor is also ready to take you back in a heart beat. You're a smart girl. You just got carried away with emotion. Come back. Please."

At this point Gabriella lost her composure and ran to the kitchen, crying hysterically with Mrs. McKinley following after her. After a few moments of awkward silence McKinley said, "That's a pretty hard sell, Mr. Peterson."

"I'm sorry, Mr. McKinley, if it seemed that way to you. But this girl can be in a heap of trouble if she does not come back with me. It's for her own sake she understands all the repercussions of her actions."

"I tell you what, Joe," McKinley said. "She seems like she's in pretty rough shape right now. What if you give her some time to work through these issues today and we can be in touch tonight or tomorrow morning. I think it may be beneficial if we talk with her alone first. Is that acceptable to you?"

"No problem, Mr. McKinley. Here's the card of the hotel where we are staying. Just give me a call tonight and let me know what is happening. If she is in agreement we can leave tomorrow."

"Okay. I'll give you a call tonight." They shook hands and McKinley showed him to the door. Peterson's smile turned to a frown as the first thing he saw from the doorway was a black BMW parked on the road outside the McKinley's house.

Chapter 56

A Familiar Face in a Foreign Land
Monday, May 26, 2003

T rying to break a window, Parks?"

A cold fear went up Ace's neck. He knew that voice. He quickly turned around and saw the menacing Tony Scalafoni coming towards him from 20 feet away. Seeing his cold steely eyes meant one thing—this was not a social call. He'd better be ready for anything.

"No, Scalafoni. Not trying to break a window. Just improving my aim. What brings you to France? I thought your sense of adventure would be driving in a parking lot without a seat belt."

"Very funny, creep. You know why I'm here. Surprised you're not running. That's something you're good at."

"You may be right. Well, can't say it's been nice seeing you. But if you don't mind, I've got things to do." Parks turned to the right as if to walk away. Scalafoni grabbed his left shoulder to spin him around.

"Hey! I'm talking to you, jerk."

Without warning, Parks swung around fast and, with all his might, nailed the mason full force on the right cheek. Blood spurted from his face as the green gem on Ace's high school ring did its nasty work. He followed that with a hard left to Scalafoni's stomach. When Scalafoni bent over from the blows, Ace kneed him in the nose, breaking it, and then turned sideways and drop-kicked him in the chest with the flat of his foot, knocking him backwards on the ground. In his rage, Ace ran to do more damage to his opponent's head while he was on the ground but seeing the blood, he just muttered, "Who's the jerk now, Mister Tough Guy?" and turned to walk away.

Suddenly, Ace felt an iron grip on his ankle. He tried to shake it off, but to no avail. A moment later he was on the grass and a bloody-faced boy of 195 pounds was on top of him swinging mallet-sized fists at his face and connecting. Scalafoni now had Ace's arms pinned with his knees and was hitting Ace at will while Ace was making a valiant effort to knock him off his stomach by kneeing him in the back with all his strength. His efforts had little effect as the other boy's solid body absorbed them like good shocks on a car.

Scalafoni raised his hand to strike again but before doing it he said, "So, pizza man. How's it feel having a pepperoni face? What the . . . ?!" A strong, vice-like hand had grabbed his wrist. The hand was massive and black in color. The mason looked further around and saw the huge physique of one Elijah Williams, in a red and black varsity jacket. He was not smiling.

"Not nice to hit a guy when he is down," Williams said simply. With a quick yank, Anthony Scalafoni found himself on the ground next to Ace and an enraged mountain of a man glaring down on him as if just waiting for an opportunity to rearrange his anatomy. Scalafoni took the safe route and just rolled a few feet, jumped up and retreated back in the direction of the BMW at a quick trot. He passed a middle-aged man in a black leather jacket walking rapidly to the scene of the fight but neither offered greetings. The man shook his head as they passed one another. A white Peugeot was parked behind the black BMW as Scalafoni ran to the driver's door, got in the car and then quickly locked the door. He was about to take off when Peterson came yelling for him to stop from the direction of the stone house. The mason clicked the door open and moved to the passenger seat as Peterson got in. Before the car screeched away, he could be heard screaming: "You idiot! You got blood on the seats!!"

Chapter 57

Friends Help Friends in Trouble
Monday, May 26, 2003
Outside the McKinley house

What in the world are you doing here?" Ace said as his friend took him by the hand and pulled him to a standing position.

"Well, I heard a friend of mine was in trouble and I thought maybe I could help," Williams said, his serious expression finally changing into a smile.

"Uncle Jerry?!"

The man with the leather jacket arrived at the scene and put his hand on Ace's upper arm and looked him straight in the eyes.

"Ace. You all right? He clocked you pretty good. I could see him waling on you from the car. Any broken bones?"

"No. I'm fine. Just glad Elijah showed up when he did." He turned to Williams. "Thanks man. You did notice his face, though, I hope. I did get him pretty good before he tripped me."

"Oh, yeah. I did notice he was bleeding pretty good. What did you hit him with? A piece of glass?" Elijah asked bemused.

"Oh, no. Just my ring." Ace held up his hand with the culprit attached. "Wasn't premeditated, Uncle Jerry. Promise."

"Right. Okay, nephew. Is there a place around here we could talk privately?"

"Yeah. Sure. Just wondering, though, if we could see Gabriella first. She's staying in this house here. I don't know what that other guy was telling her. Obviously, they were sent by Gabby's father. Wouldn't be surprised if that other guy is in the mafia."

"I don't know about that but we can see what he had to say to Gabriella," Jensen said. The trio then walked to the front door of the stone house.

Chapter 58

The McKinleys' Living Room
Monday, May 26, 2003

A ce, I appreciate your desire to see Gabriella right now, but I don't think it is a good idea. She is really broken up about everything and I think she needs some space to sort things out. My wife is with her and . . ."

"Where is she? I just want to talk to her for a few minutes. I don't see how there can be any harm in that? I'm her best friend," Ace said, abruptly getting up from the couch quickly as if to do an immediate room-to-room search.

His friend and uncle were just as fast to get to their feet and put their hands on his shoulders. Jerry Jensen spoke gently, "You'll have time to see her later, Ace. I think we should listen to Mr. McKinley for now."

"That's right, bro. Let's give her some time to assimilate things," Williams added. "You know those ladies can be kind of emotional and sometimes it's better to just leave 'em alone for a spell. And I know that from experience, believe me." His hand went to Ace's upper arm and tightened slightly as if to discourage any thoughts of bolting.

Ace looked at his uncle and Elijah, who each now held an arm, and realized it was probably smart not to press the issue.

"Yeah. I guess. Maybe. When can I see her then?" He looked at McKinley.

"Why don't you give us a call around noon and we'll see how she is doing. Okay? In the meantime you guys could probably talk down at the main house in the room next to the kitchen. Nobody should be using it now. I'm sure Sophie would be glad to give you some coffee and some Swiss chocolate. Sounds like a plan? "

"Sounds good to me," Uncle Jerry said.

"Me too," Elijah agreed.

Ace just shook his head in frustration as the four of them walked toward the door. Before leaving, Ace turned to McKinley and said, "Could you just tell Gabriella one thing for me?"

"What's that, Ace?" McKinley said.

Ace hesitated and looked down at his sneakers. He then looked up with some moisture in his eyes and said, "Just tell her that I'm sorry for what happened . . . and that I love her."

"Sure Ace. Will do," McKinley said.

Chapter 59

Facing the Truth
Monday, May 26, 2003
Missionary Base, East of Paris

Man, they really know how to make chocolate in Europe!"
Elijah Williams said, after he swallowed a piece of chocolate from the tray Sophie had brought them. The tray also
carried three small amber-colored glass coffee cups and a coffee
pot. "I dig these designs on the chocolate too." He pointed to
the remaining large bar of chocolate. "Looks like the Alps."

Jerry Jensen picked up one of the cups, poured himself
some coffee, and began sipping it. He also broke off a piece from
the chocolate bar and popped it into his mouth. The broken-
off places revealed it also had nuts.

Ace, meanwhile, took nothing and rested his head in his
right hand, elbow on the armrest, waiting for the inevitable. He
sat in a chair to the right of the couch; Elijah was on the couch;
and Jerry was in the chair to the left. In front of them was a
wooden coffee table and facing them was a large fireplace.
Sophie had a fire going before they arrived and the air was
comfortably warm.

The room was obviously a place for people to come to relax,
read or chat with friends or family. The floors were dark wood
and had recently been sanded and varnished. In the middle of
the room was an oriental-looking, dark blue, 15 x 15 foot rug.

Sun was now coming into the room through the large
vertical windows which had long white lace curtains with
designs of swans going from the top of the windows to the floor.

On the bottom of each curtain was a row of vertical strips four inches long and a quarter inch wide which descended to the floor. A large bookcase with books and various objects from around the world was set against the wall perpendicular to the fireplace on the left. To the right was another shelf which had a CD player and speakers, as well as a wide collection of CDs below it. A song by Stephan Curtis Chapman played softly in the background.

"You can thank Elijah for insisting that we rent a car instead of taking the train," Jerry Jensen began. "Somehow he felt that it was imperative that we arrive as soon as possible. Now I understand why."

Ace smiled, turned to the big man and said, "Thanks. Just like the cavalry."

"Let's just say the Man upstairs knew you needed some help," Elijah said, smiling broadly.

"I'm not sure about that but I'm glad you came when you did. That kid was getting kind of heavy on my chest."

"Looks like your face is happy about it, too," Elijah said chuckling.

Ace's cheekbones near his eyes were already puffy from the blows and it was still red from the abuse.

"Maybe we should ask Sophie for some ice," the lawyer said, pointing toward the door which led to the kitchen.

"No. I'm fine. No problem," Ace said. "I'd say he is worse off than I am, though. Think I broke his nose."

Jensen was about to say something but stopped himself. He waited a few moments before saying gently, "Well Ace, I guess it's no secret why we are here."

Ace nodded and the lawyer continued, "As you know, you are on probation for that incident that took place in the bar. The fact that you left the scene of an accident . . ."

"I had to, Uncle Jerry, there was this black guy trying to drag me out of the car and . . ."

"I understand that there may have been legitimate reasons for doing it, but the fact you did not report the accident and then fled the country with a minor does not look good in the eyes of the law. In my opinion, as a lawyer and your uncle, the best thing you can do is come back to the States, turn yourself in, and hope that the judge is lenient. I spoke to your probation officer and he said he could not promise you that he would drop the probation violation charge if you came back, but he did guarantee if you don't you can count on some jail time the moment you return to the States."

"What if I never come back," Ace erupted. "That director Polanski guy seems to have done okay in France and they never extradited him."

"Yeah, but how are you going to live in France? That guy was a famous film director. Your assets will probably be frozen and you will have to get a job. Unemployment is even higher here than the States, and you will have to get a work visa or work under the table. What kind of job do you think you can get?"

"I don't know. At least Gabriella and I will be together. We'll both get jobs."

Jensen sighed, "Ace. Think about Gabriella. She's a beautiful girl. She obviously loves you, but is this really the best for her and her family? Do you know that she could be charged with helping a known fugitive from the law? Do you want her to have a record?"

Ace folded his arms in front of him. "No, I don't. But wouldn't she get off being under 18 and this being her first offense?"

"I don't know. That depends on the judge. I can say this, though, it would go a lot better if she turned herself in, too."

"Great. And then what happens? I lose a job. I lose a girlfriend, and I might go to jail on top of that."

Elijah swallowed his piece of chocolate and leaned forward. "Ace. If you do the right thing, things will work out. I know they will. You're a smart guy. If the pizza thing doesn't work out, I'm sure there's something better for you. Remember that time I broke my arm playing football when I was a sophomore and I had to sit out the rest of the season? I thought everything was over for me. But God gave it back after I was willing to let it all go. And Gabriella is a wonderful girl. She's not going to leave you just because of this. She came with you. But Ace, if you really love her you have to think of her first. You need to make the decision that is best for her."

"Yeah. And how about her dad? He hates me. How is that ever going to work out? He'll brainwash her against me."

"Ace, trust God. If your relationship is from Him, and I believe it is, He can change her father's heart over time."

"Right. Just like He parted the Red Sea," Ace replied, smirking sarcastically.

"Exactly. God opened Pharaoh's heart to let the Hebrews go. Gabby's father's heart can't be harder than that, can it?"

"You might be surprised," Ace said.

"Ace. I don't subscribe much to this God stuff," Jensen said. "But I do think your friend here does have some wisdom in what he's saying. Think about the long-term effects of what you are doing. What is the best for the both of you in the long run?"

"What if the girl dies? What will happen to me then? Do you know how she is doing?"

"As far as I know, she is in stable condition but still in a coma. If she does die, it will definitely complicate things." The lawyer decided it best not to mention the preacher Johnston stirring up things in Albany.

"I don't know why my life has to be so difficult. I'm sick of it. First it's my dad, then my mom, and now this." At that moment Ace stood up and ran from the room. Both Jerry Jensen and Williams heard the latch on the outside door open and the heavy door close and then saw Ace pass in front of the window in their room.

"Should we go after him, Mr. Jensen?"

"No. Let's let him be for now. I think he needs time alone, too."

"You don't think he's going back to where Gabriella is, do you?

"No. But he's got some tough issues he's got to work through. I think he'll come to the right conclusions. I believe he really loves Gabriella and he'll do it, if not for himself, at least for her. In the meantime, let's just hang loose. Maybe there's someone here who could give us a tour of the place."

At that moment, as if on cue, Sophie opened the door in the middle of the wall to their left, popped her head out and said, "Ees every ting all right?"

Chapter 60

The Decision
Monday, May 26, 2003
The McKinleys' Kitchen

Well, Gabby. What's the verdict?" Ace said, standing near the window in the McKinley kitchen, first looking directly at her and then shifting his gaze away and out into the night. Gabriella was seated at the family-sized wooden table which had a typical colorful Provincial tablecloth with sunflowers and a lavender field design.

"Can't you sit down, Ace? Please." Gabriella said gently, her eyes pleading.

Ace left his sentry duty and reluctantly walked to the table. He pulled out a chair two seats over from Gabriella and sat down. He pushed his chair out from the table and folded his arms in front of his chest.

Gabriella reached out her hand to hold his but both his hands stayed in their fixed position.

"Gabby. Just tell me. This is hard enough."

Gabriella's eyes quickly watered and she withdrew her hand. "I know Ace. I know. It's hard for both of us. But . . ."

"But what, Gabby? The goon squad talked you into going back with them, right?"

"They did not talk me into going back with them. I haven't talked or seen them since this morning. I've just been talking with the McKinleys and thinking about it myself. I just don't think we really thought through what we were doing. We just did it impulsively. Ace, you're on probation. Staying here could make things worse for you and I'm not so sure I want to stay here in France for the rest of my life. I'd like to be able . . ."

"To what?" Ace stood up and opened his hands at his sides and then turned away, putting them into his pockets. "I could go to jail, Gabby. Don't you understand? At least here we could be together. We could get married like we'd planned. Your birthday is only two days away."

Gabriella got up from the table and moved towards him, putting her hand on his forearm and looking directly into his eyes.

"Ace. What kind of life would that be? Never being able to go back home out of fear of getting arrested. How would we live? What would we do for work? How about my family—my mom especially?"

Ace turned away and was standing in front of the sink. He began twirling a used coffee cup he saw in the sink. "Maybe I could get a little pizza truck like the one we saw in Châteaux Thierry. I looked and they even have ovens in those things. Brad told me the pizza isn't so good here. It's thin crusted and they don't use much tomato sauce or the same cheese we use. We could introduce the French to some real American pizza."

"That takes money, Ace. And remember what we studied in French class, about how long it takes to start a business here? It's not like the States where you can just pay a small fee and start doing business. You have to submit all kinds of paperwork and do research that can take months and months, even years. You're also not going to make the same profits in a socialistic country where you are paying so much in taxes."

Ace stopped his twirling routine and walked back toward the window. Gabriella followed.

Ace looked up toward the stars. "So when are you leaving?"

"Tomorrow morning. There's a nine o'clock plane we can take from Paris."

"Why can't we go back together? It gives me the creeps that you will be all that time with that idiot mason and the godfather."

"So, does that mean you're going back, too?"

"Might as well." He turned toward Gabriella. "What would I do without you?"

Gabriella slipped into his arms at that point and they just held each other for several long minutes. Then Gabriella pulled away and said, "I'd like to go back with you, Ace, but my dad will be at the airport and it's probably not good that he sees you right now."

"What if he says we can't see each other anymore?"

"Let's just take one challenge at time, okay?"

"Okay. I had a feeling this was going to happen. I guess we can tell the crew in the living room."

Gabriella quickly kissed him on the cheek and smiled, her face radiating a renewed joy. "Ace. Thank you. I really believe this is the right thing to do. I just know everything is going to work out. I just know it."

"Hope you're right."

"You'll see."

As they walked out into the living room Gabriella put her arm around Ace's waist and they met the waiting committee together. Jerry Jensen and Elijah Williams were sitting on the edge of the couch facing them and the McKinleys turned in their chairs to face the couple.

Gabriella looked at Ace and smiled again, with a gleam in her eye. She then faced her audience and said, "We're going back."

"Praise God!" Williams exclaimed jubilantly, raising his hands and then falling back into the recesses of the couch with a sigh of relief, at which everyone laughed.

Chapter 61

The Trial
November 2003 (Six months later)
Albany, NY

Well. You ready, Ace?" Jerry Jensen said as they sat in his Prius one block down from the Albany courthouse. A crowd had formed in front of the entrance with placards saying *Justice for Henrietta, It's time for an African American Police Chief* and *Give Him the Max.* Reverend Johnston stood in front with a wireless microphone, obviously in his element, leading the chant: "Justice For Henrietta! Justice for Henrietta!"

Several television crews with their entourages also waited at the top of the steps hoping to get a few words from any of the participants.

"I guess now is a good time as any," Ace said, scanning the sea of unfriendly faces. He was dressed in his only suit, navy blue, with a white shirt and solid maroon tie. When they both opened their doors the attention was immediate: "There he is!" "He's over there!" Johnston shouted: "C'mon everybody. Let's let our voices be heard! Here comes the coward now!" Policemen now came toward Ace and Jerry to escort them to the building. TV and newspaper reporters flashed their recording devices in Ace's face as he passed by. "Excuse me, Mr. Parks, do you have a comment for the press before the trial?" "How about you, Mr. Jensen?"

"No comment right now, people." He put his head down and muttered to Ace in front of him, "Don't say anything, no matter what they say. Just keep moving."

One middle-aged black woman in a fur coat and purple hat grabbed Ace's sleeve, locked eyes with him, and said, "You oughta be ashamed, young man, for what you did. I just hope you get all you have coming to you! That's all I gotta say!"

One enthusiastic young reporter with dark hair and glasses stuck his digital recorder in front of Ace's mouth and said, "What do you think of that, Parks?"

Ace just grit his teeth and said, "No comment." He wanted to add "slimeball" but held his tongue.

"Stand back, please!" shouted the young policeman as he noticed the reporter and the woman getting too close to the defendant. "That's right," said the other older policeman on the left. "Gotta get through, ladies and gentlemen. Let's move!"

Slowly the path cleared before the officers, and the lawyer and his client followed in their wake to the courthouse entrance.

Jessica Shaw stood to the right of the doors with her TV crew from Channel 10, reporting on the event and speaking loudly to be heard above the noise of the chanters. "Here we are outside Albany courthouse as defendant Ace Parks and his lawyer Gerald Jensen arrive at the scene. As you can see, there are a number of protesters here as well, led by the Reverend Johnston, with signs saying 'Justice For Henrietta,' 'Time For a Black Chief of Police,' and so on. Parks and his lawyers have declined comment at this time. As you know, Parks is the pizza delivery man accused of leaving the scene of an accident in which a young African American girl, Henrietta Wilson, was struck unconscious after being hit by Parks' vehicle last May and remains to this day in a coma at Albany Medical Center. Apparently, Parks fled to France with a girl, a minor, but both have since come back. We will keep you updated as the trial unfolds. This is Jessica Shaw reporting live from the Albany courthouse."

Walking into the hearing room, Jerry Jensen was surprised

to see the gallery already almost full. He saw the reporter from the *Tribune* near the front row and gave him a nod as he and Ace passed the wooden bar separating the lawyers from the rest of the room. They both sat at the table to the left. The DA, Jason Dawes III, and his assistants were seated at the right table. A court stenographer, a middle-aged woman with short, strawberry blonde hair, sat poised to begin recording the events with her small black stenograph closer to the judge's elevated platform. The jury sat off to the right side of the room, as usual a hodgepodge of body types, colors, and ages as well as levels of alertness. After waiting several minutes the judge entered the room. The room fell silent, though the chanting from outside was still faintly audible.

"All rise," bellowed the court bailiff, who was a short, bald man, a little soft in the middle. Everyone got to their feet en masse. Once the judge took his seat the bailiff said in a loud voice, "The honorable Judge Peter Fredricks residing. Please be seated." The response to this order was quicker and there was a whooshing sound from the sudden air displacement, as bodies dropped back to their original passive positions on the benches.

The bailiff continued, "The People versus Ace Parks."

The judge then brought down his gavel and said, "The court is now in session. District Attorney, Mr. Dawes, your opening statement, please."

Dawes pushed back his chair and stood up, looking at the jury and then at Ace Parks and Jerry Jensen. He was six feet, slim from many trips to the gym, dressed in an impeccable tailor-made Italian suit, confident, and deliberate as he moved around to the front of his table. An attractive young woman of about 25 and another young man a little older remained seated at the table and stared soberly at their mentor.

"Your Honor, and members of the jury. We are here today for a very serious reason. A young child, Henrietta Wilson, was playing innocently in her neighborhood on May 19, 2003 when she was struck by a vehicle driven in broad daylight by the defendant, Ace Parks, after he had just delivered a pizza to her mother. Perhaps we could understand if he was driving an ambulance, or a fire truck, or some other vehicle for emergency purposes; but, ladies and gentlemen, the urgency was not so life-threatening. He just wanted to get to his next delivery.

"I know the defense will certainly bring up that our defendant has had some rough issues to deal with—the loss of his mother in the last couple of years, no father in the household, etcetera—and we can all sympathize with him on this score.

"Yet, the evidence will show that this young man made no attempts to contact anyone. There is no record that he called the police, or 911, or even his manager. He just left a young child injured on the street. He then fled the country with a minor and never even reported the accident. Yes, you are going to hear the story that Mr. Parks ran away because someone, he says, was trying to pull him out of his car, but there are absolutely no witnesses to corroborate his story. His actions, ladies and gentlemen, were just plain wrong and must be punished according to the full extent of the law. I think, after hearing the witnesses I have summoned here today, you will agree with me that this defendant, Ace Parks, callously left the scene of a serious accident, without knowing if the victim was dead or alive, failed to report it, and then sought to escape the consequences of his actions by fleeing the country, with a minor no less. These actions, we will prove, make him guilty of a Class E Felony, and, therefore, deserving of five years in the State penitentiary.

Dawes then scanned the eyes of the jury members making sure he had direct contact to impress upon them his sincerity, walked around the table and sat down.

"Mr. Jensen, your opening statement please," the judge said nodding his head in order to look over his reading glasses.

Jensen stood, pressed his lips together, looked first to the judge and then to the jury: "Your Honor, and members of the jury, thank you for your presence here today. Both the defendant and myself are well aware of the seriousness of the charges brought against him. We are both deeply concerned over the health and recovery of little Henrietta, and only hope and pray she will experience full restoration soon.

"However, upon closer examination, the evidence will show that the circumstances surrounding the accident will reveal why Mr. Parks left the scene of the accident so quickly, and it was not as the prosecution suggests, done in a 'callous' manner, but to protect himself from bodily injury by a spectator that tried to yank him out of the vehicle. You will also learn from his neighbors, fellow employees, former teachers, and friends that he is an exceptional young man who works hard, conducts himself with utmost integrity, and . . ."

At this remark there were some grumblings from the gallery. One black teenager with a torn red sweat shirt and black jeans barely covering his buttocks yelled: "That ain't true. He ran over my cousin!"

The judge quickly laid down his gavel and shouted, "Order. Order in the court. One more outburst from you, young man, and you will be banned from this courtroom. Do you understand?"

The boy clammed up immediately, but fistbumped his friends around him as he sat down grinning like he had scored a winning basket.

"Continue, Mr. Jensen."

It was at this moment there was some loud shouting coming from outside the courthouse. The judge, obviously annoyed by another disruption, motioned to the officers in the back near the exit to investigate the matter. What the policemen saw as they exited the building was a mass of protesters, of both white and black people, yelling with their posters, "Mercy Triumphs Over Judgment" and "Love not hate." A big black young man in a red varsity jacket was leading the group along with some local ministers.

One of the officers whispered to his associate, "Isn't that Elijah Williams?"

"It sure is. I wonder what he's doing here," the other policeman replied.

The Reverend Johnston didn't miss a beat. He ran to Elijah Williams and pulled him aside and said, "Hey, Bro. What are you doing here? Aren't you on the wrong side, my man? We could sure use you with us, you know."

Williams brushed away the hand holding his sleeve and said, "No. I'm on the right side. Ace Parks is a friend of mine and you, Bro, are sticking your nose into something that has nothing to do with you. You . . ."

"Now hold on a second here, Mister Football. I am here to make sure justice takes place and to defend the rights of the powerless, the poor, and the voiceless blacks no matter where they are—Selma, Atlanta, or Albany."

At that moment Elijah Williams' cell phone vibrated in his jacket pocket. "If you will excuse me, Mr. Johnston. I may have an important call." He pulled out the Blackberry and saw it was a text from his sister's friend, Tabetha Jones, who worked as a nurse's assistant at Albany Medical Center. The text read: *PTL! Little Henrietta just opened her eyes. She's asking for food!* Elijah let out a whoop and yelled to his followers: "Henrietta opened her eyes, everybody. She's out of the coma!" The crowd went berserk with hallelujahs and praise the Lords.

Johnston stood stunned for about four seconds before he started screaming too: "I prayed for her, people—and she's healed. Glory to God!"

Williams just shook his head. He had been instrumental in

leading a weekly inter-church prayer meeting for the city, Ace, and Henrietta that pulled together at least 20 people each time they met. Many people had also signed up to fast once a week, and yet here was this rabble rouser Johnston, trying to take all the credit because he may have prayed for the girl once. Elijah had to admit, though, that God *could* heal after only one prayer. But Johnston's?

Meanwhile, on the courtroom, everyone was curious as to what was going on outside and looked in the direction of the exit for some report from the policemen.

Back outside in the town square, a young black woman in a waist-length leather coat pressed her way to Williams. With a big smile he bent down so she could whisper in his ear. After listening. Elijah's eyes widened and he nodded his head in understanding. He escorted her like a linebacker through the throng to the court's entrance. When the police tried to stop her from entering, she whispered something to them and they finally let her through.

In frustration, the judge called over the bailiff to find out what was going on. A policeman entered and shouted: "Your Honor, there is another group here now and they are saying that the girl woke up from the coma. That's why they are so riled up." This bit of news stirred up the people in the benches and a few reporters hurried out of the courtroom to get more information.

The young black woman made her way down the aisle and to the wooden bar. She waved her hand in the direction of Jerry Jensen: "Sir, sir. I have something to say that is relevant to this case. Please."

Jerry got up and went to the wooden bar. "Yes, Miss. What is it that you want to say?"

I want to say that I saw a man trying to pull your defendant out of his car after the accident. I was afraid to come forward before but I just have to tell the truth."

"Thank you, Ma'am. Please be seated. I will inform the court and the DA of your willingness to testify."

Jensen turned toward the judge and said, "Your Honor, may I have a word with you and the DA privately, please? There have been some new developments in the case that I was just made aware of."

"All right. Come forward, gentlemen."

When the two lawyers reached the judge's platform, the judge leaned closer to them.

"All right, Mr. Jensen. What do you have?" the judge asked.

"A woman just came forward and said she was a witness to the accident and saw a man try and drag my defendant out of his car. I would like permission to admit her testimony." He smiled slightly as he faced Dawes.

The judge looked to the other attorney: "Do you have any objections, Mr. Dawes?"

"Yes, as a matter of fact, I do object. The time for providing notice of defense witnesses has long since passed."

"Mr. Jensen, why is this witness coming forward so late?" the judge asked solemnly.

"I do not know, your Honor. It's the first time I have met the woman."

"All right," the judge said curtly to the lawyers. He turned toward the bailiff and raised his voice: "Bailiff, please escort the jurors out of the room. We will hear what this woman has to say without the jury present. If I determine that her testimony is not only relevant, but that she has a sufficient basis for coming forward at such a late date, I will allow her to testify before the jury."

Chapter 62

Albany County Jail
Visitors Room
Wednesday, January 19, 2004
2:30 PM

Elijah Williams sat across from Ace Parks in the visiting room, as he had done several times over the past three months. But this time, he flashed a big grin that looked as if it would erupt into a volcanic fit of joy at any moment. There were several other prisoners at the other end of the long table talking with their visitors who occasionally shot glances in his direction.

"Yo man, you look hot in orange. Maybe you should think about moving to the 'Cuse," Elijah said, giving him the once-over.

Ace's eyebrows arched in perplexity. "What are you talking about, dude?"

"Your fluorescent jumpsuit, bro. The Orange? That's what they call the Syracuse basketball team. Oh, I forgot. You're not a sports guy."

"Oh, yeah. Very funny." Ace just shook his head at his friend's dumb joke and allowed a slight smile to surface. Elijah's joy was infectious and if he didn't watch it they might both crack up laughing hysterically at the stupidest thing and be told to keep it down by the guards.

The big man's sparkling eyes narrowed after a few minutes and took on a gentler, more serious expression. "So, Ace, you ready to fly outta here today? That was a bad break to have to be in the slammer for 90 days but you made it through."

Ace shifted in his wooden seat and said, "You know, Elijah,

I've been ready to leave this place ever since I got here."

"I know, Ace. I know. But my pastor told me some good things happened while you were here."

"Yeah, as much as I don't want to admit it, I probably needed to be here to get myself straightened out. At first, all I did was kick the walls and complain to God about why He let this happen to me, especially after all the other crap I'd been through. But your pastor helped me to see things from another perspective."

"Yeah, he's good at that." Elijah said nodding.

"It also gave me time to really read the Gospels. I had never done that before. The way Jesus was with people was just amazing, and He wasn't religious at all. He just went around healing people, casting out demons, doing miracles, and confronting the dudes that thought they knew everything about God, but knew diddly squat."

"Sounds like you may have met Him yourself."

"Yeah, I guess you could say that. Just last week, after I told your pastor everything I was seeing in the Bible, he just said, 'You know you can meet Jesus and feel His peace in your heart today if you want.' I just said, 'How can I do that?' He said, 'Just agree with what the Word says—that you are a sinner and that you need a Savior to forgive you from all those things that have separated you from God—and invite Him to come in and cleanse you.' I prayed with him and I couldn't believe the peace that came over me. After a few other visits he told me there were probably some things I needed to make right if I was really serious about following Jesus."

"Like what?"

"He said he thought I should write to Gabby's dad and that little girl's mom and ask forgiveness for what I had done. I'll tell you, Elijah, it was much easier writing to that little girl's mom than it was to write Gabby's dad, but I did it. I don't know how they took it but I felt I had done the right thing when I put those letters in the mail. It's funny but sometimes it just feels good admitting you're wrong without trying to make excuses."

"That's great, Ace. You've really come a long way. I'm sure God has got some good surprises for you down the road. Speaking of surprises. I think there is someone else who'd really like to talk with you. But I think I have to vacate these here premises before number two VIP visitor can come in—so, if you'll excuse me, bro, I'll see you in a few momentos." Elijah pushed himself out from the table, stood up and walked to the locked door where the guard let him through.

Ace looked to the door expectantly when a tall girl with long black hair in a button-down, red, woollen sweater and black dress slacks was let in. She located him immediately, smiled, and bowed her head shyly as she walked to where he was sitting. The heads of every prisoner in the waiting room turned. One woman sitting across from another inmate screeched, "Whatcha looking at, mister! You want me to leave you right now?"

Gabriella's cheeks turned an immediate red as she slid into the chair that was previously occupied by a much bigger human specimen. Though Ace liked the former visitor, this one was having a much different effect on his emotions. He suddenly felt embarrassed by his clothes and situation and looked down when she sat opposite him.

She reached out and grabbed his hand with both of hers. "Hi Ace. Surprised?"

Ace's words caught in his throat. He looked up and straight into her hazel eyes and realized how much more beautiful she was in person. Of course, he'd received her letters and looked at her photo a zillion times a day, but he thought she was forbidden to see him by her father.

"Ahh . . . I thought you couldn't see me."

"I can't but . . . he made an exception for today."

"Really?"

"Yes, but he said we need to talk together and not do things behind his back. I took the day off from school and thought it would be cool to see you on the day you get out."

"Thanks, Gabby. You look great. You know, I don't know how I would have made it without your letters. They were the highlight of my day."

"And yours were mine." Gabriella said. She paused before continuing: "That was a pretty courageous thing to write to my dad. His exception today might have been because of that."

"Yeah, well, it wasn't easy but I think it was the right thing to do. How did he take it?"

"Well, he read it at least. I saw it on his night table when I went into his room to clean. I think it was well-written. You didn't try to justify yourself or anything. You just said you were wrong and that is something I think he can respect. We'll just have to keep praying and believing, right?"

"Yeah. You mean you still . . . ?"

"Don't be a dope . . . of course."

"By the way, is your dad still pushing that creep Scalafoni on you?"

Gabriella shook her head. "No. He tried once by inviting him to dinner without telling me, but when I told him how I felt about it he stopped, thank God. He just can't compete, you know, with someone else."

"Yeah, you're right. Plus you're taller than him. It could never work. How's his nose?"

"It's pretty much healed by now, but he had a bandage for quite some time, Dad said."

"That's good. Maybe that will teach him from sticking it in somebody else's business." At that moment Gabriella noticed a middle-aged man in a suit near the entrance.

"Oh, there's Uncle Jerry. He's got something to tell you." Gabriella got up from her chair.

"Gabby. Wait. Don't go!"

"It's okay, Ace. I will see you again in just a minute."

Gabriella left the room with Ace protesting her early departure. A guard let Jerry Jensen in. Jerry bounded over to Ace with the good news: "Ace. Ace. You can come with me. Your clothes and things are in the other room. Everything's arranged. The judge is letting you out a few hours early for good behavior. I thought we'd have a celebration at La Serre, that French restaurant. Everybody's invited. Robin and the kids are meeting us there."

A short time later, as the foursome walked through the correction facility's parking lot, Ace said, "Hey, you guys will get a kick out of this. You know that reporter who wrote all those articles about my accident and everything? Well, he called me the other day and he wants to write a follow-up story on my experience in prison. He says he has to do it within a couple of weeks because he got another job at a Chicago paper and has to move."

Elijah slapped him on the back and said, "That's great, bro, because now you've really got something to tell him."

Jerry Jensen cocked his head and turned to Ace with a curious expression, "Yeah, what's that, Ace?"

Elijah winked and smiled at Ace and nodded his head to go ahead and tell him. Gabriella smiled too, arching her eyebrows expectantly. Ace hesitated and said, "Ahh, I'll tell you over lunch."

"Well, I got something to tell you, too," Jensen said. "You know that detective I talked to you about? He thinks he might be able to use that analytical mind of yours to help him with some cases. Whatta ya think?"

Ace's eyes connected with Gabriella's and he said, "It sounds interesting, Uncle Jerry, but . . . I think Gabby and I want to pray about it first."

From the Author

Thank you for reading this book. I would love to hear what you thought of it and if it touched you in some way. I also would be interested in knowing if you would welcome a second book with some of the same characters from *Runaways*. Please send your comments via this email address: moviesandmemoirs@yahoo.com.

I would also like to invite you to visit my website, **moviesandmemoirs.org**, where I post weekly reviews of movies and memoirs from a Christian perspective. As of this writing, there are over 80 reviews posted. Again, I welcome feedback.

May God bless you and, if you are still running from Him, I encourage you to stop, turn around, and receive His love and forgiveness. He will lead you to a much better place.

Blessings,
Tim

"Hold fast to dreams for if dreams die,
life is but a broken-winged bird that cannot fly."
—Langston Hughes

CPSIA information can be obtained
at www.ICGtesting.com
Printed in the USA
BVOW08s0046070917
493966BV00001B/1/P